DOUBLEDAY
CELEBRATES
100 YEARS OF
EXCELLENCE

doubleday

new york   london   toronto

sydney   auckland

where you are

george constable

PUBLISHED BY DOUBLEDAY

a division of Bantam Doubleday Dell Publishing Group, Inc.

1540 Broadway, New York, New York 10036

DOUBLEDAY and the portrayal of an anchor with a dolphin are trademarks of Doubleday,
a division of Bantam Doubleday Dell Publishing Group, Inc.

Book design by Maria Carella
Illustration by Robert Hunt

Library of Congress Cataloging-in-Publication Data
Constable, George.
Where you are / George Constable.—1st ed.
p.   cm.
1. Inheritance and succession—Pennsylvania—Philadelphia—
Fiction.   2. Man-woman relationships—Pennsylvania—Philadelphia—
Fiction.   3. Dog owners—Pennsylvania—Philadelphia—
Fiction.   4. Dogs—Pennsylvania—Philadelphia—Fiction.   I. Title.
PS3553.O52L35   1996
813'.54—dc20   95-49348
CIP

ISBN 0-385-48438-0

Printed in the United States of America

January 1997

1   3   5   7   9   10   8   6   4   2

First Edition

where you are
———————————

1

She left you what?" Ellen said.

"A house," he said.

"Just her house?"

"One of her houses. The one in Chestnut Hill. She left the summer house in Maine to my sister."

"What kind of house is it?"

"Stone. It's pretty big."

"She must've left a lot of money, too," Ellen said.

Lake didn't answer. He was remembering his last visit to the house a few weeks ago: Aunt Ilsa sitting on the sofa beside the live-in nurse; Aunt Ilsa, once so strong, now wordless and trembling, shattered by strokes. The nurse would not stop talking. For an hour, she exuded cheer, a stream of babble running down the slope of the afternoon.

"What about her money?" Ellen said after the waiter brought the main course.

"Most of it went to animal charities," Lake said.

"None for you?"

"Enough to cover expenses for the house, according to the will. I'm sure she calculated the amount very carefully, knowing her."

"How much?"

"A sufficient sum," he said.

"What about your father?"

"What about him?"

"What did she leave him?"

"Nothing, I'm sure."

"How come?"

"They hated each other," Lake said. "He didn't even go to the funeral."

"He must be pissed that he didn't get anything."

"I doubt it."

"But he's the closest relative."

"She certainly wasn't going to leave anything to him. When I was eight, I remember sitting in my aunt's living room and listening to her tell my mother what a rotten, selfish person he was and how she was lucky to be rid of him. That was Aunt Ilsa's way of giving comfort after he took off."

"What did your mother say?"

"She cried."

Ellen sipped her wine. Lake ate some bread.

"And there were no other relatives?"

"Just me and Karen."

"How weird."

"What do you mean?"

"It's weird. Leaving you a house."

"I guess she felt it should stay in the family," Lake said. He decided not to tell Ellen about the exact wording of the will or the letter that went with it.

"What does your sister think? I mean, you get this big house and she just gets something in Maine."

"What would Karen do with a house in Philadelphia? The place in Maine is only a couple of hours away from her. She's probably very happy."

"You haven't talked to her?"

"No." Lake was beginning to feel uncomfortable with the conversation, but Ellen was picking up momentum.

"What can you do with the house? You don't exactly need a big house."

"I'm going to sell it," he said.

"Did you see your aunt much?" she said.

"Karen and I always stayed in touch with her. Whenever Karen came to Philadelphia, we would visit her. It was kind of a habit. And this winter I went over there a few times."

"You didn't tell me that," she said.

"There wasn't anything to tell. She was great to Karen and me when Mom was sick. I owed it to her."

"And now you have a house."

"Yes."

"But why not her money, too?"

He wanted to say: Ellen, stop it, stop it. But they had been having a nice time up until now. "I guess Aunt Ilsa considered animals more deserving than people," he said. "It's not important. How's your chicken?"

"Maybe she was of unsound mind," Ellen said. "Wills are sometimes challenged when people leave everything to animals."

"She was of very sound mind," Lake said, gritting his teeth. "Not in the last few months, maybe, but she was plenty sharp when she made the will."

"How do you know?"

"I just know."

"How much did she leave to animal charities?"

"I have no idea," he said, finally letting his annoyance show. It stopped her. After a while, he said, "So how was your day?"

"I've had better."

"Bob again?"

"Today he asked me how much math I took in school."

"What brought that on?"

"I made a mistake when I was checking some expense accounts."

"Ah."

"A totally insignificant mistake."

"You should have told him Einstein couldn't do arithmetic either."

"I'm very good at arithmetic, as a matter of fact. It's the only time I've ever made a mistake."

"He shouldn't make that sort of crack."

"I took lots of math."

Then they talked about other people in her office and about how pleasant spring can be in Philadelphia and about the food. The tension disappeared, and fondness rippled through him as she did an imitation of a salesgirl who tried to sell her some makeup in a department store. He left a big tip. Outside, a ripe moon rushed through the clouds, in a big hurry to get somewhere. He drank in the colors of traffic lights, the city sounds, the touch of warm night air. Ellen stopped to look at a window display of evening dresses. The display was backed by a mirrored wall. Lake contemplated the reflection of them peering in from the street: a happy, handsome young couple.

Later, they watched television in her bedroom. Then he stopped watching. "What are you doing?" she said as a studio audience roared. What he was doing was nuzzling her neck and tracing the inward bend of her waist, rediscovering the curve of her hip, always a surprise—an ancient wonderful surprise that focused every thought and required much more touching.

Contentment ran right through his dreams and wandered lazily ahead to greet him when he woke in the morning. It was going to be a busy day. He had to go to Baltimore and make a sales pitch to the vice president of a company that manufactured a line of gardening equipment. Selling was not his favorite thing, but he almost looked forward to it today. Maybe his good feelings had something to do with the windfall from Aunt Ilsa, but he preferred to think it was because of the weather or Ellen. She was all business now as she dressed for work.

Back at his own apartment, he changed clothes, called Mary to say he would be in the office after lunch, filled his attaché case with InstruX samples, and bounded down the stairs and out into a welcoming world. His landlady was planting some reddish-orange flowers in the tree box in front of the town house. "Good morning, Mrs. Reardon," he said.

"Good morning, Mr. Stevenson."

"The earth quickens," he said, looking at the flowers. "What are those?"

"Begonias."

"Nice," he said. "Almost the same color as the brick. It makes kind of a vibration."

She stood up and studied the flowers, frowning. Not for the first time, Lake wondered about her color sense, but she was a fine landlady, attentive to any problems with the heating or plumbing, and he would not exchange her or his second-floor apartment for anything—certainly not for Aunt Ilsa's sepulchral pile of a house.

"I'm off to see a garden-supply company in Baltimore," he said. "Can I get you something? Need any tools?"

She was still staring at the orange begonias and didn't reply. Lake felt bad about his comment. "They'll look great," he said. "It catches the eye."

The morning seethed with greenness and sunshine. After joining the flow on I-95, he opened the car windows and rode south in his own private breeze. The highway careened through run-down Chester, sped past Wilmington, and swept across the hills of Maryland in a long calligraphic stroke of concrete. Lake was aware of houses. Some sat in the distance amid barns and outbuildings. Some crouched in valleys or stood beside water. Some gathered in little clutches where country roads converged. He noted their flaws and points of appeal, training himself for the real estate transaction that lay ahead. There was a certain skill in seeing a house as an object, he realized. With houses, sentiment tended to creep in, although that seemed highly unlikely in his case.

The offices of the gardening-equipment company were sleek and surrounded by a lawn so manicured and velvety that it didn't look real. The receptionist directed him to the vice president, a man named Derek Kast, about forty years old, with a mustache and an air of impatience.

Lake gave him his card: InstruX Associates, Lake Stevenson, President. "I know you're busy, so I'll keep it short," he said. He opened his attaché case and took out some samples. "I'll leave these with you. They'll do the talking."

Derek Kast glanced at his watch.

"As I said on the phone," Lake began, "we produce instructional literature. User's manuals, owner's manuals, any kind of materials that tell an end user how to do things. How to put it together, how to operate it, what to do if it doesn't work. For any type of product or process. We'd like to do it for you."

"We create our own instructions," Derek Kast said firmly.

"They could be better."

Derek's eyes narrowed. "What are you saying?"

"It seems to me that the quality of instructional materials ought to reflect the quality of a company and its products," Lake said. "You make great products, first-class products, but I doubt that your customers would say the same thing about the instructional materials." He held up his evidence, a dense and unintelligible sheet of operating directions for a programmable sprinkler. His friend Charlotte had given it to him after she couldn't get her sprinkler to work.

"You're saying the directions are no good?"

"Not worthy of the sprinkler," Lake said. "Do you ever get calls from people who can't figure it out?"

"Maybe a couple of times."

"Do you get returns because customers broke it when they tried to use it?"

"That's never been much of a problem."

"You know your business," Lake said. "I'm going to leave these samples of our work with you. All I ask is that you compare these materials with your own."

"That's kind of an odd niche, making instructions."

"There's a real demand for it, though," Lake said. "Good instructions save a company money, and they also make money, because they help create the corporate image. But it's harder than most people think. The instructions should be simple enough so that people will read them, but they also have to be very clear and complete. If you do it right, the user can't go off the tracks. Good instructions are almost impossible to disobey."

"Disobey?" Derek said.

"It comes down to that," Lake said.

"You don't mean disobey. Misinterpret maybe."

"The motives get complicated," Lake said. "But the point is, you don't want to give the customer a chance to go wrong. That means no jargon, good illustrations, and a lot of other things."

"Well, sure."

"A trained eye can see the problems more clearly."

"I usually ask my wife to test the directions for anything new," Derek said.

"Maybe she's hesitant to tell you what she really thinks," Lake said. "Or maybe she sees a problem but doesn't know how to fix it."

"That's possible."

Lake put his samples on Derek's desk. Derek flicked idly through the pile. He glanced at the directions for furniture assembly, a blender, a toy racing car. He began to pay attention. Then he picked up an eight-page guide to vegetable gardening that InstruX had done two years earlier as a promotional piece for a seed company. He went through it slowly. Lake watched him, pleased at his choice: the pamphlet had lively typography, crisp step-by-step sequences, good pictures. It was a fine piece of work. "Being really clear and complete, that's our specialty," Lake said.

Later, after a tour of the plant, Derek accompanied Lake to the front door of the building, shook hands, and said casually, "We've got a new electric hedge clipper in the design stage right now. It's kind of a tricky piece of equipment."

"We'd like to work with you on that."

"I've been thinking that the directions should be more visual than usual."

"That's one of our strengths," Lake said.

"Give me a call in a couple of days."

"I will," Lake said. "Look at that lawn. I wish my lawn looked like that." He tried to remember what Aunt Ilsa's lawn looked like. He had never noticed.

As he turned to go, Derek said, "How did you get in this directions business anyway?"

"I always wanted to run my own company," Lake said. "I was in publishing for a couple of years, and instructional materials seemed like a logical extension." Derek seemed to be waiting for something more. Lake added, "It's probably my inner nature."

*B*ack at the office, he found everyone hard at work. He sat at his desk and looked out the window for a while, thinking about edgers and clippers and sprayers, musing on the amount of business that InstruX might get from Derek.

"Your sister called," said Mary.

"Did she say anything?"

"She asked you to call her."

Lake decided not to. He began editing the captions Danny had written for the assembly of an intricate shelving system. With a freshly sharpened Number 2 pencil, he excised surplus words, exterminated passive verbs, and inserted commas in the pauses that Danny had failed to hear. It was pleasant work, satisfying in the way that weeding probably satisfied gardeners—which reminded him that he had to learn more about gardening. On a pad he jotted: Gdning bks.

He also needed to learn a bit about dogs.

"Mary," he said, "didn't we do something on pets a couple of years ago? Have we got anything on dogs?"

Mary went to her storage area and began searching. She brought back a pamphlet, *How to Care for Your Goldfish*. "This is the only thing on pets," she said. "It isn't really ours. We only did some minor update work on it."

"I don't remember it at all."

"You took a vacation that summer. Danny did it. That was right after he came."

Lake began reading.

Goldfish are very ancient pets, dating back at least a thousand years.

What? Who cares?

The swim bladder in your goldfish functions like the ballast tank in a submarine. With it, the fish is able to rise or sink in the water as it chooses.

How? Does the fish take in water? Does it take in air? Do fish choose things?

He came to a section about cleaning gravel before putting it in an aquarium.

You can place the gravel in unused flowerpots for this task.

Why? So that the pot will drain? How many fish owners have flowerpots? How about alternatives?

Lake tossed the goldfish manual aside and resumed work on Danny's shelving-system captions, breaking them into pieces, writing stern notes in the margin. "Be direct." "Say better." "Ambig."

*W*hen he returned to his apartment that night and checked his answering machine, Karen's voice said, "Lake, call me tonight. I can't believe this."

He still hadn't figured out how to deal with the house and his predicament. Military style, he spread the pertinent documents out on his worktable and studied the legal terrain. First Aunt Ilsa's will:

> *If my nephew Lake Stevenson survives me, I give and devise my house and lot, known as 73 Peal Avenue, Philadelphia, Pennsylvania, together with all my furniture and furnishings, to him provided he agrees with my personal representative to keep, maintain, and care for, at his expense, my pet dog Randall, for and during Randall's natural life, on and in said property, excepting only any period when Randall resides at my property known as Pinecroft in York Harbor, Maine. . . .*

The terms were explicit. To get the house, he had to take the dog. He was then required to keep the house for the dog's entire lifetime: no selling allowed.

Elsewhere in the will, there was a lot of talk about money, but the money part was fine. The dog condition was the only problem. The executor, Billington Vere, had attached a document for Lake to sign:

> *I accept the house on that condition and agree to care for the dog in the house.*

Next, he turned to the personal letter that had accompanied the other materials sent by Vere. It had been written by his aunt on February 15 of the previous year, not long after he and Karen had paid her a call. They had stayed for an hour or so and chatted about old times—a routine visit, nothing special, but somehow it must have given her the idea about custodianship for her dog. She had seemed frail at the time.

Dear Lake,

I am writing you this letter about my beautiful springer spaniel Randall. His breeding is of the highest quality, as you will see from the papers I have included. He has been a friend and companion of perfect loyalty and affection. To those traits I would add gentleness, a restrained playfulness, and a natural inclination toward good behavior that is not always present in his kind and that lends particular distinction to his character.

Randall's entire life has been spent with me. If I should be taken away, I have no doubt that he would be distressed, and I have spent some time considering how I might best spare his feelings. As you must know, dogs are as attached to their homes as people are, if not more so. Randall's world is here and at Pinecroft. I wish it to remain so. For that reason, I intend to bequeath this house to you and Pinecroft to your lovely sister Karen, who has always been a young lady of good manners and pleasant disposition and a very dear reminder to me of your mother, who bore her difficulties with a dignity that I admired. It is my desire that this house be Randall's home as well as yours, and that Randall spend his summers at Pinecroft. My practice has been to arrive at Pinecroft on July 1 and return to Philadelphia at the end of August. I believe Randall would be most comfortable if that schedule could be maintained.

I have mentioned this arrangement in my will, but I wish you to think of it as a family matter rather than a legal one. Naturally I hope you will be happy in this house. It will, I think, be a considerable improvement on your present circumstances and quite ample should you marry and have a family of your own. I would advise you to approach your choice of a spouse with the utmost care and deliberation. Compatibility of temperament is the first requirement of domestic happiness, and much misery is the price of misjudging one's partner, as I have no need to tell you. I have the greatest faith in your good sense. You are your mother's child, I am glad to say.

By the time you marry and raise children, Randall may be elderly. Children, of course, have high spirits. That is their nature, but too often it is allowed to run unchecked. I ask only that their play be confined to parts of the house away from those rooms which are favored by Randall. As you will see when you come to know him better, Randall does not like noise.

These are my wishes. I will explain them to Karen in a separate letter. I feel that the matter of noise is somewhat more delicate in her case, since she can already claim the prerogatives of parenthood. If you observe that boisterousness

is a problem at Pinecroft, may I ask you to take up the issue
with your sister and see that it is remedied?

Your loving Aunt

Ilsa

It was a fairly eloquent letter, in a lunatic way.

He glanced at the document that attested to Randall's allegedly exalted bloodlines and saw that the dog was not quite six years old. Chances of death from natural causes in the near future were slim. On the other hand, things can happen to dogs. In this dangerous world, a dog's existence is not secure.

He called his sister.

"Can you believe it?" Karen said.

"Which part?"

"I'm getting a house as a summer home for a dog," she said. "I'm going to be Aunt Ilsa's dog guardian."

"Only for a couple of months a year. I'm supposed to have ten months of this Randall."

"I guess it's a small price to pay for a house."

"I don't want a house," Lake said.

"You have to admit it was very generous of her."

"Karen, we aren't the point. Don't you see what she did? She left her houses to the dog. It's all for her goddam Randall."

"For us, too."

"Yes and no. Look," he said, "what else does a dog need besides a house? A dog needs a master. So she wrote her will to give her dog a master as well as a house. Two houses and two masters, in this case. It's outstandingly clever, the work of a true dog maniac."

"I don't see it that way."

"I'm right, though."

"You're not going to turn it down, are you?"

"I'm going to sell the house."

"You can't," Karen said.

"We'll see about that," Lake said.

"I've got a problem, too," she said. "We won't be able to use the house in Maine this summer. We've already rented a place on Martha's Vineyard for July."

"I'm sure Randall would be willing to go to Martha's Vineyard instead of Maine just this once. I mean, he has to be reasonable about these things."

"We can't take him with us. There's a no-pet clause in the lease. Could you keep him this summer? Or at least for July?"

"It may not be necessary," Lake said. "By the way, have you signed the letter agreeing to the conditions of the will?"

"Not yet."

"We're going to have to sign," Lake said. "Yesterday I got a call from this guy Vere, the executor. He was a big fan of Aunt Ilsa's. Very high-minded."

"I've never heard of a will like this. Maybe the clause about the dog isn't legal."

"It's legal, all right, but I'm almost positive that it's not enforceable. I know enough about law to know that. There are no penalties for noncompliance. It's all pretty vague. This is honor-code stuff."

"It sounds quite clear," she said.

"Karen, this is a procedure that we're supposed to follow, not a procedure that we have to follow. There's a very big distinction.

Believe me, I know what I'm talking about. I'm in the business. Besides, the letter from Aunt Ilsa practically admits it's just a word-of-honor deal. If she could have made it airtight, she would have."

"I wonder if she left Daddy anything."

"Are you kidding?"

"I guess she wouldn't."

"Vere wants me to move in right away," Lake said. "At the moment, a housekeeper is taking care of the dog."

"So what will you do?" she said.

"I'll get it cleared up. The trick is to minimize the unpleasantness. We have to at least go through the motions of taking the dog. But I'm sure something can be worked out fairly soon."

"Like what, Lake?" she said. He heard a note of disapproval but ignored it.

"Dogs change masters. It happens all the time."

She was silent.

"Let me work on it for a while," he said. "Don't talk to anybody about this. We have not talked about the dog."

"All right."

"I'll get back to you in a few days," he said.

After hanging up, he stared at the letter of agreement for a long time. It was a deed of bondage, a document that sought to enslave him to a dog. But he signed it. A delay in signing might arouse suspicion. Also, there was a positive reason to sign. Restraints always energized him. He would slip out of Aunt Ilsa's snare like Houdini.

———

At lunchtime the next day, he drove out to the house. He put his mind in neutral as he approached, wanting to see it as a potential buyer might. It was impressive. It had dignity, weight, solidity; the stone construction and slate roof belonged to a more substantial age. Surrounding the property was a low stone wall topped by a wrought-iron fence, decoratively but nastily spear-tipped: Privacy was assured. An old, well-pruned oak overhung the front lawn, dogwoods were tastefully scattered about, box bushes flanked the front steps, and the lawn was neatly kept. On either side of the property were other houses of the same style, each broadcasting the same social message. The street was quiet, removed from urban annoyances. Lake figured that Aunt Ilsa's house would sell for a lot of money.

He rang the doorbell. After a long time, the door opened and a prim face peered out. "Yes?"

"I'm Lake Stevenson, Mrs. Grinnell's nephew. What is your name please?"

"Mrs. Lundquist."

"I'm glad to meet you, Mrs. Lundquist."

She opened the door. Lake stepped into the front hall. The house seemed dim; he made a mental note to have the lights on when it was shown to potential buyers. Still, there was much to attract the eye—a Persian rug on the floor, a big gilt-framed mirror on the wall, a marble-topped table with a famille verte vase on it, a splendid hanging lamp. "I came out to make sure everything is all right," he said.

"I see." She looked at him through her glasses, expressionless. She was a portrait in gray—gray dress, gray hair, gray eyes behind the lenses. Her skin was very pale, almost transparent, with fine wrinkles.

"Mr. Vere suggested that I look in," he said.

"Yes, he told me that you would," she said.

"So how are things going?" he said.

"I beg your pardon?"

"How is everything?"

"Are you referring to Mrs. Grinnell's dog?"

"No, I meant is everything okay in the house, is there anything you need?"

"Mr. Vere has made sure that I have everything I need."

"You've been coming every day?"

"Yes, I come at eight-thirty and leave at four-thirty."

"What happens to the dog on weekends?"

"I take him for boarding at the pet store on Daymond Street. We take a taxi. Mr. Vere has arranged everything."

"I see. Mr. Vere was a friend of my aunt's, I believe."

"I believe so."

"And where is the dog today?"

"In the kitchen. He doesn't like it when people come to the house."

"Who has been coming?"

"Only the mailman and the deliverymen from Stieblers. Mrs. Grinnell always ordered groceries and household supplies from Stieblers. Mr. Vere instructed me to continue. Of course, Ada placed the orders before."

"Ada?"

"Mrs. Grinnell's cook."

"I have a cook?"

"No, Ada is no longer with the household. Mr. Vere let her go."

Lake noted her use of the word "household," suggesting that the job was somehow institutional.

"Everything seems quite well arranged," Lake said.

"Mr. Vere has been very thoughtful."

"Have you been with my aunt, the household, very long?"

"Nearly two years."

"I see. Well, she was a wonderful person."

"Yes."

"A bit on the rigid side, though, wouldn't you say?"

"It's not my place to say."

"She was. Do you mind if I have a look around? You go on with what you were doing."

She disappeared through a door at the back of the hall. He strolled into the living room. It was all very familiar, hardly changed from his childhood days: the ormolued table; the chintz sofa and velvet-covered chairs; the huge brass andirons behind the fire screen; the portrait of Uncle Paul over the mantelpiece, looking like a silver-haired raptor; the silk curtains; the lamps and tea caddies and Queen Anne candlesticks—all still here, his aunt's world, laden with time and memory. On the big table in front of the windows stood an array of photographs, some with his aunt or Uncle Paul in them, others showing people and places he didn't recognize. Lake picked up one, a picture of a springer spaniel sitting on a cushion near the helm of a big sailboat, looking very self-satisfied. The sainted Randall vacationing in Maine.

He sank into a chair. What he remembered most vividly of his childhood visits to this house was the urge to escape from the living room as quickly as possible. He and Karen had always slipped away to play in the attic while the adults talked: two little kids, light and expansive, rising out of a denser medium and floating upward. Even now, so many years later, he felt an urge to head for the attic refuge and renew his acquaintance with its musty treasures—cast-off furniture and boxes of odds and ends. Aunt Ilsa had probably never gone there; she had never known that there were things in this house that could be assembled into a palace or fort, especially if you had a little sister to help with the work and praise your creative genius.

He wandered out of the living room, exploring. Everywhere were signs of suspended domestic ritual—candles on the dining-room table waiting to be lit, a television in the library waiting to be turned on, a letter opener on the desk waiting for the mail. He went upstairs and investigated the bedrooms and dressing rooms and bathrooms. The closets were empty: at least his aunt's clothes had been taken away.

Then it was time to interview Randall in the kitchen. As he pushed through the door, the dog rose stiffly from the floor and gave a couple of lukewarm wags. He was brown and white, with floppy ears, brown eyes, a big pinkish nose, and a lugubrious expression.

"Hello, Randall," Lake said pleasantly.

The response was a perfunctory wag.

"Having a little nap?"

The dog ambled over and sniffed at his pants. He then turned around, went back to his spot, and lay down. Lake was content with this behavior. Randall was not a sociable dog, not even a likable dog. Definitely a disposable dog.

He looked in the refrigerator. Empty. He opened a closet door and saw a very large bag of dog food—enough to last many months, it seemed. "No such luck, Randall," he said.

The dog did not bother to lift his head, but his eyes followed Lake, monitoring the situation in a bored way. Deciding that communication with Randall should be kept to a minimum in view of what the future held, Lake left the kitchen, let the door swing shut behind him, went through the pantry and dining room and into the hall, and called to Mrs. Lundquist. She appeared at the top of the stairs. "Yes?" she said.

"I'm leaving now, Mrs. Lundquist. I'll probably be back this weekend."

"Will you be wanting the dog then?"

"No, do the usual boarding. I'm not sure of my schedule." He thought for a moment. "What did Mr. Vere say to you about the dog?"

"He told me you would be keeping the dog here, in accordance with Mrs. Grinnell's wishes."

"Right, that's right. But I'm not sure when I'll move in. So if you would just continue as you are, that would be good."

"All right."

"I'm sure we'll be very happy here," he said, thinking: While it lasts.

2

*H*e returned to the house with Ellen on Saturday afternoon, parked in the garage, and escorted her around to the front so that she would have a proper entrance.

"My, my," she said as they approached the front steps.

"A journey back through time," he said.

In the hall, Ellen stood stock-still, like some hunting creature, then headed for the living room. He followed. She inventoried with her eyes, touched curtains with a fingertip to judge the weight, trailed a hand along the back of a chair as she passed, peered out a window. Lake sensed that everything was being fitted into some highly developed mental model that he could never begin to comprehend.

"It's very auntlike," he said.

"It's not very you," she said.

"Definitely not."

"Who's that?" She pointed to the portrait over the fireplace.

"My aunt's husband, Uncle Paul. I never really knew him. He was much older. It was a second marriage for him."

"He looks like a captain of industry."

"He was a banker."

"Captain Paul," she said. "Was he the one with all the money?"

"Most of it."

"Look at those killer eyes."

"His killer instinct was underdeveloped, actually," Lake said.

She resumed her survey. They went into the library. She sat in a leather chair to test it, then moved to the chair behind the desk and pulled open a drawer. Lake could see that it held some sheets of paper. Probably it was just blank stationery, but he suddenly felt he should have spent time checking out the house on his own before bringing Ellen here. She opened another drawer.

"I haven't taken title yet," he said.

Ellen glanced up.

"I won't actually own the house for another few weeks, when all the legal stuff about the estate has cleared."

"But you said you were thinking about staying here."

"The executor wants me to, this guy Billington Vere. He thinks the house should have someone in it. It already does, in fact."

"I know."

"How?"

"Everything is dusted and polished."

He hadn't noticed. "There's a housekeeper."

Ellen led the way into the pantry and began opening drawers and cupboard doors. She proceeded into the kitchen, studied the stove, flipped up the trash-can lid with the foot pedal, checked the refrigerator. "How often does the housekeeper come?" she said.

"Every day."

"She must bring her own lunch."

"I guess."

Ellen opened the closet door and saw the bag of dog food. "What's this?"

"There's a dog. My aunt's dog."

"What's going to happen to it?"

"That hasn't been figured out yet."

"They should give it to the city pound for adoption. Where is it now?"

"At some kennel not far from here."

"Maybe the kennel can get it adopted."

"I'll look into that."

They went upstairs. Ellen was enjoying herself, he could tell. In his aunt's bedroom, he saw the flash of her hair reflected in a mirror, lifting sideways as she did a kind of pirouette; he became conscious of the bed, but he didn't want to think about that right now. "Want to see the garden?"

"Sure."

They went downstairs and out the garden door and onto the terrace.

"Hey," she said. "Wow."

"Major maintenance," he said. "Let's go."

"Why not stay awhile?"

"I don't want to hang around here," he said.

"I do." She took his arm. They stood for a moment, still looking out on the garden. He grew restless and led her into the library and turned on the television set, and they watched the news. When the program was over, he said, "You must be getting hungry. Let's go."

"Let's order a pizza."

Later they talked for a long time as color drained from the sky outside the library window and the leaves sagged black in the stillness. An airplane dragged its noise over the house and left it in a deeper hush than before. Lake sat at one end of the sofa and Ellen at the other.

"That must have been your aunt in the photographs on the table in the other room," she said. "Very thin and elegant."

"That's her," he said. "She was an interesting character."

"What was she like?"

"Opinionated."

"That's all?"

"She was a person who knew her own mind and made sure you knew it too. But we got along okay."

"You said she didn't get along with your father."

"No."

"How come?"

"He misbehaved."

"Why don't you ever talk about him? What did he do? What's so terrible?"

"He does whatever he feels like doing. Usually women are part of it."

"Is that why your parents split?"

"He got involved with his best friend's wife. There was a big uproar."

"I bet," she said.

"Then he did it again after he moved to Greenwich. He sort of makes a career of it. Right now, he's between marriages."

Ellen was silent.

"What are you thinking about?" he said.

"Nothing. Work."

"Being in this house isn't very relaxing," Lake said.

"I feel relaxed."

"I'll feel relaxed when I sell it."

She didn't reply.

"So what are you thinking about work?" he said.

"We had a big reshuffle yesterday. Bob was promoted to CFO. Now I'm working for Harry McQueen. He got Bob's job as controller."

"Well, you're rid of Bob."

"Yes."

"That should make life easier."

"Harry McQueen is an asshole."

"It's better than having a sadist for a boss," Lake said.

"But."

"But what?"

"Bob was letting me do some financial analysis. I thought he was trying me out for something. I thought he liked my work."

"Did he ever actually say so?"

"Yes."

"He did?"

"He said I was doing a good job."

"When was that?" Lake said.

"A few weeks ago, in my evaluation. He said I have a lot of promise. I always thought that at least he was honest."

"You think he isn't?"

"Yesterday some people were talking about him. Edith said she didn't understand how someone could be so positive in evaluations and so negative the rest of the time. He didn't even bother to tell anybody he would be leaving the controller's department. It was like instant sayonara. So long, peons. The rocket is leaving and unfortunately there's no room for you on this trip."

"Bob isn't worth hating," Lake said.

*F*or the next two weeks, he was too busy to think much about the house. A manual for some software was moving through the last stages of design and editing. Danny grappled enthusiastically with the project, working late every night and spending days talking on the telephone with software engineers.

"Where did you learn to speak that language, Danny?" Lake said.

"You pick it up. It's just logic."

"I'm appointing you Vice President in Charge of Logic."

"Is this a promotion?"

"It's an empty title."

"It sounds like a promotion."

"You're always jumping to logical conclusions. But it doesn't work with me, because I'm President in Charge of Nonlogic. I specialize in logical flaws."

"What's the flaw?"

"I'm the president."

Mary said, "He's not really insane, Danny. He's perverse."

On a Wednesday morning, Lake devoted half an hour to analyzing a booklet on worker safety in a lumberyard. It had been produced by someone in the lumber company and was riddled with problems—cryptic warnings, a blaming tone, afterthoughts. At one point a phrase seemed to link higher pay to faster work. A plaintiff's lawyer would love it.

The phone rang and Mary said, "Someone named Vere."

Lake picked up. "Good morning, Mr. Vere."

"Good morning, Mr. Stevenson." Vere's voice had a slight quaver of age, but it was firm underneath. "I'm calling to make sure there are no problems."

"None at all," Lake said. "I've been to the house a few times. This is a busy period for me."

"Of course."

"I appreciate how you've taken care of everything."

"Mrs. Lundquist seems capable," Vere said. "I trust the dog is being cared for."

"Yes, Randall is fine. In good spirits, considering."

"Losing an owner is quite traumatic for a dog, I would think."

"He's handling it well," said Lake. "No credit to me. I haven't been able to spend as much time with him as I would like."

"Your aunt had a deep feeling for dogs."

"I know that."

"She valued their loyalty."

"It's easy to tell that Randall has a faithful nature," Lake said.

"But it's typical of your aunt that she regarded the relationship in terms of mutuality. She was a remarkable woman. We were great friends, you know."

"I thought so. Yes, she was special."

"She had a rare feeling for what is right."

"Right," said Lake stupidly.

"I will never forget what she said to Laura after she had a car accident. My wife, Laura. She said, 'The first day you're on your feet, you come driving with me, and we'll drive through that intersection twenty times until you know it wasn't your fault.' It wasn't, you know. They had changed the timing on the light."

"I see."

"That was a little more than a year ago."

"They should have put up a sign or something."

"It was typical of your aunt's kindness. But I'm rambling. I only called to be sure you don't have any questions or problems. You should receive title in just a few days. This has been an unusually simple estate, and I'm delighted we've been able to wrap it up so quickly. We can work out the last details next week. Do you expect to move in soon?"

"As soon as I can manage it," Lake said.

"I trust your sister is well."

"Yes, she is."

"I must call her. Incidentally, I'm pleased that we will be neighbors."

"What?"

"I live in Chestnut Hill, too."

"Ah."

"If you need any help or advice, you must let me know. As a neighbor."

"Great. I will."

"I'll be in touch next week."

"Nice talking to you," Lake said. As he hung up, the phone almost slipped out of his sweating palm. He had let things drift. He needed an action plan for the house and the dog.

Mary said, "Shall I order in lunch?"

"Yes. No. I might go out for a while and walk around."

"Which one? Yes lunch or no lunch?"

"Yes lunch, but I might go out and walk around for a while and then come back."

"I'm ordering tuna fish. Yes or no?"

"Yes."

"Yes white toast or no white toast?"

"Okay, Mary. I've got a lot on my mind." He began to formulate an approach to the dog problem. The first principle was to have all the facts. Should he ask some lawyer whether the will was enforceable? He rejected that idea. It wasn't, he was sure—but getting approval to sell the house might involve going to court and being accused of bad faith. Vere, for one, would probably never see it from his point of view. Such messiness was unnecessary, however. The straightforward, simple way to remove the difficulty of the dog was to remove the dog.

Another good principle was stealth. To avoid any glitches or suspicions, he had to operate under deep cover and not reveal his intentions to anyone. Unfortunately, he had already mentioned to Karen that he might do something about Randall. That was probably a mistake, but he could trust Karen. Besides, he had been vague. Besides, they were in this together.

Another good principle was to be aware of fringe factors. Did Mrs. Lundquist care about the dog? He suspected she didn't, since she kept him locked in the kitchen. But maybe she saw herself as a protectress of the house. He would have to ease her out of the picture somehow. Maybe he should also try to get a better read on Vere. On the other hand, that was probably an acquaintanceship best left unpursued.

Then there was the matter of pacing. He was determined to get rid of the house as soon as possible, but he must give the appearance of sincere compliance with the will, briefly anyway. That would require living in the house for a while: minimally, two or three weeks of time with the dog, then a few more weeks after the dog disappeared—a decent interval, sufficient to erase all hope of Randall's return.

The key question was how to get rid of the dog. In theory, death was an option, but no matter how he felt about Aunt Ilsa's machinations, he couldn't do that. On the other hand, he could easily see himself losing a dog. Many people lost their dogs. It was commonplace. Life went on.

Some possible methods of losing a dog were: (1) deposit the dog in another state and drive away; (2) tie up the dog to the gate of the city pound at 4 A.M. and drive away; (3) take the dog for a walk and become separated.

Lake liked the walk-and-separation idea. A walk ending in the loss of a dog had no criminal overtones, no signs of malice aforethought. It would be an act of fate, more or less. That was the way.

Randall's destiny was to get lost. Someone would find him, and all parties would be happy thereafter.

He looked up and saw that Mary had resorted to one of her favorite communication tactics: a Lake tableau. She was sitting motionless at her desk, chin in hand, staring dreamily into space. Her free hand held a pencil that was pointed off into space. In front of her, facing Lake's desk, was a cardboard sign with large block letters:

LAKE THINKING

"Okay," he said, "I'm going back to work."

She took the sign down and turned to her computer.

"This place is like one long mutiny," he said. "It's a good thing I have great leadership skills."

"Right," said Mary, but affectionately.

"*D*id Vere call you?" he said to Karen on the phone that night. "He told me he was going to."

"Yes, we had a long talk this morning."

"What about?"

"Mostly Aunt Ilsa and how she was such a special person and how much she cared about animals. I think he really admired her."

"No doubt."

"He told me it would be all right to skip this summer with the dog," Karen said. "I explained about the Martha's Vineyard lease.

He said he thought you might be willing to keep Randall for the summer just this once."

"He thought wrong."

"He told me you seemed fond of the dog."

"The dog is retarded."

"What are you going to do?"

"A new destiny will unfold."

"Lake."

"What?"

"You're getting peculiar."

"Look. I don't want the house. The dog is the only obstacle to selling it, so the dog will have to cease to be an obstacle. There are some perfectly decent ways of handling that. It's a question of being fair to all concerned. By the way, don't say anything to anyone about any of this."

"You don't have to keep telling me. I heard you the first time."

"Good."

"But I would like to know about the new destiny," she said.

"The details haven't been worked out. You don't have to worry, though. No harm will come to Randall."

"I certainly hope not."

He changed the subject. "How should I go about selling the house? You've done it. I've never owned a house."

"Call some real estate agents. Pick one."

"Is there any way a sale can be done privately?"

"Maybe an agent will know exactly the right buyer. But if you sell it, people are going to find out sooner or later. Sales are reported in the papers, not to mention moving vans and all that."

"But it's possible to be discreet?"

"I think so."

"How do I find a good agent?"

"Ask around."

"I can't ask around. That's exactly what I can't do. Not now, anyway."

"I know one real estate agent in Philadelphia," Karen said. "I think *you* know her."

"Who's that?"

"Jennifer Dee. We went to school together. Don't you remember her? We were friends."

"Sort of dark hair?"

"Yes."

"She can't have much experience in real estate if you were classmates."

"She's been doing it for three years. She's probably a terrific agent, and she's very nice."

"Maybe," he said doubtfully. "Anyway, there's no hurry. I'm going completely underground on this. Remember, we haven't talked."

"You'd better not do anything bad to that dog, Lake," she said.

Lake hung up, thinking: Was that a threat?

*O*n a Thursday in late May, he drove to Chestnut Hill for a pre-move inspection. He was now the legal owner of 73 Peal Avenue, with all its furniture and furnishings, plus one expendable dog. He felt prosperous. InstruX Associates was doing well. The proceeds from the sale of the house would make him highly liquid. As he drove, he transposed his future self to the leather seat of a large Mercedes sedan, whispery quiet, with Vivaldi on the sound system and several hundred horsepower underfoot. He could also see himself in something sportier—perhaps a Porsche, maybe red. Also, he might travel. He and Ellen would go skiing next winter; they could take up scuba diving. The Caribbean beckoned, awash with sun and rum.

In the meantime, he would operate the house in a businesslike manner. He decided to dispense with the gardening service and cut the lawn himself. Mrs. Lundquist would be reduced to a couple of days a week, sufficient to keep the place cosmetically clean. That meant he would have to take over most of the dog care, of course, but a brief bout of dog ownership wouldn't be much of a burden. Dogs sleep a lot. They have simple tastes in food. They don't get sick. You only have to walk them once or twice a day. A slow-witted, lethargic dog like Randall would be no trouble at all.

He let himself in the front door with his key. "Mrs. Lundquist?" he called. The house was silent and chilly.

After a while, he heard footsteps approach the head of the stairs. Mrs. Lundquist peered down. "Yes?"

Lake wondered what she did up there. Why was she always upstairs?

"How are you today?" he said in his friendliest fashion.

"I'm well, thank you."

"Do you have a minute?"

"Yes." She came down.

"Where's Randall? In the kitchen, as usual?"

"Yes."

"Maybe I'll take him for a walk. I'm going to be moving in

permanently tomorrow, Mrs. Lundquist. I'll only be bringing my clothes at first. I think I'll probably have a decorator look the house over before I do the full move. I may want to make big changes."

"I see."

"I have to talk to you about something else. I won't be needing you five days a week. This is kind of abrupt, I realize, but I figure it's best to come straight to the point." He was watching her closely. She remained expressionless. "I'll be much more self-sufficient than my aunt was. I'm sure you understand. I want you to know I'm very grateful that you've been here during this transitional period, but I think two days a week should be enough from now on. Mondays and Fridays, let's say. Starting next week. With notice, of course. Let's say two weeks at the usual full wages, but you can switch to the new schedule next week. How would that be?"

"I see."

"See what?"

"I'll have to think about it."

"When can you let me know?" he said. "If you don't want to do it, I'll understand."

"Perhaps you'd like to find someone else."

"No, no, it's not that—you're perfect. I'm sure you do an excellent job. I can see you do. But I live a different way from my aunt." Realizing she might misinterpret this, he added, "I'm used to being on my own. I like to do a little cleaning now and then. It's good exercise."

She stared at him.

"With me pitching in," he said, "two days a week ought to be enough."

"This is a large house."

"Think it over and let me know. I'll be at my office this afternoon and tomorrow. I assume you'll come tomorrow, right?"

She didn't reply.

"Here's my card."

She took the InstruX card and examined it for booby traps—tiny razor blades soaked in curare, messages from the Antichrist.

"I'll give Randall a walk," he said. "Where do you take him?"

"I let him out in the yard."

"He never goes farther than that?"

"No."

"How long do you leave him there?"

"For twenty minutes in the morning and twenty minutes before I leave."

Ah, thought Lake. The dog problem might be solved by simply opening the gate and releasing Randall into the outer world. It was the sort of innocent mistake a first-time owner might easily make.

"Thank you, Mrs. Lundquist. You've been very understanding."

He went to the kitchen. "Hello, Randall," he said. The dog lay on the floor, sunk in his usual torpor. He didn't even bother to wag his tail. "We've got a problem, Randall, and you're it," Lake said. "Our time together is going to be brief."

To keep things friendly, he stroked the top of Randall's head. The cranium was quite small, with not much room for brains. Probably nine-tenths of the brain tissue was devoted to analyzing smells. That left one-tenth for all other senses and any logical functions. Lake estimated that only about a hundredth of the total brain volume was assigned to handling relationships with other creatures such as humans. Considering the cranial capacity, Randall's goldfishlike behavior was not surprising.

"Come on," he said. Randall followed him to the front door, down the steps, and out onto the lawn. "Remember," Lake said, "freedom is a precious gift."

Randall lifted his leg on a box bush, turned to sniff the bush, turned and lifted his other leg, sniffed at the bush, sniffed at the grass, looked around. So far, he had gone about six feet from the front steps. Casually, Lake walked down the path, opened the gate, and stepped aside. Randall appeared not to notice the route to freedom. The dog's obtuseness was a problem.

Randall devoted himself to investigating the bushes along the right side of the house, reading leaf and soil with point-blank nosework. In the meantime, Lake inspected the perimeter of the property, looking for a weakness in the fence, anything that might lead to the disappearance of a dog, even if Randall was unlikely to use the getaway route on his own. The fence was intact everywhere.

In the garden, little bushes and yellow and pink things were in bloom, and also some tall blue things, and the beds were neatly edged and weeded. It made a pleasing sight. He sat on the terrace, imagining his aunt whiling away the afternoon with a book, taking tea and saying the occasional fond word to the springer spaniel sleeping at her feet. He saw it in mezzotint, a scene from a distant time. The likeliest and most appropriate buyer of the house, he felt, would be an older person, a little tired, no longer part of the hurly-burly of the world. As for himself, he would be merely a transitional moment in the history of the house, a sort of catalyst who would disappear the moment 73 Peal Avenue was back in proper hands. That was a good way to look at it, he felt: to sell the house was to restore the natural order of things.

After a while, he retrieved Randall. He noticed a slight jingling and reached down to identify its source. On the dog's collar was a tag that said: *RANDALL Mrs. Ilsa Grinnell 73 Peal Avenue Philadelphia PA 19118*. It would have to be removed. As he closed the kitchen door, he said, "Soon you'll get a much longer walk, Randall." The dog wagged his tail.

Lake's next stop was a hardware outlet that sold lawn mowers. The choice was more extensive than he expected, and the price tags were uniformly astounding. A salesman came over as Lake examined the row of machinery.

"Can I help you?"

"I need a lawn mower."

"How big is your lawn?"

"About half an acre, I guess."

"This tractor is one of our best-sellers."

"I don't need a tractor."

"A large rotary, then," the salesman said. "This one is a good machine." He pointed to a massive red rotary mower with a chute to catch the grass.

"How about the old kind you push?" said Lake.

"A reel mower?" the salesman said with distaste. "That's in another department. You're going to need more than that."

"I can handle it."

Five minutes later, Lake was the owner of a reel mower that cost less than one visit by the gardening service, was environmentally friendly, and would provide aerobic benefit to the user. He drove back to Peal Avenue, unloaded it in the garage, bolted on the handle, and took it for a test run in the garden. He liked the smooth sound of metal scissoring against metal. He liked the way grass flew out the back as the wheels sped along and the blades spun. This was not a proper test, since the lawn had been cut a day or two before, but he was satisfied that the mower was a fine piece of engineering.

It didn't mow a very wide swath, however. Lake cut along the edge of a flower bed and back. He misjudged the overlap and left a mohawk stripe between the cuts. He mowed the stripe and made a few more up-and-back runs, until he had sweated through his shirt. A quick survey of the amount of lawn still left to be mowed—not counting the grass in the front of the house—indicated that cancellation of the gardening service would be a bad move. He put the mower in a corner of the garage and headed for the office, reminding himself that small miscalculations occur in every campaign. Only the big decisions mattered.

Mrs. Lundquist did not call that afternoon. Lake drove out to Peal Avenue the next morning to feed Randall in case she had not showed up, but she was there, dusting the living room.

"Good morning," he said.

"Good morning."

"I was hoping to hear from you."

"I had intended to leave you a note."

"What will the note say?"

"I will be here on Monday."

"Good. Fridays as well?"

"Yes."

"Good."

"I spoke to Mr. Vere," she said.

"Why?" said Lake. "Vere is out of the picture now. He has nothing to do with this house."

"He's been very thoughtful."

"I know that, but he's out of it now. This is between us."

"Mr. Vere spoke to me several weeks ago. He asked me to call him in case there was any change in my employment. Mrs. Vere has been needing some more help in her house."

"What does Mrs. Vere have to do with it?"

"I will be going to her on Tuesdays, Wednesdays, and Thursdays."

"You'll be working for the Veres?"

"On Tuesdays, Wednesdays, and Thursdays."

He digested this news, hardly believing it. Vere had suborned his housekeeper. He had put her in his employ and now would be able to keep tabs on Lake without even lifting the phone. For a moment, he thought about firing Mrs. Lundquist then and there. But on what grounds? He couldn't accuse her of disloyalty. He couldn't say that he had decided to take over all cleaning himself.

"That's very nice," he said.

"Mrs. Vere has difficulty getting around. She was in an automobile accident."

"So I understand."

"Will you be paying the notice next week?"

"The notice?"

"You said you would give me notice for the three days you won't be needing me."

"Ah, the notice."

"And I will need some Johnson floor wax and some Top Job."

"Okay, okay, I'll get it. Leave me a list of whatever you need and I'll buy it this weekend."

She returned to her dusting. Lake left without bothering to check on Randall. In his irritation, he was inclined to drop the walk-and-separation option and switch to a plan that involved violence. He was tempted to strike soon.

3

The whole day was a dead loss. On his desk was a manufacturer's rough draft of assembly instructions for an outdoor barbecue grill.

The manifold pipe ought to slip into the right front notch and the ignition wires will be loose beneath the burner (if applicable).

He glared at the words, knowing he would have to send Danny to the plant to figure out what was intended.

Note: the front flange should bottom out on the edge of the post when rotated to engage the rear flange.

Danny's trip would be billable, but Lake hated to have him out of the office, since it meant that Lake would have to deal with the software engineers on the computer project. He decided to record all conversations with them; later, Danny could interpret.

Seal joints with a compound unaffected by liquefied petro-leum gases or any other chemical constituents of the gases.

He finally shoved the draft away; he had more pressing problems to worry about. The Lundquist-Vere alliance was a serious complication. Mrs. Lundquist would be in a position to give Vere regular briefings on everything Lake did—how he treated the dog, whether he was actually moving in or just faking it, everything. Twice a week, on Mondays and Fridays, Lake would have a viper in his house, slithering about, its tongue licking the air. Three times a week, the viper would slither over to the Veres with evil reports. Was it possible Vere had planned this maneuver from the beginning? Lake decided the executor could not be that clever.

He called Ellen. "Hi. You busy?"

"Very."

"Still have to work late?"

"It looks like very late."

"Call me later, if you can. I'll be at my aunt's house to-night."

"Your house, you mean."

"My house, I mean."

"I still don't understand why you want to spend time there if you're going to sell it."

"I want to make sure I know what I'm selling. It won't be for long."

"You might get to like it."

"I won't get to like it."

"I think it's great."

"Then it'll sell fast," he said.

"I have to get back to work," Ellen said. "Bye now. Wait a minute."

He waited, hoping for a change of mind.

"I just had a thought," she said.

"Good," he said.

"No—another kind of thought. Listen. You have a house. You're moving in for a while. You should have a housewarming."

"A housewarming?"

"A party."

"I don't want a party."

"We'll give a party in your new house."

"Ellen, no."

"I've got to go."

"No party," he said. "It would be disrespectful. Maybe in a few months, but not now. No party."

"Think about it," she said.

*B*y the time he reached the house, he was in such a bad mood that he didn't bother to check on Randall. Instead, he watched the news on television, all the way through the movie reviews and minor local fluff. After a while, guilt about the dog began to creep over him and contaminate his justifiable annoyance at Mrs. Lundquist and Vere and even Ellen. He went to the kitchen, liberated Randall without a word of greeting, and returned to the library. Randall followed close behind; he lay at Lake's feet, composed himself in a ball, and shut his eyes. "Don't get too comfortable," Lake said. He reached down and worked the tag off the dog's collar, putting it in his pocket. "Now you don't belong to anyone," he said. "You're nobody's dog."

Later, feeling bored, he began rummaging through the cabinets beneath the library shelves. They were filled with labeled folders and boxes—his aunt's archives. Several boxes were devoted to financial records, which might provide a future evening's amusement but didn't interest him now. In one box was a trove of travel literature about austere places like Greenland or the Faeroe Islands, well suited to his aunt's temperament. Another contained a harvest of garden-club newsletters. He glanced through folders filled with animal-charity documents and perused a clip file of newspaper and magazine articles dealing mainly with canine behavior. In the margins of the articles were his aunt's comments: *precisely;* or *an ignorant conclusion;* or *springers far superior.*

Many boxes in the cabinets were filled with correspondence— mostly letters from friends, chronologically organized. He scanned a few of the letters; they were chatty, not very interesting. One box of correspondence was labeled "Institute of Animal Understanding." Unable to resist the name, Lake pulled the box out, took it to the desk, selected a few letters, and read them with growing wonderment. Each bore the letterhead *Institute of Animal Understanding,* and each was from a man named Ernest Jeffords—evidently the director of that organization.

Dear Mrs. Grinnell:

Please allow me to extend my sincere thanks for your generous contribution to our special drive. Your support of the Institute is greatly appreciated. Research into animal communication has reached an exceptionally fruitful stage, and—as you know—our regard for Dr. Stapleton's work is unqualified. Your donation will do much to sustain his efforts.

May I say, too, that the Institute always values your thoughts about animal intelligence, so commonly underestimated. You are entirely too modest in your self-appraisal. Many important advances in our understanding of nature have been made by individuals who lacked formal scientific training. The 19th-century British physicist Michael Faraday is an example. As you no doubt know, he lifted the veil on many electrical and magnetic phenomena. He possessed little formal mathematical training, but his intuitive abilities more than made up for this deficiency. Why should it not be the same in our arena of investigation?

I was fascinated by your description of how you choose a new puppy. To observe a litter of six-week-old pups and somehow "just know" what that puppy will become is, I think, an experience many of us have had yet cannot ever quite explain. You, however, ask this intuiting process to bear a weight that is quite extraordinary. Until now, I had not been aware of your preference for having only one dog at a time. The selection of a puppy from a litter must thus be an experience of great intensity for you, the stakes being so high, as it were. (I myself have four dogs of various breeds, the oldest now 12, the youngest 1 year.) I rejoice in your saying that you have never erred. In my own case, I must confess to erring more than once, very likely because I did not allow myself to "just know" but lapsed into reasoning, analyzing the pros and cons, and so forth.

You speak of the choice of a puppy as "mutual recognition," a "call." I would very much like to hear more from you about this. We know that animals and people understand one another in ways that can seem almost telepathic. Your idea of "recognition" is breathtaking.

I did not quite understand your point about a similar "recognition" when you purchased your summer house in Maine. Are you saying that "calls" come to you whenever you make important life decisions?

Whatever its extent, I take great pleasure in hearing that you possess this gift. No one could be more deserving.

I will, of course, keep you fully informed about activities at the Institute and particularly about the progress of Dr. Stapleton. In the meantime, may I thank you once again for your generosity and for being such a good and unfailing friend to our cause.

Yours sincerely,
Ernest Jeffords

This man, Lake surmised, was addicted to his aunt's money. He would do anything to keep it flowing in his direction.

The next letter was dated a month later.

Dear Mrs. Grinnell:

Forgive the tardiness of my reply to your letter. It is due in part to the press of work at this time of year and also to a need to give careful thought to your amplification of the idea of a "call" or a "recognition." These matters are, I confess, beyond the usual scope of my studies. I am flattered that you think I might have something to say about them.

Subject to your correction, I gather the sequence of events was as follows:

You and your husband spent summers in Maine for several years and had become very interested in the history of the state, especially the very early history. One day, walking near a headland, you "felt" a call. (How very interesting that you use the word felt.*) You sensed something in the land there, a "presence." Subsequently, you discovered the property was for sale and purchased it, knowing you were supposed to have it.*

I may have confused these events somewhat because of the manner in which you described them in your letter—in a fashion I might characterize as poetic, in the best sense of that term. I was not certain what you meant by "a field of hidden life," for example, although you are quite correct in noting that Michael Faraday too studied invisible fields— electrical in his case. Also, I did not understand your reference to a "Pinecroft." Is Pinecroft some coastal feature? Is it a house?

You are right in surmising that I have an interest in historical matters. Maine's history is indeed fascinating, not least because the earliest chapters are wrapped in mystery. It is not unthinkable, I suppose, that Indian magic could be associated with that spot. I might also mention the voyage of some Irish monks led by St. Brendan, said to have taken place long before Columbus. According to legend, they sailed far across the North Atlantic in a small vessel and fetched up on an unknown shore. If I recall correctly, their adventure included many magical events, rather Celtic in flavor, although the monks were Catholic, naturally. Perhaps they landed in Maine. Perhaps some touch of magic lingers where they came ashore. Who knows? You may have sensed it these many centuries later.

This takes us far from the usual concerns of the Institute, of course, but the phenomenon of "recognition" does seem to have some application with animals, as you noted in your very interesting letter about choosing puppies. Indeed, it has occurred to me that your thoughts about the selection of a pet may perhaps point toward a research program that the Institute could initiate and support.

Yours sincerely,
Ernest Jeffords

The next followed in mere days:

Dear Mrs. Grinnell:

I was frankly upset by the tone of your most recent letter and must protest that you are quite wrong to think that (1) I believe you to be a Roman Catholic; (2) I implied that you are of Irish descent. *It was not my intention to suggest a connection between yourself and St. Brendan. I was merely musing about a possible spiritual or even supernatural aspect of the early history of Maine. Please accept my apologies for infelicitous phrasing. I would not for the world offend one who has been so generous and steadfast in supporting our cause and whose ideas I have always found so stimulating.*

Your pride in your Norwegian forebears can only be commended. Did you know, by the way, that Scandinavians settled in Ireland in the first millennium of our era? Dublin began as a Viking community. Who is to say that Norwegian blood did not run in the veins of those bold monks who voyaged across the North Atlantic to an unknown landfall?

Yours sincerely,
Ernest Jeffords

Lake kept reading.

Dear Mrs. Grinnell:

This is written in some haste, since I am off to California for two weeks.

No, I am afraid that the springer spaniel breed did not originate in Norway, nor among the Vikings who settled in Ireland. All the authorities seem to agree that their line began in Spain in the Middle Ages.

Sincerely,
Ernest Jeffords

The next few letters were desperate attempts to regain favor, a campaign that apparently succeeded when his aunt asked Jeffords about the possibility of dog reincarnation and he promised that the Institute would sponsor research into that very interesting idea— with her financial assistance, of course.

Lake closed the box in disgust.

*S*leep that night was thick with dreams. The worst one was about a strange remaking of reality. In the dream, he saw houses, buildings, streets, alleyways, but they had no human meaning. They were a dog's world, full of smells and dangers and things to chase. He had to wake up to escape.

He stared into the darkness, knowing he was in foreign space. The tentacles of the dream reached toward him. He got up, intending to splash cold water on his face in the bathroom. He took a few steps and ran into a wall, banging his head. Then he remembered that he was in his aunt's bedroom. Where was the bathroom? Where was the bed that he had just left? He stood still, trying to reassemble his knowledge of this terrain. Gradually the elements came together. The bed was behind him. The bathroom was on the other side of the bed—exactly the opposite of the layout of his own bedroom in his own apartment. It was all wrong.

But hitting his head had at least fended off the dream, and afterward he slept deeply, not arising until eight o'clock. An orchestra of bugs and birds filled the morning with sound. He opened the curtains. Sunshine poured past him, flooding into every corner of the room, splashing off the glass top of the dressing table, surging into the depths of the mirror. Even on the best days, his apartment never received this kind of light.

He wandered downstairs and looked for coffee in the kitchen cupboards. The cupboards were empty. That wasn't a surprise, but he resented it.

He hunted for Randall and finally found him in the library, topping off his ten hours of nighttime sleep with a morning nap. Lake went straight to the front door, swung it open, hustled Randall out, shut the door, and went upstairs to dress. He drove to a 7-Eleven and bought English muffins and instant coffee and a newspaper. When he returned, he found Randall near an azalea bush, vacuuming the ground with his nose. Lake made a cup of coffee, toasted his muffin, and went out onto the terrace to read the newspaper. Randall came over and sat beside the chair, expectant.

"What is it?" Lake said.

Randall maintained his laserlike gaze.

"What do you want?"

The reply was an intensification of the stare to a level of hope and need that could burn through any defense. Lake tore off a piece of English muffin and gave it to Randall. The dog gobbled it down and waited for more.

"No more," Lake said, and put the newspaper between himself and the pressure of those begging eyes.

The Saturday edition included a real estate section. He looked through it for anything that might relate to Chestnut Hill, but the section was almost entirely devoted to new houses, advertised in language that was both lush and seductive. The words spoke of exclusive communities, grand foyers, immense living rooms, ducal dining rooms, sweeping staircases, luxurious master suites. Amid the phantasmagoria of adjectives floated pen-and-ink pictures of cozy town houses, maple-shaded colonials, and pillared Georgian edifices with rooms beyond counting. As for the outdoors, the ads offered stately exteriors, lawns that seemed to go on forever, access to boundless parkland, vistas of water, promises of unassailable privacy. It was a vision of housing heaven.

From the depths of memory came something his kindergarten teacher once said. Lake remembered her as a kindly woman with a soft voice. She told the children that heaven was a happy land where everyone got to live in a big house. Someone in the class asked the teacher how many people could fit in heaven. "Everyone," she said. "But only if they are good."

He watched Randall for a while. The dog was now working his way around the base of a beech tree, absorbed in his nosework. Lake sipped coffee, read the sports section, gazed at the flowers, and let his mind drift. The house was all wrong, but it was peaceful. Probably he should spend less time here. Peace could be insidious. It was the opposite of action. A man of action kept his distance from peace.

Lake decided to let Randall spend the whole day outside to develop wilderness skills, just in case the disposal took a bad turn. He went upstairs to make the bed, since he and Ellen might come back here tonight. But why would they? He would much rather go to her place. He liked her apartment. But he made the bed anyway.

Then he conducted a search through the other rooms on the second floor, looking for a small, portable television set that he recalled seeing when he and Ellen had walked around the house. He found it in the bedroom at the far end of the upstairs hall. This had probably been the nurse's room during the last month of his aunt's life. An easy chair was pointed toward the television: that explained why Mrs. Lundquist spent so much time upstairs. He took note of the channel selector, planning to check the TV schedule to see whether the chosen channel carried a lot of soap operas. He was sure it did. The woman was sly, but he could handle her, and he could handle her spymaster, too.

Disinformation was the key—disinformation and a natural sequence of emotions. She and Vere would have to be convinced that Lake was making 73 Peal Avenue his lifetime residence. Mrs. Lundquist would observe abundant signs of friendliness toward Randall—friendliness ripening into true affection. She would then be a witness to Lake's distress when the dog disappeared. That tragedy would go far toward explaining why Lake had to sell the house quickly. Even Vere would understand that—with Aunt Ilsa's wishes undone by fate—73 Peal Avenue could only be a place of pain.

As a first step toward establishing a settled-in look, he drove to the supermarket and ranged up and down the aisles collecting cans of soup, soft drinks, cold cuts, boxes of cereal, trash bags, dishwashing detergent and dozens of other purchases that seemed likely items for a well-appointed kitchen. He piled two carts high with food and supplies, sufficient to suggest long-term occupancy. He bought a giant bag of dog food, which would raise the inventory to a wildly overstocked level. He bought ten bottles of Top Job, an amount that would indicate to Mrs. Lundquist that he expected her to be cleaning the house well into her dotage. The total outlay came to more than two hundred dollars, but he figured it was a good investment: Mrs. Lundquist's reports to Vere would describe a young man whose domestic instincts had enabled him to make the transition from a small apartment to a large household with remarkable ease.

After Lake unloaded the bags, he drove to his apartment, where he selected enough clothes to make a dent on the vacant closets and drawers in his aunt's bedroom. By the time he returned to the house and put everything away, it was three o'clock. He saw Randall puttering around outside and went hunting for a leash. It was time to reconnoiter. They set out on a walk.

The ideal method of disposal, Lake figured, would be to lose Randall during a completely routine outing. Dog and master would be walking along, perfectly content in each other's company; master takes off leash to let dog enjoy himself more fully; dog chases animal or follows scent while master is not looking; when dog is out of sight, master hurries off, making minimal noise but moving at high speed; master goes home, leash in hand, sorrowful expression on face; tagless dog seeks out new master and, with any luck, lives happily ever after.

Of course, the release would have to occur far enough away so that the dog could not find his way home. Lake was not sure how far that was, although Randall's low intelligence and lassitude suggested the distance need not be great. He walked for about fifteen minutes, following a random course to prevent Randall from memorizing the route. But Randall was unconcerned with navigation; he was experiencing a succession of adventures—squirrel sightings, another dog barking at him, the reading, here and there, of olfactory messages. At many points along the way, he added territory to his personal holdings.

They came to a little park, and at once Lake felt this was a suitable place for dog and master to part ways. At the far side of the park, beyond a field, was a patch of woods, just the sort of obscuring terrain where the master could slip away without his dog noticing. Best of all, other dog owners frequented this park, which meant that Randall's lack of a master would be quickly noticed and protective measures taken.

In the center of the field stood a middle-aged man and two girls who looked like college students. Their dogs swirled close by. Lake headed in their direction. Suddenly Randall jerked the leash out of his hand and sped toward a large, blondish dog. Lake let him go and strolled over to the group. He wanted to see if any of these people recognized Randall or had known Aunt Ilsa.

"Hi," said the girls. The man gave Lake a nod of greeting and glanced at Randall, saying, "How old is he?"

Lake surmised that this was a standard opening gambit in dog-owner conversations. "Five, almost six," he said. "How old is yours?"

"He's a real old soldier," said the man, gazing fondly at his dog, a big one with silver-flecked red hair. "Almost twelve."

"That's old," said Lake.

"But still going strong," the man continued, somewhat defensively. "Still likes to run, don't you, boy?" As far as Lake could see, the dog showed no signs of liking to run. He stayed right by his master, who stroked his grizzled head.

One of the girls said, "What's your dog's name?" She looked good in her purple tee shirt.

"Randall. How about yours?"

"Chloe."

Chloe was the blond dog that Randall had charged off to see; now he was sniffing her indecently. "Nice name," Lake said. "What kind of dog is she?"

"Yellow Lab," she said, in a tone suggesting that this should be obvious to anyone who called themselves a dog owner.

"I don't know too much about dogs," he said.

"That's a great-looking springer."

"Yeah, he's not so bad. I'm taking care of him for a while. Have you seen him at this park before?"

"I don't believe so," she said. "No, I'm sure I haven't."

Lake was prepared to let the conversation drop, but she said, "I'm Holly. This is Tina, my roommate."

"I'm Luke."

Holly was friendly and perky; she seemed to do all the talking for the two of them. "This is a great park for dogs," she said. "I come here all the time."

"On weekdays, too?"

"I have plenty of free time. I'm an aerobics instructor. I'm thinking of going back to school next year, though."

"I'm sort of in that line of work."

"I think I've seen you at that fitness club in Wyndmoor."

"No, I mean I'm in the instruction business. I create instructional materials. Mostly directions for how things work."

"What kind of things?"

"Every kind," he said. He decided that it was best not to talk about himself, considering future events. "How old is Chloe?" he said.

"A little over two."

He glanced over and saw that Randall's lust had become flagrant. "Sorry about his behavior. He has an impetuous personality."

"That's all right. She can take care of herself." Just then,

Chloe whirled on Randall and charged at him, snarling. He skittered out of the way, then slunk up to her again to continue his attentions.

"Do the dogs here ever stray?" he said. "It's a big space."

"What do you mean?"

"Do they ever get separated from their owners—you know, go poking around in the woods, lose their bearings?"

"I've never heard of it, but I guess it could happen. Sable took off once—Tina's dog."

"Only for an hour," Tina said. "He chased another dog. I drove everywhere looking for him. I spotted him going around the back of a supermarket."

"He didn't try to find his way home?"

"I think he panicked. I was really terrified. Sable is my munchkin, aren't you, Sable?" Sable was black and feral-looking, with predatory eyes.

"I wonder how Randall would handle the situation if he got lost," he mused.

"You have a tag on him, don't you?" Holly said.

"Not yet. I'll get one."

"He's a great-looking dog. You should definitely get a tag on him. A lot of people would like to have a dog like that."

"They might not try to find the owner, you mean?"

"Maybe," Holly said.

"But they'd probably take good care of him, right?"

Holly seemed puzzled. Tina said, "I was terrified that Sable would be hit by a car."

"Randall's not exactly a rocket scientist," he said, "but he knows about cars." He saw some other dog owners approaching.

"I've got to get back. Come on, Randall." He grabbed the leash and hauled him away from Chloe.

"Bye, Luke."

"Bye, Holly. Bye, Tina."

Thinking about the conversation on the way home, he concluded that the release would have to occur on a weekend, when plenty of people would be in the park. At worst, Randall would end up in a pound, where adoption was a certainty. But maybe one of the dog owners would take him in. A tagless dog of such high quality would probably find a new master instantly. All of the facts of the case pointed toward a rapid installment in a new home, a home where his presence would be truly appreciated, a more loving situation altogether.

*L*ater, sitting in the library, he grappled with his conscience. Abandoning the dog in the park was likely to reduce Lake's chances of having a nice house in heaven; that much seemed clear. And there was always the possibility that Randall would do something stupid and get himself hurt. Aunt Ilsa, of course, was the architect of this predicament. By placing dogs before people, she had created an impossible bind.

As Lake mulled the moral issues, Randall went over to the leather chair and stood in front of it. He looked back at Lake in a speculative way. He looked at the chair. He turned to look at Lake again, as if trying to make up his mind about something. Lake watched, fascinated. Suddenly Randall hopped on the chair, curled up, and shut his eyes, as if to indicate that—although he had just committed a crime in full view of the authorities—any protest would be in vain and the matter was closed.

Lake admired the dog's nerve. During the stern regime of Aunt Ilsa, hopping up on a chair would surely have been a felony. Randall had sized up the new owner as more liberal. The dog was more perceptive than he had thought.

As Lake reflected on the strictness of his aunt, the moral fog began to lift. He realized that Randall actually had been a prisoner here. The dog had been trapped in this house for his entire life—cosseted, maybe even doted on, but denied the free play of his instincts. He had been given no chance to hunt, to explore. He had known nothing but rules and boredom and confinement. For five years, he had been enduring slow emotional starvation. It was a life that he surely would have rejected had he been given a choice.

With that thought, the moral landscape changed. There was another way to look at the issues. Lake would shift the burden of choice to Randall. He would take Randall to the park, let him play to his heart's content, help him understand that there were alternatives to Peal Avenue. Then, in full view of the dog, with nothing shifty about it, Lake would start toward home. At that moment, Randall would have to decide whether to follow him or not. It would be a gift of freedom in the truest, most basic sense: the freedom to choose.

He was pretty sure what Randall would decide. Judging from today's expedition, the dog would choose the park. But the important thing was that the decision would be his. And if, contrary to all expectations, Randall decided to follow his master home, Lake would make arrangements for some sort of outplacement. He would install Randall in a distant kennel until an adoptive parent could be found.

Lake reviewed the procedure as Randall slept in the leather chair. He concluded that, under the circumstances, it was quite ethical—a form of canine empowerment, if you looked at it from the proper angle.

4

So what did you do today?" Ellen said as they drove to the restaurant to meet the Allens.

Because he couldn't tell her about his moral deliberations, he said, "I was busy around the house. It's ridiculous living in that much space."

"Space is nice."

"Think of all the energy wasted on lighting and heating rooms you use two minutes a day."

"There's no such thing as too much space."

"If everyone felt that way, we'd be in real trouble," he said.

"You're in a pleasant mood."

Lake tried to think of a comeback, but his heart wasn't in it. "I didn't realize how complicated this house thing was going to be," he said.

"You're making it complicated."

"What does that mean?"

"You have a funny attitude about it."

"I'm just not ready for this."

"For what?" she said.

He thought: For *this;* for the dog problem; for the lawn that was too big to cut without investing in a tractor; for the bathroom being on the wrong side of the bed; for Ellen's seeing the house as something more than a financial windfall. She hadn't mentioned the housewarming again, but he was sure she would.

A housewarming was not a totally bad idea, he realized. It might be seen by Mrs. Lundquist and Vere as evidence of commitment to his new residence. But what kind of a party could you have in a house like that?

"You know, I might take more vacation this summer," he said. "I was thinking it might be good to go to somewhere like Nantucket for a week or so in July or August. We could probably still get a house rental."

"Uh-huh."

"How does that sound?"

"Don't forget we're supposed to spend the Fourth with Susan and Charlie."

"I was thinking of maybe the last week of July and the first week of August."

"I might not be able to."

"Why? Is that budget time?"

"I might be in school."

"School," he said blankly.

"I'm going to take some classes."

"In the middle of the summer?"

"Beginning this summer. In about three weeks."

"What classes?"

"I'm going to get an MBA."

"You what?"

"A business degree."

"I know what an MBA is. Why do you want to do that?"

"Why not?"

"An MBA is a long program."

"Five or six years if you do it with night courses."

"Six years?" he said, barely comprehending.

"Or five."

"When did you decide this?"

"The last couple of days. I've been looking into it."

"You really want an MBA? I mean, you're in the controller's office. You don't need a whole MBA for that."

"Lake."

"When at night?"

"Tuesdays and Thursdays."

"Until what time?"

"About ten o'clock. Also, I would have a fairly big homework load."

"For six years."

They drove on in silence. Finally Lake said, "So you've definitely decided to do it."

"I haven't signed up for the classes yet, but I'm going to. Why does it bother you so much?"

"No reason. If you want to, you should."

She looked straight ahead.

"You never once mentioned it," he said. "You didn't say a thing."

"I'm telling you now."

"It's none of my business, is that what you're saying?"

"No, I'm saying it's business. It's my career. You don't ask me how to run your business."

"I talk to you about it all the time."

"No, you don't."

"I do."

"You only think you do," she said.

"Well," he said, tired of arguing, "you'll end up running the company."

"I wouldn't want to."

"I thought you liked it."

"A business degree gives you options."

"Do you get any time off at all?"

"Sure. Between trimesters."

"Maybe we could go on that vacation between trimesters."

"Maybe you should go anyway," she said. But she softened. "I could come up for a weekend."

"No, that's no good."

"You should go. You never take vacations."

"I don't like to. Certainly not by myself."

"Maybe you should try it."

"What are you saying?"

"Nothing. Maybe you should try it, that's all."

"Maybe I should," he said. Black feelings were stirring in him—inky currents with no name. "Why are we arguing like this? Let's stop arguing. Listen, I guess I was insensitive."

"I hate it when you say things like 'Certainly not by myself.' I hate that."

"But it's true."

"I know," she said.

"I don't see what's wrong with it."

"I know."

"You think it sounds selfish."

"How do you think it makes me feel?"

"I'm not sure," he said.

"I'm going to ask Bob about the MBA program," she said. "Did I tell you he wants to have lunch?"

"No."

"He called out of the blue on Friday and said let's have lunch. I think that's very nice."

"What does he want to have lunch about?"

"Just to catch up."

"And you're going to do it?"

"Of course."

"I didn't know Bob was so friendly."

"It's not that he's so friendly, but we're friends. He would never have asked me to lunch when I was working for him. That's the way he is."

"So you're telling me that the way he was treating you then was friendly?"

"It wasn't unfriendly."

"I must have misheard," Lake said.

"I never said it was. He's very demanding, but never nasty or anything like that."

"Ah."

"I learned a lot from him."

"Didn't you tell me his life is messed up?"

"He's separated from his wife, is what I said. But that's settled down now. He's going out with someone who just got divorced, some lawyer, Marion. I think he's known her for years."

"When did he tell you all this?"

"When I was still working for him. He's a good person, in fact."

Lake didn't answer. They pulled up in front of the restaurant and left the car with the valet parking attendants.

Charlie and Susan were already there, sitting at a table in back and sipping drinks. "Hi." "Hey." "Hi." "Hi." Then Lake settled in, smiling and feeling unhappy with himself and with everything.

"How are you two?" Charlie said. Susan was looking at Ellen.

"Great," Lake said.

"Nice tie," said Charlie.

"Thanks," Lake said.

"This place has atmosphere," Charlie said. "How did you find it?"

"We just walked in one night. What's that green paint on your hand?"

"I spent the day painting a bathroom," Charlie said.

"Lacquer," said Susan.

"I thought you were looking for another apartment," said Ellen.

"We are. But I couldn't stand the bathroom anymore."

"We were just talking about that," Lake said. "About how much room is the best amount to live in."

"How many rooms, you mean?" said Charlie.

"Right," Lake said.

"As many as you can get," said Charlie.

"That's what Ellen said. But why would you want more than you need?"

Charlie didn't answer. Ellen and Susan began talking about an art exhibit. It occurred to Lake that Ellen had told Susan about his aunt's house. "Did I tell you I inherited a house from my aunt?" he said to Charlie.

Charlie feigned surprise. "Fantastic," he said.

*B*y dessert, Lake's restlessness had lifted. They talked about the Phillies, movies, potholed streets, the Fourth of July weekend. The waitress poured the last of the wine. Ellen was laughing with Susan about how Charlie accidentally painted his shoe. Lake thought about lacquer; he grew aware of the shine of Ellen's hair, honey yellow, with lustrous shadings from dark to light.

"Ellen's going back to school," he said.

"You are?" said Susan.

"At night," Ellen said. "For an MBA."

"Great," said Susan.

"It'll take a while."

"But that's great," said Susan.

"I should probably do it, too," said Lake.

"I can't see you with an MBA," Charlie said.

"No, I mean take some courses. Expand the brain."

"Like how?" said Susan.

"Philosophy, maybe. I like philosophy." It was true. He had

liked philosophy in college. Maybe a course in philosophy would be good. He pictured himself arguing a point of ethics with a professor. The professor was saying: That's very perceptive, Mr. Stevenson. The other students were listening respectfully.

Charlie looked at his watch. "We better get going," he said. "It starts in ten minutes."

Lake said, "Ellen and I want to have a housewarming at my aunt's house."

"That's a great idea," said Susan, as if she already knew about it.

Ellen glanced at Lake, her eyes slightly narrowed. He decided that, later, after the movie, after they said goodbye to Susan and Charlie, he would apologize again about his reaction to the MBA news and say "I was a fool" or something along those lines, except less Hollywoodish. He would think of something.

*A*s they pulled up in front of Ellen's apartment building, he said, "Listen, I know I was kind of insensitive before."

"Don't worry about it."

"I was a fool."

"What are you talking about?"

"I was a fool to suggest that movie."

"Isn't that overstating it a bit?"

"It was the worst movie of all time, including movies made in Bombay."

"It wasn't that bad."

"I was a fool." He kissed her with confused feelings. She

wasn't the only one who didn't know what he was talking about. He didn't either.

By the following weekend, things were almost back to normal. After dinner on Friday night, they went to Peal Avenue and made love in his aunt's bed, playfully, enjoying one another, lost in the sounds and surging pleasure. Afterward, sensing a presence, he rolled away from her warmth and looked over the edge of the bed. The dog was lying on the rug, oblivious to all the commotion.

The next morning, they talked about the party. Lake wanted to have it the following Saturday. "Spur of the moment," he said. "That's always fun and relaxing." He wanted to get it over with and move ahead with his plans, but he said nothing to Ellen about that.

"Too soon," she said. "Two weeks from now at the earliest."

"Let's make it casual. A spontaneous get-together. Nothing too serious."

"What did you have in mind?"

"Six or eight people. We could eat out on the terrace if the weather is nice. A quiet evening, in the spirit of the house."

"A house doesn't have a spirit. You make the spirit."

"Right, okay. Maybe ten people, but very casual."

But he could see she would insist on doing it her way. She was going to force him to celebrate something he wanted to push out of his life with all possible speed.

In the end, they compiled a list of more than thirty people. Then Ellen said, "We could invite Bob. And Marion."

"Bob? Bob at work?"

"Sure. You'd like him. If we're having your friend Bill, I don't see why we can't have Bob and Marion."

"Marion is the lawyer he lives with?"

"He goes out with her."

"I don't quite get the connection to Bill."

"You used to work with him at that publishing company. That's the only reason you know him. He's a business friend."

"He's a friend friend."

"So is Bob," she said. "Let's ask him."

"Okay, what the hell."

"He probably won't come."

"I'd like to meet him," Lake said.

They began to talk about food. "We'll have it catered," Lake said. "They'll take care of everything."

"You and I can do it. I can easily make some casseroles and things that day."

"Let's have it catered. Then you won't have to worry about anything. Give yourself a break. They do it all."

"It's not a problem."

"Look," he said, "the caterers supply everything—plates, glasses, forks, the works. There's nothing to clean up afterward."

"You want them to provide all that? Do you have any idea what kind of china and silver you have?"

He knew. He had done a rough inventory, because it would all have to be sold at auction; but he didn't want to say that, so he shook his head.

"Come with me." She led him into the pantry and started opening cupboards. "There," she said. He surveyed the stacks of plates, the rows of cups hanging from hooks, the serving dishes and the tureens, the gleaming ranks of wineglasses, champagne glasses, sherry glasses, water goblets, tumblers. "That's yours," she said. She pulled a gold-rimmed dinner plate off a shelf and held it out to him. "That's yours."

He took it gingerly in both hands. "But we're not giving a fancy dinner party," he said. "It's going to be a bunch of people sitting around. The caterer's equipment will be fine. Nothing will get broken, nothing to clean up."

"Forget the caterer."

"It makes sense to keep things simple if I'm selling the house."

"I'll tell you what. Forget the party."

"I'm just trying to make it easier."

"This isn't a museum. What do you think, people are going to trash it? They're going to smash the china? Give me that." She grabbed the plate out of his hands and put it back on the shelf.

"Of course not. But this whole deal is a temporary situation. You know that."

"Why don't you give a temporary housewarming in a hotel?"

"It isn't exactly a housewarming, since I won't be here long. It's just a party."

"Forget the party."

"I don't want to forget it."

"Forget it."

"Let's start over," he said. "Erase all this. Let's go right back to the beginning. We're giving a party. It's going to be a nice party. It's not going to be catered. No caterers will get anywhere near this party. We'll do everything ourselves, and it will be fun."

"I doubt it."

"Trust me," he said.

"I don't see why."

"Ellen, we're always arguing."

"I've noticed."

"I'd like to stop."

She glared at him. Then she said, "All right." But she was angry the whole morning.

*O*n Monday, in the middle of reviewing a draft of operating instructions for the new electric hedge clipper, it suddenly came to him that he was letting events slip out of his control. Maybe that explained why he was feeling uneasy all the time. Mrs. Lundquist would soon begin to wonder why he wasn't moving any furniture in; the dog was acting more chummy each day; and he and Ellen were giving a housewarming in a house that had nothing to do with his life. He had to move ahead, or things would get worse. He had to take at least the first steps toward selling the place. He called Karen.

"Hi, it's Lake."

"How's the dog?" she said.

"I'm just calling to say hello."

"No, you aren't. You never call to just say hello. What have you done with the dog?"

"Nothing. Randall's fine."

"You've changed your mind?"

"What mind? It seems to me that we talked about the dog in a vague, generalized way. You shouldn't read anything into it."

"You'd better not do anything to that dog."

"The secret of your involvement is safe with me," he said.

"I'm serious."

"I need the name of the real estate company your friend works for."

"Jennifer? I think I've got her work number. Hold on a minute."

While he waited, Lake studied the engineer's diagram of the hedge clipper. It looked like the maw of a great white shark boring in for a taste of human flesh. He would have to talk Derek into letting InstruX redo all of the art. Karen came back on the phone and gave him the number.

"I'll probably ask for someone else at the agency," he said.

"Why? I'm sure she's good."

"It's better to keep friends out of this," he said. Then he realized how sinister that sounded. "You're right," he said quickly. "I'll call her. There's no reason not to."

"I certainly hope not."

"Can she keep things confidential? At this stage, I don't want anybody to know I'm planning to sell."

"Ask her."

"I remember her as being kind of talkative."

"Don't take advantage of her, Lake."

"I won't. Look, I probably won't even call her. I'll get an agent out of the Yellow Pages."

"Fine."

"I may be near Martha's Vineyard this summer. I could stop by."

"That would be nice," she said with extreme coolness.

———

*L*ake called the real estate brokerage. He intended to ask for the senior member of the firm. Then, feeling that Karen was watching him in that way of hers, he changed his mind at the last second. "Jennifer Dee, please."

"Thank you, I'll see if she's in."

A voice-mail message came on the line. "This is Jennifer Dee," it said. "I'll be out of the office this morning and back at two o'clock. Please leave a message and your number and I'll call you back."

Lake hung up. He replayed the voice in his mind, weighing it. She sounded reasonably professional.

At two-thirty he called again. This time she came on the line in person.

"Hi," he said. "This is Lake Stevenson. Karen's brother."

"Hi."

"I'm sure you don't remember me. I was the guy playing music upstairs."

"How's Karen?"

"She's fine."

"I haven't seen her in a long time."

"Right. Listen, I'm thinking about selling a house."

"Uh-huh."

"It's in Chestnut Hill. Does your agency cover that area?"

"Yes."

"I need some advice about what's involved in selling and so on."

"All right."

"Can this be confidential?"

"Of course."

She sounded sincere, but he decided that some protective ambiguity was in order. "I haven't made up my mind," he said. "I may want to stay in the house. It's my aunt's house, actually. I inherited it."

"I see."

"I assumed I would live there, but it may be too big."

"Mm."

"The real estate market isn't great, I hear."

"It's a little soft," she said, "but things are moving. How many rooms does the house have?"

"I have no idea. A lot."

"The upper end of the market is still fairly strong."

"This is the upper end, I think. How do you go about setting the price?"

"We would look at it, then make a recommendation. Perhaps you already have a price in mind."

"Who is we?"

"My partners and I."

"I don't want a lot of people involved."

"There are only a few of us. I could come and take a look by myself, if you like."

"That sounds better. Can it sell quickly?"

"That depends on a lot of things. Price is the most important."

"You mean I should price it low for speed?"

"I'm not saying that at all. I'm saying a house won't sell if it's overpriced."

"I like the idea of speed," he said.

She didn't say anything.

"Also, I wouldn't want to stir up the neighborhood with for-sale signs and people going in and out all day."

"That's not necessary."

This was very good news. A tactical shift occurred to him: Perhaps he could sell the house without Mrs. Lundquist and Vere even knowing it was on the market. Then, when they found out, any protestations would be moot. Yes, that was the way, he decided. He would keep Mrs. Lundquist around so that she could testify to his distress at the loss of the dog, but the house would be sold secretly. Neither she nor Vere would find out until he was ready to move back to his apartment. It was an excellent plan, designed for minimal headaches.

"Also," he said to Jennifer Dee, making rapid adjustments, "I wouldn't want the house to be shown on Mondays or Fridays. A housekeeper is there on those days. I don't want to upset her. She's old."

"That shouldn't be a problem."

"Can you keep other agencies from finding out about it?"

"The listing usually goes on the computer, the multiple-listing system. But exceptions can be made."

"I would want to make them."

She was silent. Then she said, "Is there anything else?"

"Just that I would like the whole thing to be handled as quietly as possible. Privacy is in the spirit of the neighborhood, I think. Also it's a question of respecting my aunt's memory. She only died about two months ago."

"I understand," she said.

"This is just fact-finding, of course."

"You may want to talk to some other brokers," she said.

"You mean you aren't interested?"

"I didn't say that," she said. "You asked for my advice. It's important that you be comfortable with the broker you choose and with the listing price."

"Okay, I'll check around. It's a great house," he said. "It's full of beautiful furniture. I'll bet it sells in a flash. When can you come look at it?"

"I could do it this week."

"How about tomorrow?"

"I'm tied up most of the day. I could come by at four o'clock."

"Good," he said. "It's 73 Peal Avenue. Stone, with green shutters and an iron fence."

"What was your aunt's name?" she said.

Why did she want to know? Would she put out the word that Ilsa Grinnell's house was coming on the market?

"Ilsa," he said.

"I mean her last name."

"Stevenson," he said. It wasn't exactly a lie: Stevenson was her maiden name. He sensed Jennifer was writing something down— presumably a memorandum of this conversation. He would have to be careful. "I'm not committing myself to anything," he said. "This is all completely hypothetical."

"I understand."

"See you tomorrow then." He hung up.

It was going to be simple, unless she lowballed on the price. The only other requirement was to dispose of Randall so that he would be legally in the clear, and he foresaw no difficulties there.

The conversation with Jennifer Dee had gone so well that he was only mildly irked when he came across one of Danny's witticisms later that afternoon. On a provisional layout of the assembly instructions for the outdoor grill was a picture of a screw being driven into the burner box to fasten the handle. The caption read:

With a twirl of the driver, insert this screw.
If you do it right, you'll never need glue.

"Danny."

Danny came over. Lake pointed to the caption.

"Look at that," said Danny. "It must be the poet coming out in me again."

"Don't do it, Danny. You could forget and it would get printed this way."

"The picture," Danny said. "There's something funny about it."

Lake looked. It seemed all right.

"Something about that screw."

Lake studied it. The threads were angled the wrong way. "Paul."

The designer came over, all innocence. "Don't do it," Lake said, pointing. "I don't want you guys to do anything like this again. It's dangerous." He waved Paul away. "See this?" he said to Danny. He indicated a caption on another layout; he had circled it in blue.

Before your first use, turn the heat control to high to temper
the grill.

"Turn it to high for how long?" said Lake. "For thirty seconds? For a day? Until it melts?"

"For fifteen minutes," said Danny. "Sorry, that's my mistake. It's a typo. It was supposed to be in there."

But Lake felt a speech was in order. "You've got to spell everything out," he said. "You've got to spell out every single step of the procedure. Otherwise the person reading the manual will go flying right off the tracks. You've heard me say this a thousand times before, but I'm saying it again because it's the essence of our business. If you give a person the smallest opportunity to mess up, they'll take it."

Danny, looking contrite, was inching away from the desk.

"You know why?"

Danny shook his head.

"Because they want to," Lake said.

"They want to?"

"Deep down, they *want* to do it wrong. They *want* to disobey. It's human nature. Half the people who read these instructions would turn the grill to high heat for a nice safe two minutes. A quarter of them would run it on high until there's nothing left in the propane tank or the house burned down. The rest would stare at the grill for a year, wondering what to do. And you know what? No one would operate it for fifteen minutes. Not one single person."

"Gotcha. Sorry."

"Enough about that," Lake said. "Listen, you did a good job on this. Seriously. I checked the material you had to work with."

"Thanks."

"The meter in the second line of the poem was off, though."

———

*A*t 3:45 the next afternoon, Lake took a bowl of water and a dish of dog food up to the attic. It seemed much smaller than when he and Karen had played there as kids, but otherwise it was mostly the same—a jumble of boxes, trunks, furniture, old etchings, rugs. A sheet-covered chair that had once served as his throne was still there. The smell of camphor was the same. The same weak light percolated through a round window at the far end of the attic. It was a fine place to sequester a dog. Prudence suggested that Jennifer Dee should know nothing of Randall, since his continued existence was legally incompatible with even contemplating the sale of the house.

"Come on, Randall," he called. Silence. He went down to the second-floor hall. Randall was lying at the foot of the stairs. "Come on," Lake said, clapping his hands encouragingly. Randall did not move. Apparently the attic was not part of his territory. Lake picked him up. "It's okay," he said. He carried the wriggling dog upstairs and put him down beside the food and water. Randall's nose was furiously working the air. Lake found a small rug and spread it on the floor as a bed.

His watch said 3:55. "Hold it right there," Lake said. He left, shut the door behind him, pounded down two flights of stairs to the kitchen, grabbed a package of sliced ham from the refrigerator, and raced back up to the attic. Just as he arrived, he heard the faint chime of the doorbell. Randall barked. Lake dropped the ham into the dish and tiptoed away. He closed the attic door tight, then closed the hall door at the foot of the attic steps. With double soundproofing, the secret of Randall would be secure. He hurried to the front door.

He expected to recognize her, and he did, but only vaguely. She was very pretty—dark-haired and fine-featured in a French sort of way. "Hello," she said, holding out her hand.

He began to remember her from long ago—a kid running around the house in Haverford with Karen. "Come in," he said. He was still breathing hard from the sprints up and down the stairs. "I was moving some things in the garden," he explained. He gestured at the hall. "Well, here it is."

"It's lovely," she said.

"Yup."

She waited.

"How do we go about this?" he said.

"Let me be sure about what you want," she said. "You're thinking of listing the house with us."

"Right."

"You don't have a particular price in mind."

"No."

"The first step would be for our firm to recommend a price. I would also recommend that you give it to us as an exclusive, which means that we represent you for a fixed period and you agree to pay us a fee of six percent at settlement. You have to sell it through us during the period agreed upon."

"Right."

"You would sign a listing contract."

"Fine," he said. "But if we agree, I want to talk to you about some special provisions in the contract."

"All right."

"About confidentiality."

"I'd like to look around."

"Do you want me to come along?"

"If you don't mind."

"It's a great house," he said, leading her to the living room first. "This is all my aunt's furniture. I haven't touched anything, but you can probably see that."

She didn't answer. Why had he remembered her as talkative? When she talked at all, it was in businessese. "You know, I hardly recognized you," he said. "It's been a long time."

She nodded.

"But I guess that works both ways," he said.

"You and Karen look a lot alike," she said.

"I suppose we do."

"What are the taxes?"

"I'm not sure. I'll have to find out."

"I can look it up," she said.

He had forgotten about public records. "You know," he said, spotting a problem, "yesterday I told you my aunt's name was Stevenson. I meant to say Grinnell, Ilsa Grinnell. Her maiden name was Stevenson." He led her through the library, through the dining room, through the pantry, and into the kitchen. Suddenly he remembered the bags of dog food in the closet. He casually leaned against the closet door, but she made no move to open anything. Her method of examining a house was a steady, rapid scan—so rapid that he was not even sure she was paying attention.

"Is there anything else I can tell you?" he said. "It's oil heat. The furnace is almost new. The house has been very well maintained. Did you see the roof? Slate."

"Yes, I saw."

"All the gutters and downspouts are copper."

"Mm."

"It's kind of old-fashioned, I know."

"It's lovely."

"But the wiring and plumbing are quite new. That's a good selling point, right?"

"It helps."

"So how do you like the real estate business?"

"I enjoy it."

"You've only been doing it for a couple of years, I guess."

"Three years."

"My aunt left Karen her summer house in Maine, did I tell you that?"

"I'd like to go upstairs."

"She's going to keep it."

They wandered through the rooms on the second floor. As they left the nurse's bedroom at the end of the hall, a thump sounded from the ceiling. She stopped, listening. Lake heard a clicking noise, very much like dog toenails on wood.

"I think some squirrels got in under the eaves," he said. "I'll have to call an exterminator. Come on, I'll show you the cellar. The furnace is almost brand-new, and you can see the plumbing down there." He hurried her away.

After they looked at the cellar and the garden and the garage, she walked around the side of the house to the front path, no longer scanning. She stopped on the path and turned to him. "Could I have your telephone number?"

Lake fumbled for a business card. He tried to read her expression. It seemed neutral, even indifferent.

"It must be strange, evaluating houses all the time," he said.

"It's interesting."

"How did you get into the business?"

"A friend suggested I try it. What kind of work do you do?"

"I create instructional materials."

"That's interesting. I'll get back to you on Thursday or Friday." She held out her hand. He shook it. Afterward, the feeling of her hand clung to him for a while. The small bones.

*T*he next step was to make sure that Jennifer did not lowball on the price for a quick sale. He knew he could ask Vere what value had been placed on the house in the estate appraisal, but such an inquiry would alert the enemy. Indirect methods would have to do. He selected a big residential real estate firm from the Yellow Pages and telephoned. "I'm interested in buying a house," he told the person who answered.

She put him on hold. Another voice came on, saying, "Mrs. Evans. How can I help you?"

"I'm interested in buying a house in Chestnut Hill. Is there a simple way I can find out about the general range of prices? I'm not ready to look at houses. This would be just to get oriented."

"I could put together some current listings for you."

"With pictures?"

"Yes, that's probably the easiest way to start, Mr.—"

"Stevenson."

"Certainly, Mr. Stevenson. How do you spell your name?"

At once, Lake regretted having taken this approach. Even on the furthest extremes of the house-selling campaign, every little step seemed to require falsification. "S-t-e-p-h-e-n-s-o-n," he said. "I don't want to take up much of your time, since I may decide not to buy. If I could look at the listing sheets for a few minutes, I might get a sense of whether it's possible or not."

"Do you live in Philadelphia now?"

"I'm being transferred here," he said. "Could I come by your office today? I'll only need a couple of minutes. This is strictly for perspective."

"Would three o'clock do?"

"Fine."

"My name is Margaret Evans. Could you tell me what size house you are interested in?"

"Large."

"Do you have children? I don't mean to ask personal questions, but it would help me pick out the sort of thing that might be suitable."

"One child, but he doesn't need a playroom or anything. He's quite sedate."

"I'll pull some things together."

"*O*h," she said, when he appeared at her alcove. "You're younger than I expected."

He assumed a steely demeanor to silence any further chitchat of that sort. She was a large woman, fidgety. He sat in the chair beside her desk and began leafing through the photocopied listing sheets she had assembled for him.

"Could I ask what your price range is?" she said.

Lake was busy memorizing. Some of the prices were astronomical, with zeros stretching toward infinity. Two houses looked roughly like his. He skimmed the facts and figures, frowning outwardly and rejoicing inwardly. The asking prices on the houses would fund a lifetime of annual visits to scuba-diving school in the Caribbean, or—better still—would allow InstruX to expand into video and other growth areas.

"What?" he said.

"I was wondering about your price range."

"Lower than this, I'm afraid."

"Where are you transferring from?"

"Alaska."

"I thought real estate was expensive in Alaska."

"Not the part where I live."

"Chestnut Hill is one of the most expensive neighborhoods. Perhaps I could make some other suggestions."

"I'll have to think it over. Thank you very much, Mrs. Evans. This tells me what I need to know. If I decide to buy, I'll get back to you. But I may rent. It's likely that I'll rent for a while."

He saw that she was going to offer to help find him a rental place. He thanked her again and hurried away, feeling guilty about the deception but soothed by all the zeros.

———

*J*ennifer did not call on Thursday. That night, as he walked Randall, he pondered her failure to get back to him promptly. Maybe she was not an aggressive agent. Maybe she was feigning a lack of interest to set him up for a lowball bid. Maybe suspense was simply part of the dramaturgy of real estate. With her, you couldn't tell.

At exactly eight-thirty the next day, Mrs. Lundquist arrived as he was bringing Randall back from a trip around the block. "We've had quite an outing," he said, moving at a fatigued pace to suggest that they had been walking for miles. "Did you go to the Veres' this week?"

"Yes."

"How is Mr. Vere?"

"I haven't seen him."

"If you do, give him my best. Tell him we're all fine here. Randall seems to be adjusting well."

"Yes."

"Why don't you let him spend some time outside today, Mrs. Lundquist? I think fresh air agrees with him." He unclipped the leash. Randall drifted away. Lake headed for his car.

*T*hat afternoon, Mary said, "A Jennifer Dee."

Lake picked up the phone. "Hi," he said.

"We're ready to recommend a price."

He braced himself.

She named a figure almost a hundred thousand dollars higher than he expected. "That seems in the ballpark," he said.

"If you decide that you're interested in working with us, I'll draw up an exclusive listing contract. Or a private exclusive, if you want. That would keep it off the computer."

"I need a little time. Also, as I said, I'll want some special clauses in the contract if I do go ahead."

"We can talk about that, certainly."

"You think this price will move the house?"

"I do."

"Should I get some opinions from other brokers?"

"Obviously I think you should go with us."

"The other day you advised me to check around."

"The other day we were just chatting. Now I'd like to sell your house."

The words bothered him, but he didn't know why. "Let's talk about the contract," he said. "My problem is, I want everything to be very quiet. I'd rather not have anyone know the house is being sold, if that's what I decide to do. No signs or advertising."

"We'll stipulate that in the contract."

"I also want to be able to cancel the agreement at any time."

"That's a problem."

"It's a sensitive situation, and I want to be able to withdraw the property from the market if necessary."

"Why?"

"My aunt's memory and so on. It's possible her friends might get upset about the house being sold at this stage. It's hard to explain, but there are very delicate feelings involved. I won't consider selling unless I can put a stop to things if I feel it's necessary. I don't expect to do it, but I want an out if I need one."

"In other words, we're supposed to invest our time and work hard at finding a buyer, but even if we find one who's completely qualified and willing to pay the asking price, you can simply say you're no longer interested in selling. That's not so good from our point of view."

"It's just a precaution."

"I'll have to talk this over with my partners."

An hour later, she called back. "Okay," she said. "This is unusual, but okay."

When she said that, Lake knew she considered the house highly desirable; he was sure of it. His campaign was unfolding beautifully, and now he even had a contractual exit if things grew too hot for some reason. "Why don't you draw up the contract and send it along," he said. Then it occurred to him that Mrs. Lundquist might be intrigued by an envelope bearing the name of a real estate firm. "Send it to my office. But you may not hear from me for a while. I've got to clear some things up."

"Okay."

"I've got a crazy question," he said. "Do you know any good caterers?"

"For what?"

"A buffet kind of party, not too fancy."

She gave him a name. He was hoping for a change of heart from Ellen, but he knew he couldn't reopen the catering subject with her directly. She would somehow have to see the logic of it on her own.

5

*T*hat night, he found an invitation lurking among the bills and junk mail that Mrs. Lundquist had left on the hall table. *Cocktails; the Veres; June 20; RSVP.*

He studied the invitation. Why would they invite him for cocktails? Maybe he was already under suspicion and Vere wanted to conduct a face-to-face interrogation. He would say that he couldn't make it, that his schedule was jammed, that he expected to be in China that weekend, drumming up business for a new line of instructional materials in Mandarin.

On the other hand, perhaps he should accept. It would give him a chance to rave about the house and proclaim his growing fondness for the dog. Yes, that was the right move. The house exceeds my wildest expectations, he would say. Plus: I can't believe how a dog slips into your heart.

He called. "Mrs. Vere, please," he said when a woman answered.

"This is Mrs. Vere."

"It's Lake Stevenson, Mrs. Vere. I'm calling about the invitation for June 20. I'd love to come."

"I'm so pleased. Your aunt was such a good friend. I'm glad you have the house."

"I still can't believe my luck," he said. "And Randall as a bonus."

"Randall?"

"Aunt Ilsa's dog."

"I see, yes, of course. I'm delighted you can come. We're having a few neighbors over. Billington thought you might enjoy meeting some of them. But it won't be just us old fogies. There will be a few young people, too."

"Please give my best to Mr. Vere. Thank you for taking on Mrs. Lundquist, by the way. There really wasn't enough work for her here."

"She's a great help," Mrs. Vere said.

Lake thought: She's an informer, is what she is. But Mrs. Vere would know nothing about that. "See you on the twentieth," he said.

*M*eanwhile, there was the matter of his own party and Ellen's continuing failure to see the logic of having it catered. He tried to nudge her in the right direction. One night he pointed out an inspirational picture in a food magazine—a table laden with a huge roast, a salad extravaganza, cheeses, breads, and other temptations, all aglow under a forest of candles, with flowers everywhere. "That must have been a lot of work," he said.

"Not exactly real life," Ellen said.

"The article says it's someone's house."

"It's a photo shoot. They bring in a whole team of people to do it."

"Sort of like caterers, you mean?"

She didn't answer. Then she said, "I like the tablecloth. Maybe your aunt had a lace tablecloth we could use."

"I doubt it."

"I'll have to check," she said.

Lake put the magazine away.

When Ellen cooked dinner at the house to get the feel of the kitchen, he tried another approach—helping her, using as many mixing bowls and measuring cups and pots and skillets as possible, dirtying as many whisks and spoons and knives and spatulas as he could, piling equipment high in the two sinks. "Look at this mess," he said. "There's got to be a better way."

"The better way is for you to clean up as you go."

Later, she made a list of things for him to buy for the party. It was two pages long.

"I may not have enough time," he said. "Maybe we're being too ambitious here."

"Make time," she said.

He considered disabling the stove. Without a stove, she would have no choice but to call a caterer. But he couldn't go that far.

She was watching him. "What's your problem?" she said.

"What problem?"

"You resist every single thing that has to do with this party."

He gave up. "I don't connect with this house," he said.

"Why don't you give it a chance?"

"Can you see me living here?" he said.

She didn't say anything. She was looking at him, but really she was looking at something else beyond. She was forming a thought.

"Never mind," he said. "It doesn't matter."

*W*hen the day of the party came around, she was a whirlwind of efficiency. Her energy swept him up and spun him through the errands of the day. He bought ice, washed glasses, set up a table in the library for drinks, fiddled with the placement of furniture in the living room, straightened pictures, selected music. He washed lettuce, cut bread for croutons, cleaned bowls as she used them. Randall followed him everywhere, alert to the opportunity for food.

Ellen sent Lake out for more cream and some thyme. As he emerged from the supermarket with his purchases, the man who helped load bags said to him, "Been seeing a lot of you today."

"We're giving a party."

"That's good. I like a Saturday-night party."

"We'll see," Lake said.

"I was having a party last week and the police came to shut me down."

"What was the problem?"

"Too much noise, they said."

"Ah."

"I told them we'd hush up."

"So what happened?"

"They went away."

"I guess they're fairly reasonable about these things," Lake said. "You can't stop people from partying."

"Then they came back and shut me down."

"You're kidding."

"Took my brother away."

"Boy, that must have put a damper on things."

"It did. It did."

"We're having a kind of quiet crowd," Lake said.

"Got to keep the windows closed. Keep the doors shut."

"I'll do that. Anyway, I have a dog that doesn't like noise."

"Must be a police dog."

"He's too small. You wouldn't be interested in a dog, would you?"

"Don't need a dog."

"Well, I've got to get back."

"You have a good time, now. You hear that knock on the door, you say, Man, this is the wrong place. No misbehaving here."

The discussion reminded Lake that Randall's presence was not essential tonight. The fewer people who knew of his existence, the better. "I'll put the dog upstairs later," he said to Ellen when he got back.

"He won't be in the way."

"He's highly susceptible to noise."

"Peel these, will you?"

He peeled and washed and toted and fetched. Pots bubbled on the stove and in the oven. A salad grew. On a gold-rimmed plate, transparent slices of ham made an iris. She produced cauliflower florets and a dressing from somewhere. A box yielded a vast pastry covered with kiwi and peaches. The house filled with delicious smells.

From pantry drawers and cupboards came delicate glass dessert bowls that sang when you touched them, intricately chased saltcellars with cobalt glass liners, a treasury of silver platters and silver serving dishes, piles of linen, endless china. Lake spent forty-five minutes polishing silver, amusing himself by calculating how much it would bring at auction. Ellen found a lace tablecloth and spread it on the dining-room table. She went into the living room and countermanded his shrewd rearrangement of furniture, but he didn't mind.

Soon the afternoon was gone and the sky had turned pearly. He wandered out into the garden and listened to the birds discussing their affairs. He felt good. Ellen was upstairs dressing. Maybe tonight would repair whatever was broken between them.

Then it was seven-thirty, with Randall stashed away in the attic for safekeeping and music playing softly. The doorbell chimed and the guests began to arrive: Ed Sparkman and his wife first, and then Ellen's friend Ruthie and someone Ruthie introduced as Morgan or Morton, then a stream of people, and then, after eight, Bob and his alleged girlfriend Marion—Bob tall, with dark wavy hair and an aloof smile, straight out of a men's fashion magazine in his striped tieless shirt and his wide-lapelled jacket and his pants of exotic corduroy and his feet shod in some sort of black Italian loafers, probably made from the hide of an almost-extinct lizard: Bob not looking like a finance department guy at all, not even a little bit. But Lake merely registered these facts. By then, having gained buoyancy from a glass of sauvignon blanc, he floated on the surface of the party, riding the conversational chop.

———

"*J*ulia, Ed, how are you?"

"Are we early?"

"No, no, right on the button, come in."

"We're early."

"You're not."

"He's so compulsive."

"If someone says seven-thirty, am I supposed to assume they're lying?"

"Come in, come in."

"Look at this place, oh my God, look at this. Lake, this is incredible."

"Well."

"It's incredible."

"It's my aunt's house. I just moved in."

"I love this carpet."

"She died a few months ago."

"The mirror. Is it an antique?"

"I think so."

"It's got to be. Look at the glass. It's an antique."

"Come on in. Let me get you a drink. Julia, what would you like?"

"My God."

"Ellen will be down in a second."

"I knew it. We're early, Ed."

"You're not."

"Who's that?"

"My Uncle Paul."

"I see the resemblance."

"We weren't related."

"He has the same expression. Same eyes."

"He was an uncle by marriage."

"Are you going to keep him up there?"

"I haven't thought about it. Why?"

"Just curious. He fits."

"Maybe I'll leave him there. I haven't decided."

"*H*i, you two."

"Ellen, I love that dress."

"Thank you."

"I can't believe this place."

"Lake inherited it."

"I know, I heard."

"*S*usan, let me get you a drink."

"So this is the house."

"Yes."

"Ellen described it to me. It's really beautiful."

"Good Monopoly move, Lake."

"Thanks, Charlie."

"You look right at home."

"I don't know about that."

"*L*et me get you some more wine."

"No, thanks. You know what I hate?"

"What?"

"Low ceilings."

"My old apartment had low ceilings. It's not so bad. They grow on you."

"These ceilings are eleven feet high, maybe twelve."

"They are quite high."

"I'm a decorator."

"You came with Steve?"

"With Bill. Do you know what the fabric on that chair is?"

"No."

"It's Clarence House, I'm pretty sure. Are you going to redecorate?"

"I suppose."

"Let me know if you need help."

"Okay."

"You'll want to do something about those curtains."

"I will?"

"To lighten up the room."

"Too dark, you think?"

"Definitely."

"You're right. They have to go."

"And those lamps."

"I see what you mean. Sort of old-fashioned."

"We can salvage a lot of what's here."

"Maybe a clean sweep would be better."

"You'd be surprised how easy it is to completely change the feeling of a room just with colors and textures."

"I favor a clean sweep."

"*E*llen looks so great."

"How are you, Ruthie?"

"She seems so happy."

"Yes, she does."

"Who's that person Ellen's talking to?"

"Marion somebody. She came with Bob, the guy from her office."

"Oh, Bob."

"You know Bob?"

"I may have met him once."

"Where was that?"

"When I was meeting Ellen at her office, I think."

"And he was hanging around?"

"No, I mean he was just there."

"You know Ellen is enrolling in night school?"

"She's so bright."

"Bob suggested she should, right?"

"I think he encouraged her, yes."

"Good for him."

"She's been thinking about it for a long time, you know."

"A good man, Bob. An encouraging sort of man."

"What do you mean?"

"What does Morgan do?"

"Morton."

"What does Morton do?"

"He works for WJVJ in ad sales."

"I'll have to talk to Morgan about video."

"*L*ake, in five minutes, pass the word that people should go into the dining room."

"Can I help?"

"Just start people toward the dining room in five minutes."

"I'll encourage them in."

"Have you been drinking?"

"A glass or two."

"No more wine."

"Not a drop."

"Go talk to Ruthie. She hates the guy she's with."

"It doesn't matter. He's a good man. He's in video."

"Five minutes."

"*L*ake, can I take a peek upstairs?"

"Sure."

"I'm dying to see the whole house."

"Go anywhere, Charlotte."

"Do you love it?"

"Love may not be the precise word."

"You must be thrilled. You must wake up every morning and say, Did this really happen?"

"Maybe it hasn't sunk in."

"I'd be ecstatic."

"This house would fit in your garage, Charlotte."

"I hate my house."

"I'd offer you this one, but I don't think Frank would approve."

"*B*ob, how are you doing?"

"Lake."

"Right."

"Nice place. Must have been built in the twenties."

"I'm not sure."

"It was."

"How do you know?"

"It's obvious."

"So you and Ellen work together."

"We did. You've got something on your jacket there."

"A stray fusilli."

"Ellen's a good cook."

"How do you know she cooked this?"

"She told me."

"But it was probably obvious."

"What do you do, Lake?"

"I create instructional materials. I have a company called InstruX."

"Family business?"

"I started it. You think I should put that on my card? Founder and Chief Executive Officer?"

"I wouldn't."

"I don't know. I wouldn't want there to be any doubt about the founder."

"What are your sales?"

"We sell editorial services."

"Revenue. What are your revenues?"

"Oh, about fifty million, maybe fifty-one. I'm kidding. A bit less than that. There are four of us at this point. What do you know about instructional video products?"

"Not a thing."

"Probably not needed in finance."

"No."

"Especially if you have an MBA."

"Who's that person?"

"Just some banker. My aunt's banker. Her husband."

"What bank?"

"Who knows?"

"I like his pocket watch."

"Yeah, that's a style that should come back."

———

"*H*ello, beautiful Charlotte. Did you look around?"

"You haven't moved in yet. None of your things are here."

"The movers are coming next week."

"It's so much work moving."

"I may reschedule."

"*L*ake, did you lose this?"

"What is it?"

"Some sort of letter."

"Where did you find it?"

"Under the cushion of that chair. Some money fell out of my pocket. I picked up the cushion and there it was. Who's Randall?"

"My aunt's dog."

"I can hardly read it. Something about the chair and Randall. She wrote this?"

"Yes."

"Look at the handwriting. She must have been in bad shape."

"She was."

"You never saw it before?"

"No."

"I guess she stuffed it under there."

"I think that must have been her way of sending it to me. It was all she could do by then."

"This word looks like 'untrustworthy.' "

"It is."

"You can read it?"

"Perfectly."

"Well, I'm just delivering the mail."

"I'd better start looking around the house. Maybe there's more."

"*N*ight, beautiful Charlotte."

"Night, Lake."

"Give my best to Frank."

"Where's Ellen? I want to say good night."

"Haven't seen her."

"There she is. Good night, beautiful Lake."

"*T*hanks, Lake. I love your house."

"Good night, Ruthie. So long, Morgan. I'll call you."

"What?"

"We have to talk about video. I'll call you."

"*T*errific party."

"First of many."

"—weak man."

"What?"

"Next weekend. The Phillies. Sunday, remember?"

―――――――

"*B*ye."

"Lake?"

"Bye."

"Who are you talking to?"

"Oh, Ellen."

"Who were you talking to?"

"Myself. Checking the acoustics."

"Are you drunk?"

"Certainly not."

*T*hen, without looking at his watch but knowing it was late and possibly close to the end of time, he wandered around picking up glasses and napkins and plates and carrying them into the kitchen, where Ellen was up to her elbows in soapsuds. He dropped a plate. Tiny shards of white china and gold rim scattered across the kitchen floor, proving what he had said about the caterers: it never would have happened, there wouldn't have been any breakage or cleanup, no need to care about anything. Now he had to find all the pieces.

Ellen said, "Lake, go to bed."

He went to bed.

6

*H*e woke up in the morning with Ellen not there and someone else's brain inside his skull, because it hurt horribly and he never had headaches. On the other hand, he didn't usually drink that much either, so it could be his brain after all. Furthermore, it wanted to punish him by a verbatim playback of all the things he said last night. He rushed into the shower and stood under a hard, hot spray.

Afterward, he looked at the crumpled letter Steve had found under the cushion in the living room. It was written on his aunt's embossed stationery, the handwriting unmistakably hers—an erratic, ravaged version of the handwriting in the letter that had accompanied the will. She must have written this note after her first or second stroke, when she could still move around a little bit and could still think, after a fashion. It said:

My dear Lake Randall must not be allowed on chairs. One day I found him asleep on this one. I punished him and thought he had learned his lesson. But I have found the cushion depressed on several occasions since then. It is not like Randall to be untrustworthy perhaps he did not fully understand. If you find him on this chair you may be sure that he knows better.

Lake felt sad, picturing her trying to get the words down, trying to tell him about Randall. He put the letter in his top drawer, under his socks.

*E*llen was in the kitchen, lining up glasses on a counter. "Let me help you," he said.

"I'm almost finished."

"How long have you been down here?"

"About an hour."

"You should have waited."

"No problem."

"Stop. I'm going to do the rest."

"You can help by drying plates."

"I broke a plate last night."

"Yes, you did."

"I wasn't really drunk."

"No."

"I was stupid."

"You seemed fine."

"I said idiotic things all night."

"Don't worry about it. You were fine. Everyone had a good time."

"They did?"

"It was a good party," she said.

"You think so?"

"I enjoyed it."

"Maybe we should give more parties," he said.

"Lake."

"What?"

"I think we should take some time off from each other."

"I knew you were going to say that."

"You think so, too. Anyway, it's what we're going to do."

"I should have helped you more."

"It has nothing to do with the party. The party was fine."

"Why don't we sit in the garden and relax."

"No. I want you to drive me home after we finish cleaning up. I've got things to do."

*H*e had things to do, too, although their nature was unclear at first. He read the paper, annotated layouts for the software project, watched a baseball game on television, and thought about Ellen and Bob and Ruthie and Charlotte and how an unstructured day was his favorite kind of day as long as he had someone to share it with. But he had no one and wanted no one.

Randall seemed to sense that something was wrong and stuck close to Lake. Much later, in the silence of the house, Lake looked at the dog, and a thought suddenly came to him, imperative, irresistible. He thought: Randall, we should take some time off from each other. And he thought: Starting now. He would forget about giving Randall a choice of destinies. Life did not always offer choices.

At eleven o'clock that night, he escorted Randall to the front gate. He pushed him out and swung the gate shut. "May the force be with you," he said. He went back inside and sat in the library. It was easy; he didn't feel like a rotten person at all.

As the minutes ticked by, he focused on what he would say to Mrs. Lundquist in the morning. "He ran away," he might say. "He got through the fence somehow. I've been up half the night looking for him." He might interrupt his explanation to call, "Randall! Here, Randall! Come on home, boy." He could say, "I'm going out to drive around the neighborhood and search for him." Yes, he could say that. But of course he would drive to work. Later in the day or the next day or Wednesday at the latest, he would contact Jennifer Dee and tell her to quietly proceed with the sale of the property. With luck, everything would be wrapped up in a few weeks.

But even as he considered how to break the news to Mrs. Lundquist, he was listening, wondering where the dog was, wondering if Randall was dumb enough to run in front of a car, seeing him caught in headlights or limping dazed through dark alleys. The chances that Randall knew how to scavenge food from garbage cans were nil. All that stood between him and dying were his good looks; but within a few days or even hours, Randall would be so unkempt and frantic that no one would want him. "My God," people would say when they found his body. "Who would do this to a dog? What kind of horrible person?" Someone else would answer, "A vicious

person. A person without a shred of decency. It's hard to imagine
how a person like that could live with himself."

Even anger couldn't excuse an eviction in the middle of the
night, he knew. He would have to find Randall. With luck, the dog
was still somewhere in the neighborhood, gathering his nerve to
strike off into the unknown.

At the very instant that Lake realized that he must undo what
he had done, he heard a bark—a single matter-of-fact bark, very
much like Randall's. It sounded close. Lake went into the living
room, turned the lights off, crept to a window and peered out.
Randall was standing at the front gate, looking directly at him. The
dog hadn't moved a single inch. He had been saved by his total lack
of initiative.

Lake went out to him. "Very clever, Randall," he said. The
dog walked up the path with a triumphant step, and later he followed
Lake to his bedroom and settled down to sleep as if nothing had
happened.

*N*ow, however, the battle was joined. Henceforth, Lake resolved, it
would be fought on absolutely fair terms. There would be no forc-
ible eviction, but he would reinstate the plan to allow Randall to
select his own future. Place: the park. Procedure: Lake would walk
off in full view of Randall, and the dog could stay there or not,
whichever he chose. Day: next Saturday, when there would be
plenty of dog owners around, ensuring Randall's rescue. Time:
morning, so that Randall would have a whole day to make new

arrangements. Contingency action: stash Randall in a remote kennel if he declined his chance for a fresh start in life.

Yet doubts once again gathered like a fog, blurring the moral landscape. Lake attempted to regain the high ground by thinking about indentured servitude and slavery and his aunt's certainty that anybody could be bought. But nothing was clear.

Meanwhile, Randall pulled out heavy weapons. Every morning that week, he sat at Lake's side and waited for his piece of toasted English muffin. Lake recognized that aeons of bonding skill lay behind this ploy, but Randall's polite manner and sincere appreciation of the muffin were impossible to resist. Then Randall launched a similar dinner ritual. Lake tried to indicate that dinner was an improper occasion for food sharing, but once again he caved in under the pressure of the eyes. It had to be admitted: he enjoyed Randall's company. He liked Randall's mad wagging when he returned home at the end of the day.

One evening in midweek, Randall drew Lake into a game of keep-away with a stick. Lake spent half an hour chasing him around the property. The next day, he stopped at a pet store on the way home to buy a Frisbee. At the store, he spotted a book on springer spaniels and bought it, figuring it might contain some useful information. After a session with the Frisbee, he and Randall retired to the library, and Lake leafed through the book. It was full of saccharine sentiment about the breed, but he skimmed past that part and homed in on a section about dangers faced by unsupervised pets.

Are you aware that a dog left to roam in a wooded area or field could become infected with any number of parasites if he plays with or ingests some small prey, such as a rabbit, that might be carrying these parasitic organisms?

The chances of Randall catching a rabbit were slim. He read on.

The springer spaniel is essentially an outdoor dog. For generations he has been bred for hunting, rejoicing in the freedom of fields, woods, and streams.

Furthermore:

Springers are very rugged and can withstand all kinds of weather.

Lake took comfort in this. If the experts regarded springers as physically equipped to live in the wild, his disposal plan had not been so iniquitous after all.

*A*t lunch the next day, he and Bill talked about publishing pet books. It was a huge market, Bill said.

"I looked at one dog book recently," Lake said. "Very low-grade information. Mostly about how terrific the breed is."

"That's the usual formula."

"This book actually talked about a dog's merry tail signaling his excitement. I quote. His merry tail."

"What kind of dog?" Bill said.

"It had long hair," he said evasively.

"What color?"

"I don't remember."

"I think you should forget about pet books. It's not your thing."

"InstruX would do it differently. No sentiment. Nothing but facts."

"It's not what the market wants."

"Look, why not sell pure procedure and technique? You've got to feed your dog or cat or fish. You've got to give the dog or bird a bath. You've got to clip their wings or watch out for diseases. People would be grateful for straight talk."

"You don't give birds a bath."

"Whatever. Your cat."

"You don't give cats a bath."

"Your horse, for Christ's sake. Your hamster."

"None of the above."

"I know you give horses a bath. You spray them with a hose."

"I seriously doubt it."

"I've seen it done. At the zoo. It may not have been a horse, maybe it was an elephant, but it's the same idea."

Bill shrugged. "How's Ellen?" he said.

"Fine."

"I didn't get a chance to talk to her much the other night."

"Yeah, well, she was busy with another conversation anyway," Lake said. "It's finished with Ellen."

"You two seemed good together," Bill said.

"We drifted apart, as the saying goes."

Bill nodded.

"It was probably more my fault. I let it happen. I don't know why, I just did."

"It's usually both people," Bill said.

"How's Sarah? She wanted to redo my house."

"What's your plan with the house?"

"I may get rid of it."

"Keep it," Bill said.

"Why?"

"You and that house go together."

"You're out of your mind."

"Seriously."

"It's a total mismatch. It's the biggest housing mismatch in the history of mankind."

"Maybe not as much as you think."

"I want to talk some business. What would it take to bring you to InstruX? We're expanding. We're going to get into all kinds of new things."

"I like where I am."

"I want you to imagine a set of circumstances that would persuade you to come. Anything at all. Just let your imagination go."

"Triple my salary. Give me half the equity."

Lake was pleased: Bill was willing to imagine.

*T*hat night, after a Frisbee game with Randall and a shared meal of hamburger, Lake decided to search for more messages from Aunt Ilsa, convinced that her crumpled note about Randall's craving for chairs was part of a larger communications strategy. She was, after all, a Stevenson, and Stevensons were known for their persistence and follow-through.

It was impossible to know where to look. Who could predict the mail-delivery policies of a woman who would stuff a note under the cushion of a chair? He decided to start in the cellar and work his way up.

He soon hit pay dirt. In the top of a box containing some Christmas things, he saw a red velvet stocking with a piece of paper protruding from it—Aunt Ilsa's creamy stationery. Her handwriting leaped wildly across the paper, as though registering an electrical storm in the brain. The note said:

This is Randall's stocking

He had to hand it to her. She did have foresight. She wanted to make sure that when Christmas came around, Lake would hang Randall's stocking by the chimney with care. Unfortunately, Santa would not find Randall at Peal Avenue this year.

In a closet on the first floor, Lake discovered a small basket filled with dog toys—a bone made of cloth, a ball with a bell in it, leathery sticks for chewing. Presumably Aunt Ilsa felt that the use of these things was self-evident, since he could find no note.

He checked under the cushions of every chair and sofa in the living room and library, but found nothing. Then he saw a glint of creamy white behind the amplifier of the sound system. He tried to guess what it would say. Probably something like "Do not play music in this house at night." But it said:

Randall likes Mozart. Beethoven makes him restless

He went through the desk drawers. In the center drawer was another note:

Lake Green Grove Mr Witter

The handwriting was the worst yet, careening across the page with minimal control. Somehow, he figured in the message, but "Lake Green Grove Mr Witter" held no meaning, except as a measure of the frailty of flesh.

He searched the dining room and pantry and kitchen, finding nothing. He continued the hunt on the second floor, beginning at one end of the long hall and progressing to the other, checking every bedroom, bathroom, dressing room, and closet. Nothing. After "Lake Green Grove Mr Witter," her strength had winked out.

*S*aturday drew closer—the moment of truth with Randall. For moral buttressing, Lake studied the portrait of Uncle Paul over the mantelpiece, recalling how he had always deferred to Aunt Ilsa, sitting quietly while she and Lake's mother talked. Despite his hawklike appearance, the man had lacked backbone. He made a mental note to meditate on Uncle Paul's deficiencies when Saturday came around.

No matter how Randall's fate was resolved, Lake was determined to stick to his overall schedule for getting rid of the house. On

Thursday, he called Jennifer. "I think I'll put the house on the market next week."

"Have you signed the contract?"

"I'll sign it tonight and date it for next Tuesday."

"Shall I come by and pick it up?"

"I'll put it in the mail. Remember, this is very confidential."

"I understand, but I can't guarantee complete secrecy. The house has to be shown, after all."

"Discretion is all I ask."

*F*riday came. After breakfast, he awaited the arrival of Mrs. Lundquist, ready to lay the groundwork for his grief at the loss of Randall. Through the living-room window, he saw her approach up the path. He went to the door and opened it. "Good morning, Mrs. Lundquist," he said.

"Good morning."

"A great day," Lake said.

"Yes."

"If you're in the kitchen, Mrs. Lundquist, you may notice that Randall has a bigger-than-usual amount of breakfast in his bowl. He's full of energy these days."

She didn't reply.

"You should see him sniffing the air," Lake said. "He seems restless."

"Mrs. Grinnell used to leave for Maine about now."

"He's probably getting itchy."

"I understood he would be going to your sister."

"That's off. Randall stays with us, I'm glad to say. Now, Mrs. Lundquist, since I know you pay particularly close attention to cleaning the upstairs, I wanted to mention something. You may notice an unusual amount of dog hair in my bedroom. That's because Randall has been sleeping there. It's really something the way dogs attach themselves to a new master."

"Yes."

"And vice versa," Lake said. He sensed the beginnings of suspicion and changed the subject. "Have you found any notes around the house? When my aunt was ill and couldn't talk, she wrote some notes. Little messages. Her handwriting wasn't so good by then."

"I did find one or two pieces of paper."

"What did they say?"

"It was difficult to read them. They didn't seem to say anything."

"Where were they?"

"One was in that closet."

"With the basket of dog toys?"

"It may have been. I believe it was."

"If you find any more notes, would you save them for me? Most of them seem to have something to do with Randall, so naturally I'm very interested in them."

"All right."

"Have you ever heard of a Mr. Witter or Green Grove?"

"I don't believe so."

"No matter."

"Mr. Stevenson, I noticed on Monday that the tag has fallen off the dog's collar."

"I'll get a new one next week," he said. She was a sharp-eyed devil, but Lake figured that her noticing the missing tag worked in his favor. She and Vere would realize that, without a tag, the lost dog could not be returned to his owner. In effect, Randall would have to be considered legally dead.

*F*inally Saturday arrived—hot, with great fluffy clouds and rich summer smells. Lake began the day by standing in front of Uncle Paul's portrait and musing on the man's weakness. Then he and Randall headed off for the park. Lake told himself that he would just let the situation develop: he would keep an open mind.

He was surprised to find a dozen dogs and their owners already on the scene, Holly and her Labrador among them. "Hi, Luke," she said.

"Hey, Holly." She was wearing jogging clothes and had her hair in a ponytail. "How's Chloe?"

"You remembered."

"Sure."

She smiled at him, but it was a distracted smile.

"Big crowd here today," he said. They stood together off to the side of the main group.

"Yes," she said. But she wasn't listening.

"How's the aerobics trade?" he said.

"Okay."

"How's Tina?"

"Tina's fine."

Lake started to move away. Then it occurred to him that something might be really wrong. "Is Tina all right?" he said.

"Sorry," she said. "Tina's fine. I'm a little stressed out."

"How come?"

"Family stuff."

"Nothing serious, I hope," he said.

"My parents," she said with a shrug.

"What are they doing?"

"I just got off the phone with them. It's like the tenth call in the last two days. You don't want to know."

"I do," he said.

"They want me to go back to Missouri. I'm supposed to leave here and go back to the middle of nowhere and get a job. I could work in my stepfather's store, my mother says. It's a town with four hundred people. I don't know why I'm telling you this."

"Say you won't do it. You've got a job already."

"They don't think teaching aerobics is a job." She looked away, seeing Missouri.

"That's ridiculous," he said.

"You have no idea what it's like trying to talk to them."

"Holly, you should just refuse. That's one thing I know about. Explanations aren't that important."

She seemed embarrassed, and they edged back toward the main group. "I've got to give Randall some exercise," he said.

"You should come to the park more often," Holly said.

He couldn't tell her that his visits to the park would end on this day.

But the conversation had removed any remaining possibility

that he might leave Randall here. He felt bad for Holly, with her future so uncertain. He couldn't do that to Randall. Putting him in a kennel until the house was sold was the only solution. After that, Randall would live with him in his apartment. They were stuck with each other.

Still, because he had invested so much mental energy in his plan, Lake wanted to see what would happen when Randall faced a choice of park or home. It was a matter of clinical curiosity. "Let's go, Randall," he said. He led him to the far side of the park, and they played with the Frisbee for a while. Randall kept glancing over at the other dogs. "No," Lake said each time he moved in their direction.

When Randall refused to continue with the Frisbee retrieval, Lake walked to the edge of the trees and sat down. Randall sat beside him, still watching the other dogs with longing eyes. Lake stroked his head. Then it was time for the test. "Randall," he said. "I'm going to leave. You can come if you want. It's up to you."

He stood. Randall lay down, tired from the Frisbee game.

Lake walked ten feet away. Randall closed his eyes.

"I'm leaving, Randall. Stay or come. It's your choice. Pay attention."

Randall went to sleep.

Lake went over and nudged the dog with his toe. "That's pathetic," he said. Randall rose and trotted after him.

*T*he schedule had to be obeyed, however. When Mrs. Lundquist arrived on Monday, Randall would have to be gone. On Tuesday, the house would go on the market. None of that could be changed. Back home, Lake looked up "kennels" in the Yellow Pages. Dozens of them were advertised. The listings spoke of wooded acres, expert grooming, on-the-premises veterinarians, training programs, air conditioning. One facility called itself a country club. Another described itself as a ranch. He studied the listing for the Valley View Pet Hotel. The place seemed to have everything, and the advertisement said that inspection visits were welcome. "Bring your Best Friend for a look, too," it said. Lake called to get directions.

They drove for a half hour through the summer morning. Randall sat in the front seat, watching the city open out into a world of big lawns and fenced fields. A country road led over a narrow bridge and up a hill, then tipped down toward a valley quilted with farms. A sign said "Valley View Pet Hotel." Lake followed the driveway to a low white building, tidy, with several cars out front. Lake snapped on the leash. "What a view, hey?" he said to Randall.

But things went badly from the start. As they approached the building, Randall planted his feet, terrified by something. Lake hauled him through the door. He became aware of muffled yips and barks and whines and howls emanating from somewhere nearby. To give Randall time to calm down, he paused by a bulletin board covered with postcards and letters. One postcard said:

Dear Bimi,

I hope you are having fun at the pet hotel. I hope you are being a good puppy. Yesterday I went to the beach and I swam in the waves. Today I am going fishing with Daddy. Be a good puppy and eat your food or I will be mad.

A woman behind a counter said, "Can I help you?"

Lake dragged Randall to the desk. "That's a cute note about Bimi on the bulletin board," he said. "The little kid's puppy. What kind of dog was Bimi?"

"There are so many. I really don't remember."

Lake felt a strain on the leash. Randall was pulling toward the exit with all his strength. "I'm interested in boarding my dog," he said. "Maybe fairly long-term."

"Certainly. How did you hear about Valley View?"

"The Yellow Pages."

"Shall I tell you about our special programs? We have hiking and play programs as well as training sessions. Of course, we do grooming, too. It's all explained in this booklet, with all the rates."

"You have hiking for dogs?"

"Of course."

"Is that different from just letting them walk around?"

"They hike with a camp counselor."

"Did you hear that, Randall?" he said. "A counselor." But Randall's tail was down, his eyes wild. "I think all that barking has upset him," Lake said. "What's back there?"

"The kennels. Each dog has his own private exercise area. We clean them twice a day."

"Can I take a look?"

"Certainly."

She opened a door behind the counter. The barks and yips and howls rose to a deafening level. Ahead stretched a long line of cages holding dogs of every type—big ones, little ones, shaggy ones, short-haired ones, some clawing at the grillwork of wires, some pacing frantically, some catatonic. "Very clean," said Lake.

"Our grooming room is over there."

Lake wasn't paying attention. He had his hands full with Randall, whose feet were skidding on the linoleum floor as he attempted to escape from this place.

"My dog isn't too comfortable here," Lake said.

"The presence of so many other dogs sometimes disturbs them at first," the woman said. "They get used to it."

"He may not be ready. We'll think about it," Lake said. But the verdict was clear. Randall tugged Lake out the door and down the path to the car, his legs taut with effort, pulling so hard that he was choking himself. "It's okay," Lake said. "That's no place for a dog."

*O*n the way home, he remembered that he was due at the Veres' for cocktails that evening. The prospect was less appealing than ever, and he contemplated claiming a sudden illness or calling to say he was stranded in Akron. But he decided to march into the fastness of the enemy. Why not? Since it was settled that he would be Randall's permanent master, he had no reason to feel guilty. Home would not be where Aunt Ilsa had decreed, but, in the final analysis, it was none of Vere's business. This was Stevenson versus Stevenson.

He still needed a way to make Randall vanish, of course. All afternoon, he waited in vain for inspiration. Finally, driving over to the Veres', he opted for a temporizing tactic: His apartment would be Randall's hideout on the days when Mrs. Lundquist came to 73 Peal Avenue. He would take Randall there on Sunday night and take him back to Chestnut Hill when the coast was clear on Monday night. Then he would do it again for Mrs. Lundquist's Friday visit. It would be inconvenient but effective: as far as Mrs. Lundquist and Vere were concerned, Randall would cease to exist.

The Vere house was of the Aunt Ilsa type, but even bigger, with a circular driveway and a many-chimneyed roofline that suggested scant concern for saving the world's forests. An Asian woman opened the door and steered him in the right direction. He walked into a sea of voices, spotted a white-jacketed bartender across the room, and navigated toward him. A serving tray floated past. He plucked a small tartlike thing from the tray and pressed on. As far as he could tell, he knew no one here, not a single soul out of the whole babbling throng. But probably that was just as well. "White wine, please," he said to the bartender when his turn came. The bartender poured generously, and Lake was grateful.

He looked for Vere, trying to recall the seamed, aquiline, chilly face, last seen at a funeral. A fortyish woman touched his arm. "Are you Peter McClellan?"

"No, I'm Lake Stevenson."

"I must find Peter."

"I don't know him," Lake said.

"We were talking about England," she said, indicating her conversational partner, a stylishly dressed woman who looked bored. "The prices. Awful. I don't know how they live. Have you been there recently?"

"No," Lake said.

"Awful, Marjorie," she said to the bored woman, at the same time indicating to Lake with a swiveling motion of a shoulder that his part in the conversation was finished.

He moved on, sipping the wine. Someone lurched into his path. "Sorry," said a gray-haired man.

"My fault. I'm Lake Stevenson."

"Perry McClellan," the man said. "Lake Stevenson, eh? Son of the same, no doubt."

"Right."

"I haven't seen your father in years. Hope he's behaving himself." He peered at Lake and stroked his chin, evidently remembering something.

"I don't see him much either," Lake said.

"Lives in Greenwich now? Didn't I hear that somewhere?"

"Yes."

"I heard something about him up there," Perry McClellan mused. "Can't think what it was. Quite a fellow, your father." He winked.

"So I'm told."

"I'll bet you have a way with the ladies, too, eh?"

"Not really," Lake said. He had to get away from this man. "You have a son here, right?" he said, to change the subject.

"Peter. You know him?"

"No."

"Over there." He pointed.

Peter McClellan was standing in a group of middle-aged men. He was in his late twenties, with tortoise-rim glasses and slicked-down hair. When the group laughed, he laughed loudest and longest of all. Lake headed in the opposite direction.

He heard two men talking about real estate and eased over. "—five million underwater," one was saying.

"More," said the other.

"Hi, I'm Lake Stevenson."

"Nice to see you."

"You were talking about real estate," Lake said.

"Are you in real estate?"

"In a small way, mostly residential," Lake said.

Just then, a white-haired woman approached. "You must be Lake Stevenson."

"Yes, I am."

"I'm Laura Vere. I'm so glad you could come."

"It was nice of you to invite me."

"Your aunt was the dearest friend. We miss her dreadfully. Are you happy in the house?"

"I haven't been there long, but I think it'll work out fine," said Lake.

"I'm so glad. Have you met David Dugan? He just moved to Chestnut Hill, too."

"No, I haven't."

"Let me introduce you." She led him toward the center of the room. "David, this is Lake Stevenson. You two are almost next-door neighbors."

David Dugan was in his fifties, an orthopedic surgeon. Encouraged by Lake's questioning, he talked about hip replacements for ten minutes. Then Mrs. Vere reappeared and drew Lake away to meet someone else. Faces began to blur. He lingered in a conversation about the abysmal state of Philadelphia politics, then drifted through the crowd, chatting here and there. Mrs. Vere intercepted him again. He readied himself to say, Sorry to hurry away but it's been a delightful party, good night, thanks, but she beat him to the punch. "Billington, it's Lake Stevenson," she said.

"Hello, Mr. Vere," Lake said.

"Glad you could join us," Vere said. He had a lofty, austere manner, like someone on the lookout for moral bankruptcy.

Lake groped for words. "I've been meeting my neighbors," he said. "A hospitable bunch."

Vere studied him.

"One feels welcome," Lake said.

"There is a certain neighborly spirit."

"It's almost like coming home."

"You lived here as a child?"

"No, in Haverford."

"I thought so."

"But Aunt Ilsa's house is full of memories. Too many, I sometimes think."

"How is that?" said Vere.

"In a way, she's still there," Lake said. "All the furniture, all her things. I haven't changed anything yet. It would be like moving her out."

"Yes, Mrs. Lundquist mentioned to my wife that you haven't made many changes," said Vere. "But you'll soon feel at home."

So, thought Lake. He had been right: Mrs. Lundquist was indeed an informer.

"I guess moving into someone else's house is a kind of psychological hurdle," Lake said. "You have to make it over an ownership barrier. I think I'm getting there. I'm at mid-hurdle, you might say."

He was pleased by his hurdle metaphor. When Vere learned that the house had been sold, perhaps he would take Lake's delicately balanced mental condition into account, realizing that the loss of a dog would come as a doubly dreadful blow to someone whose state of mind was not firmly grounded.

But Vere seemed fixated on neighborliness. "You must know Peter McClellan?" he said. "He's about your age, I believe."

"I haven't had a chance to talk to him."

"A nice young man."

"Laughs easily," Lake said.

"What?"

"He has a great sense of humor."

"I see. Your sister is well, I trust."

"I trust she is," Lake said. He glanced at his watch. "I must be off, Mr. Vere. Thanks very much for having me. I'll get over that hurdle with the house, I'm sure."

"I hope we see you again soon."

"I hope so, too," Lake said.

He found Mrs. Vere, thanked her, and charted a course for the door. But before he got there, he saw Jennifer.

It startled him, and he was inclined to whiz by without saying hello. After all, he had accomplished his mission—had performed commendably, in fact. But he felt that he and Jennifer were allies, in a way. Besides, just looking at her was enjoyable. Anyway, he liked her. He hadn't thought about that before, but it was true; he did.

She was talking to an older woman but smiled at him as he approached.

"I'm Lake Stevenson," Lake said to the woman.

"I'm Eleanor Winter," the woman said. "Jennifer, it's lovely to see you. Now I must find Charles."

"How are you?" he said to Jennifer.

"I got the contract," she said.

"The very confidential contract," Lake said, "the one that assumes a sort of attorney-client confidentiality?"

"Right."

"What brings you here?" he said.

"I came with a cousin. Over there." She pointed to a clot of people around Mrs. Vere.

"If you're in real estate, it's good to meet lots of people, right? Isn't socializing an important part of it?"

"It doesn't hurt."

"That's a beautiful scarf."

"Thank you."

"Red," he said, suddenly feeling tongue-tied.

"Yes."

"And gold."

"That too."

Lake licked his lips. For some reason, his brain had ceased to function. Finally he said, "Do you live in Chestnut Hill yourself? I never asked you."

"No, I share a house in Merion with some friends. Six of us."

"A lot of people."

"It's not dull," she said.

"I'm more solitary myself," he said.

"Two of them are moving out," she said. "They're getting married."

"Were they involved before, or did that happen at the house?"

She started to laugh but didn't.

"Just curious," he said.

"I promise everything is legal. She's a lawyer."

"What do the others do?"

"One is a trainee stockbroker, and one's in advertising. And, let's see, a graduate student, and one is looking for a job."

"It's like a whole urban society in miniature," he said.

"It is, isn't it? I never thought of it that way."

Lake was aware of her dark hair, the shape of her lips, her beautiful brow, all the sculptural delicacy that God gave women to destabilize the mind of the male. She had a way of talking that was serious, but with a faint feathery tickle in it. He had lost track of what he was saying and had to take a stab. "So you'll have more space," he said.

"Yes, but we may not fill it."

"I have an apartment in a town house, the second floor. Had. Well, still have."

"Will you go back there?"

"Yes."

"That makes it easy," she said.

"I'm thinking of going to Nantucket in a couple of weeks," he said, in connection with nothing.

"Could you give me a number? I may have to reach you."

"I'd like to stay in touch," he said. Then, because that sounded strange, he said, "This is a nice party."

"I'm glad I came," Jennifer said. "My grandmother looks much better."

"Your grandmother?"

"She was in an automobile accident. She's never been quite the same."

A premonition formed—dark, turbulent, flashing in its depths.

"Who's your grandmother?" he said.

"My grandmother Vere."

"Mrs. Vere is your grandmother?"

"Yes."

"And Vere is your grandfather? Mr. Vere."

"I promise they are," Jennifer said. She appeared to think something was funny.

"This is news," he said. "About the Veres, I mean."

"You seem surprised."

"Not at all. It's just that I didn't know."

She was watching him.

"I have to go," he said. "By the way, to get back to what we were talking about a minute ago, I cannot stress too strongly the confidentiality of our agreement. No exceptions at all. I hope you don't mind me hammering at that. For reasons of respect and people's feelings and so forth."

She nodded.

"So long," he said.

"Bye."

He walked out with his thoughts racing. This latest Vere connection was worse than the Lundquist link. As a matter of fact, it seemed like a species of treachery, although he wasn't exactly sure who should bear the burden of blame.

Such moments come in every war, he later reminded himself. The essential thing was to stay calm and to hold your course. For an absurd and reckless moment at the Veres, he had thought that he might ask Jennifer out someday, because he enjoyed chatting with her, even if he couldn't think of what to say. But that would be a bad move, especially in light of the family tie. Everything in the house-selling campaign had to remain businesslike. This was a time for monkish focus.

The following afternoon, the Phillies won, coming from behind with two walks, a single, and a double in the ninth. "Stupid to leave him in," Steve said. "You could see his control was gone." But Lake hadn't been paying attention to the game. He found the roar of twenty thousand ecstatic voices oppressive and was dully conscious of the space beside him where Ellen should have been sitting.

He had a long Frisbee session with Randall that evening. Then, after filling a garbage bag with dog food, he drove Randall to his apartment. He would announce the loss of the dog to Mrs. Lundquist the next morning, on schedule. Randall rode on the front seat like a princeling.

Lake parked in front of the town house and gave Randall a quick walk up and down the sidewalk to introduce him to the locale. Randall sniffed at the ivy Mrs. Reardon had planted in the tree box instead of the begonias. After all the necessary claiming of property rights, they went upstairs. "Make yourself at home," said Lake as he swung his door open. Randall followed him toward the kitchen.

The place felt small. Lake had always thought of his apartment as impressively big, but after the opulent caverns of Peal Avenue, it seemed squeezed and even a bit drab. The department-store furniture looked like department-store furniture. The posters were clichés. He didn't even like his old still-life photographs—the geometric pictures of machinery and vintage carpenter's tools and junkyard objects that he had taken when he was sixteen. That's what happened when you lived somewhere else for a while. It changed your eye. But he had no doubt that he would quickly regain his pride in the apartment when he moved back in. And Randall would be around to liven it up.

He decided that he would import a few choice articles from Peal Avenue after the house was sold. Most of the furniture and furnishings would be sent to auction, of course, and he would give Karen whatever she wanted. But the library desk might look good here, and some of the chairs, and he liked his aunt's paintings. In fact, it might be a good idea to put most of the contents of the house in storage, just in case he ever moved to a bigger apartment.

Someone knocked on the door. When he opened it, Mrs. Reardon was standing there, scowling. "Mr. Stevenson," she said, "did I see you come in with a dog?"

"Yes. Don't worry, he's friendly."

"I assume you know that you are not allowed to bring a dog here."

"I what?"

"If you read your lease, you will see that no dogs are allowed in this building."

"This is a very civilized dog. He won't bother anyone."

"Mr. Stevenson, I suggest you look at your lease."

"I didn't notice that clause when I signed it. We'll have to renegotiate. He's going to be living here."

"I'm allergic to dogs."

"I'll keep him out of your way."

"You will take the dog off the premises right now. This minute."

"I can't, Mrs. Reardon. The dog has nowhere to go."

"That's not my problem, Mr. Stevenson." Then she sneezed. Lake suspected it was for dramatic effect, but he couldn't be sure. "I want that animal out of here now," she said.

"This is a very valuable dog," Lake said. "Any threat to this dog's well-being, such as throwing him out on the street, raises some fairly large financial issues that I think you ought to be aware of."

"Out of here right now."

"Don't you have pills for your allergy?"

"Out." She sneezed.

"He's not a very big dog," Lake said.

"If the dog is not gone from the house in one minute, there will be trouble, Mr. Stevenson."

"There already is trouble, Mrs. Reardon. I'm unhappy about this. I seriously question what kind of place it is that has no room for dogs. Dogs have been human companions for thousands of years, maybe millions, how should I know."

"You've got one minute." She stalked away.

"Come on Randall," he said. "This is a fucking disaster."

"*H*e's gone," Lake said to Mrs. Lundquist when she arrived on Monday morning. "I can't believe it. Randall disappeared." He looked past her, as if scanning the horizon for a glimpse of brown and white that would restore happiness to his world.

"Where did he go?"

"I don't know how it happened. He was outside. The gate was closed, I know it was closed."

"Perhaps he'll come back. He has to eat."

"Mrs. Lundquist, I've been looking for him for almost twenty-four hours. I'm afraid there's not much hope. I never did get a new tag for him. I was planning to do it this week."

"I don't think he could open the gate by himself," she said.

"Of course he couldn't. I've checked the gate many times myself."

"I always kept an eye on him when he was outside," she said.

"I know that, Mrs. Lundquist. You were an excellent guardian of Randall. But I wanted him to have more time outdoors. I thought it would be good for him."

"I don't believe the dog would wander off."

"I agree with you," Lake said. "He was taken. I think he was stolen right out of the front yard. It happened when I was making breakfast yesterday. He didn't make a sound. I had no idea he was in danger."

"Someone took him?"

"What else?"

She appeared to be assessing the likelihood of a kidnapping, not favorably. "I'm sure he'll turn up, Mr. Stevenson," she said. Her words seemed somehow pointed.

"Please keep an eye out, Mrs. Lundquist. Leave the gate open."

"All right."

"I'll call the police, of course."

"That would be a good idea," she said.

Lake didn't like that comment at all. He headed toward the garage. Randall awaited him there, perched happily on his front-seat throne in the car, always ready for an adventure. "Lie down, Randall," he said. "Be inconspicuous."

"What's this?" said Mary.

"This is a dog," said Lake.

"I know that, but what's he doing here?"

"He'll be spending the day with us. In fact, he'll be a regular for a while."

"I didn't know you had a dog."

"This is not necessarily my dog."

"Whose dog is it?"

"Think of his status as indeterminate. Think of him as a stray."

"He's a very good-looking stray."

"Yes, he's quite handsome."

Randall walked over to make friends with her, gazing into Mary's eyes as she rubbed his head. "What a nice dog," she said. "What's his name?"

Lake was ready for the question. Last night, he had tried out various new names on Randall, saying them aloud in a normal voice to see if he responded. The name Ralph produced no reaction. The name Bongo drew a blank. Then, after further tries, Lake had found a winner—a phonetically similar name that Randall accepted as a substitute.

"Renard," he said to Mary, using the French pronunciation, which had yielded best results in last night's tests.

"Renard? As in fox?"

"Yes."

"You're no fox," Mary said in baby talk, continuing to rub his head. "You're a dog, a beautiful dog."

"He's quite foxlike, in fact," Lake said.

Mary began to make cooing sounds.

"He's just visiting," Lake said. "I thought he might humanize the place."

Danny came in, half an hour late and bleary-eyed. He walked over and gave Randall a pat. "How come you brought your dog, Mary?" he said.

"He's Lake's dog."

"Please," Lake said. "Let's not get into these fine points of ownership. He's an office dog."

As the day proceeded, Randall proved to be a very good office dog. He lay sleeping beside Lake's chair, occasionally rousing himself to sniff wastebaskets or pay a call on Danny or Paul. He seemed especially fond of Mary, who responded with further head rubbing and baby talk. Lake considered the performance of both of them to be mawkish. "Is the dog distracting you, Mary?" he said.

"Has Renard been fed?" said Mary. "I could buy a can of dog food at lunchtime."

"He eats dry dog food."

"Want me to buy some?" she said.

"He doesn't get a midday meal."

"He looks hungry."

"He's not. I know his eating habits very well."

"Are you hungry, Renard?" cooed Mary.

"Come here, Renard," Lake said.

"I could take him for a walk."

"I'll take him for a walk," Lake said firmly.

A moment later, hearing the telltale cough that usually signaled a Lake tableau, he looked across to her desk. She was frozen in a pose of ogrelike malignance, her mouth a snarl, her fingers twisted into claws. The block letters on the cardboard sign in front of her said:

LAKE THE CRUEL

But he ignored her, and office relations with the dog settled into a stable pattern, with Randall occasionally circulating to receive pats and promote bonding in his expanded pack. Lake monitored office productivity out of the corner of his eye. There was no significant falloff. If anything, morale was up.

Jennifer called at three. "My partners will view the house at ten tomorrow morning, if it's all right with you."

"Do they understand about confidentiality?"

"They understand," she said. "I don't know if you know anything about our firm, but you picked the right one."

"Good."

"I'll also show it to a client later tomorrow. I've been working with her for a while. This is the sort of house she's interested in."

"Is there any way of telling her the house is just sort of for sale, I mean it might be for sale, but it's a shade less than official."

"It is or it isn't," she said. "You've got to make up your mind."

"Okay, it is."

"Fine."

"Call me afterward and tell me how things went," he said.

"All right."

"Or I could call you."

"I'll call you," she said.

*T*hat evening, he examined the house to make sure it looked its best. As far as he could tell, Mrs. Lundquist was doing a competent job on her shortened schedule. He had done some vacuuming himself to remove dog hairs that might alert her to Randall's nighttime presence, and he had kept the food dish scrubbed to maintain an appearance of disuse. Lake wondered if Randall sensed that he was a fugitive. It was a hectic existence for him: visiting a kennel and then an apartment and leaving both in haste; spending his days in an office and his nights at Peal Avenue; being smuggled out of the house on Monday morning and sneaking back in at night.

In the course of his inspection, Lake noticed that the channel on the portable television upstairs had been changed—proof that the cleaning duties were not straining Mrs. Lundquist. He looked at the TV schedule in the newspaper to see what played on that channel. There were hours of soap operas. He didn't care, really, since she would soon be out of his life, but he switched the selector to another channel as a quiet warning.

As the day wound down, he sat on the terrace and watched some robins and a mockingbird fooling around. The grass had just been cut and had a moist, fresh smell. Some tall, whitish flowers stood serene in the evening light—lilies, he thought, although maybe they were irises. In any case, they were good flowers. He stayed there for a half hour, then moved to the library and listened to music, throwing in a Mozart clarinet quintet for Randall.

At work the next day, his thoughts regularly turned toward the house and what was happening there. He pictured Jennifer's fellow agents roaming through it, probably making cutting comments. He imagined Jennifer saying to her client: I know this place is old-fashioned, but at least it's structurally sound.

Derek Kast called in midafternoon. "I like what you did on the Hedgemaster," he said.

"I hoped you would," Lake said.

"Excellent graphics."

"Our design department is top-quality, I think," said Lake, trying to transmit a mental image of an army of designers and graphic artists, rather than just Paul, with his earring and wild tee shirts.

"In a couple of places, the tone gets kind of ominous," said Derek.

"We always try to tell it straight," Lake said. "It's one of our absolute principles."

"Anyway, it's good. I'd like to talk to you about doing some other work."

"I'd be very interested," Lake said.

"I'll be out of town for the next couple of weeks. Can you get down here the third week in July? Actually, I may be in Philadelphia around then. We could discuss the possibilities."

"I'll come there," Lake said.

They settled on July 25. Lake, pleased at this further freshening of the financial wind, wondered if InstruX should move to more glamorous offices. It might be a good idea, especially if video developed as a new line of business and Bill agreed to come on board.

At five o'clock, Jennifer called. "You wanted a report," she said.

"How did it go?" Lake said.

"Fine. My partners are enthusiastic. The woman I showed it to in the afternoon didn't say much, but that's the way she is. I think she's interested."

"She didn't say much? She must have said something. You can't walk in that house and say nothing. What did she say? She said she hated it."

"No, she didn't."

"You're keeping something from me."

"It was one of three houses I showed her today."

"Did she rank them? How did my house come out?"

"No, she didn't rank them," Jennifer said.

"How about your partners?"

"They think the price is right."

"I see, they walked all around the house, then came out and said the price is right. I don't understand real estate agents. You're like the rest of them, I have to tell you. You walked through the house in about five minutes and didn't look at anything and a few days later you finally delivered your commentary, which was, if I recall, a price. But I guess that's what it takes to be in real estate."

"No."

"No what?"

"No, that isn't what it takes. What if I told you that the wallpaper in the front hall is ghastly?"

"What's ghastly about it? I think it's outstanding wallpaper. I really like it. How can you say it's ghastly?"

"It's not," she said. "It's quite lovely, in fact. But do you see what I mean about telling you everything people say?"

"Ah."

"We haven't set up any appointments for tomorrow. I'll let you know if we do."

"I've got a question. How come you didn't insist that your partners view the house before your firm recommended a price? Isn't that how it's done?"

"It's the usual way, but I persuaded them to make an exception."

"Why?"

"Just a feeling I had."

"What feeling?"

"Instinct," she said. She hesitated, then added, "You have very strong concerns about privacy."

"But you understand my reasons."

"Not exactly," she said. "Anyway, that's beside the point."

"It's not beside the point. I want you to understand."

"Tell me again."

Lake reached inward for a powerful speech about his aunt's memory and respectfulness and propriety. But he couldn't say the words. They wouldn't come out. He cleared his throat. She waited. "I'll do a better job of explaining someday," he said finally. "It's kind of complicated right now."

After a moment, she said, "It's a big thing, selling a house."

"It is."

"I'll let you know when I have some news," she said.

"Sorry about badgering you before. This house thing makes me edgy."

"That's normal," she said.

"You don't have to keep me informed about appointments. Go ahead and show it whenever you want. I don't need to know all the details. The important thing is to sell it."

"I'll be in touch," she said.

"I'll be calmer," he said.

*S*he called again on Thursday afternoon. "Hi, this is Jennifer," she said. She sounded happy.

"How are you doing?" he said.

"Quite well, I believe. We've shown it to about a dozen people. There's definitely some interest."

"Wow, you've been busy. What's that noise I hear in the background?"

"I'm calling from my car."

"You have a car phone?"

"It's a lifesaver in this business."

"Maybe I should get a car phone. I definitely think I should. Then you could call me in my car, and we'd be even. I don't like to give anyone an edge in mobility."

"Why not?"

"Track was my sport," he said. "I ran the mile in high school and college. The person with greatest mobility is the winner."

"I'm calling because I'd like to bring two people to the house at ten o'clock on Saturday morning. One is the person who saw it the first day. She wants her husband to look at it, and he can only come on Saturday. Incidentally, this will be the first time she has asked him to look at a house."

"That's a good sign?"

"It might be."

"You said you've been working with this client for a long time."

"Yes, but strictly speaking, she's not a client. You're the client. We represent you."

"I like the sound of that."

"Ten o'clock Saturday morning, then?"

"I'm going to be there," he said. "Is that okay?"

"It's all right with me if it's all right with you."

"And I'll have a guest."

"I can reschedule," she said.

"You won't bother this particular guest."

"Ten o'clock, then."

*A*t lunchtime on Friday, he visited a drugstore and studied the boxes of women's hair coloring. He chose dark auburn. The box promised "natural-looking gray coverage," which seemed appropriate for Randall, since the white sections of his hair were no doubt the equivalent of human gray hair. That night, Lake put on an old undershirt and blue jeans and rubber gloves, lured Randall into an upstairs bathroom, shut the door and went to work.

He filled the applicator bottle and squeezed coloring gunk onto the white stripe on the top of Randall's head, keeping it well away from his eyes. He then applied some of the liquid to his white chest, and he spread a batch on one of his shoulders. Holding him in the crook of an arm, he lathered it all up. At first, Randall attempted to struggle free, but he gave up after a while. "Don't worry," Lake said, "you'll look great." They sat in that position for forty minutes; Lake endured it only by telling himself it was a superhuman feat. He wished he had brought the little television into the bathroom to help pass the time. A tip about the boredom problem should have been part of the hair-coloring instructions, he felt.

> *Tip: Provide for entertainment to avert boredom. A small,*
> *portable television set is recommended if circumstances make*
> *it impossible for you to turn the pages of a book.*

The job was completed by a rinsing in the bathtub, which violently ended all cooperation from Randall. Later, inspecting his work, Lake saw that Randall's dark patches were now two-tone and that the auburn on his formerly white chest had a strangely splotched appearance. Still, he judged the treatment a success: No one could mistake this dog for his former self. "Takes the years off," he said.

While Randall dried, Lake called Karen in Martha's Vineyard. "I trust you are well," he said in greeting.

"What?"

"I'm merely passing along a question from Vere. 'I trust your sister is well,' he said. I was at a cocktail party at his house last weekend."

"And what did you say?"

"I said I trusted likewise. Listen, I'll be in Nantucket in a couple of weeks. Can I come over to the Vineyard for a visit?"

"Just give me some advance notice."

"I've put the house up for sale, by the way, but it's not public knowledge. In fact, it's sort of an undercover operation."

"You certainly move fast. What have you done with the dog?"

"You have my personal guarantee that the dog is fine. Randall is no more, but the dog is fine and will stay fine."

"I don't think I want to hear about this."

"You don't have to worry. I have one problem, though. Jennifer is the agent."

"Why is that a problem?"

"Vere is her grandfather."

"No. Oh no. I knew I was forgetting something."

"I just found out."

"I never should have suggested her," Karen said in dismay.

"Who could have guessed it? It's not your fault."

"Change agents, Lake. Mr. Vere is going to be seriously upset when he finds out you've sold the house."

"I can't help it. He shouldn't have let Aunt Ilsa write a will like that in the first place."

"And how do you think he'll feel if he finds out that Jennifer was involved with the sale? He'll think she was in on it somehow."

"But she isn't."

"This is wrong," Karen said. "You should change agents. That's the least you should do."

"I can't. I've signed a contract."

"Then tell Jennifer about the will. Tell her that her grandfather is the executor. Let her make up her own mind about what she wants to do."

"She might talk to him about it, and then he would get all excited."

"Tell her. You have to."

Lake pondered this. It would be the stupidest thing he could possibly do. Even if Jennifer didn't alert Vere, she might cancel the deal; and she was bound to dislike him for his deviousness. "You really mean it, don't you?" he said.

"I really do."

"No other way."

"No other way," she said.

"I can't believe this is happening to me."

"Do it."

"I'll think about it," he said. "I've got another question, while we're on the subject. Does Jennifer go out with anyone in particular? I mean, is she involved with anyone? Do you happen to know?"

Seconds ticked by as Karen processed the query. He could feel powerful waves of suspicion radiating from Martha's Vineyard to Philadelphia at the speed of light. Finally she said, "Why do you ask?"

"I'd like to know."

"That's why you called, isn't it?" Karen said.

"It's a perfectly innocent question."

"Sure."

"So is she involved with anyone?"

"I'll tell you after you tell her about the will."

"I'm only planning to admire her from a distance. Seriously. I'm just curious."

"There was somebody for a while," Karen said, "but he went to California. It wasn't working out anyway."

"She lives with a bunch of people in a house," Lake said.

"I never should have suggested Jennifer."

"Yes, you should have. It was a good suggestion, except for the grandfather thing, and that's nobody's fault. Don't worry. I'm devoting my life to work."

"Good."

"You never believe me," Lake said.

"I believe you most of the time, but only because I know when not to."

He didn't like that answer, but he had to admit that she was a good sister. "I'll figure out some way of telling her about the will," he said. "But right now, I can't see how."

"Do it."

At exactly ten o'clock on Saturday morning, the doorbell chimed. Lake, joined by Randall, went to the door. He swung it open, hostlike. Jennifer glanced down at the dog in surprise, then addressed Lake in her most professional tone. "I hope we're not interrupting anything." Behind her stood a tweedy man and his tweedy wife. "This is Mr. and Mrs. Dankmyer," she said. "This is Mr. Stevenson."

"Good morning. Come in," Lake said. The couple followed Jennifer in. Their manner was distant, as if to suggest that the house was now anyone's territory, theirs as much as his. "I'll be out in the garden," Lake said. "Take as much time as you want."

He read the paper in the garden for a half hour. Then, assuming that they had left, he went back indoors. Randall trotted off toward the living room, and Lake followed. Jennifer was there, standing in the middle of the room, her arms crossed.

"You're still here," he said.

"They're upstairs."

"I figured they'd be gone by now."

"Do you want me to hurry them along?"

"No, it's not that. They didn't seem very interested."

"I don't know about him, but I can tell you that she's interested. I'm sure of it."

"Could have fooled me," Lake said. They stood silent. He tried to think of how he might broach the subject of her grandfather's connection to his aunt and this house. He would have to begin with that, and other facts would follow in due course. He would need to explain it in stages, so that she would understand how he really had no choice—how the will was a form of bondage, probably unconstitutional, a violation of the Fourteenth Amendment.

"I didn't know you had a dog," Jennifer said.

"I'm taking care of him for now. He's the guest I mentioned."

"I see."

He waited for her to ask who the dog belonged to, but she didn't. He decided it might be better to preempt the question. One last little lie would be necessary, although it wouldn't exactly be a lie: it was more like a metaphor. "My aunt used to have a dog like this one," he said. "His name was Randall." He went to the table by the window and picked up the photograph of Randall sitting in a sailboat in Maine. He handed it to her. "That's her dog. This one's name is Renard. Same breed, except Renard is swarthier."

"Hello, Renard," she said, bending over to give him a scratch.

"Do you like dogs?" Lake said.

She nodded.

"Did you have one when you were a kid?"

"A Lab."

"Springers are great dogs. They're very resourceful."

"You should get one," she said.

"I have one."

"I thought you said you were taking care of this dog for someone else."

"I may end up keeping him."

She said nothing.

"Do you mind having him in the house when you're showing it?" he said.

"No."

"Maybe he's a plus. Lends a domestic touch. But you'd rather not have him here, right?"

"I didn't say that," she said. "It doesn't matter one way or the other. He's part of the general mystery."

Lake blinked. "What do you mean?" he said.

"I'm sorry, I didn't mean to say that. You're being quite mysterious about this dog, that's all. It's fine." She shook her head, as though shaking off some small irritant.

"The general mystery," he said.

"Please forget I said that."

"It's okay," Lake said. "I know what you mean." He put the photograph back on the table and adjusted its position. He could hear voices upstairs. The Dankmyers would be coming down in a minute. As he looked at the photograph, shame suddenly seized him, and he felt himself flush. He thought: Why now? Why after all these weeks of maneuvering? But the feeling was so strong that he knew it had been hiding in him the whole time.

Jennifer turned toward the door.

Lake said, "Can I talk to you about this sometime? The mystery."

"Sure."

"There isn't any, really. It's more like a bind, and I'm not quite sure what to do about it."

She watched him.

"That would be good," he said.

"What would?"

"Talking," he said.

She didn't seem to know how to respond. Then he saw a flicker of alarm. He wanted to stop, but he couldn't.

"Could we talk about it over dinner?"

"I don't think so."

"I wish we could."

"I don't think it would be a good idea."

"You're right," he said. "Probably it wouldn't."

Her hair was slightly astray; her expression was caught between anger and perhaps some sadness. Lake let the shame come. It burned in his face, merciless. He reached down to pat Randall, trying to conceal the stricken feeling. Jennifer was already halfway to the door.

Afterward, the feeling dulled, but it didn't go away. He packed a suitcase, left a message on the office voice mail, and drove away from Chestnut Hill with Randall, going north—to Nantucket, if possible, but anywhere at all would do: away from this house, this version of himself. He pulled into the first stop on the turnpike, called the Nantucket Chamber of Commerce, and asked for the telephone numbers of some bed-and-breakfast places. After more calls and some discussions about pets, he located a place to stay. Late that afternoon, he parked his car in the steamship lot on Cape Cod and bought a one-way ticket to the island. He found a seat on the top deck of the white ferry. The big diesel engines growled to life, and he and Randall headed out across Nantucket Sound. Gulls rode the air above the deck, crying piteously. Randall watched them as they swung close and swooped away and swung close again. Their yellow eyes watched back.

8

"You're lucky we had a room," said Mrs. Hayes. "Usually we're booked at this time of year. We had a cancellation just last night."

"Luck is my middle name," Lake said. Immediately he regretted the wisecrack: They had grown easy with each other in their twenty minutes together, sitting in the parlor of her bed-and-breakfast, conversation ebbing and flowing as she knitted. "Actually," he said, "my middle name is Drew."

"Drew."

"A maternal relative. But quite a lucky person, in some ways. I'm not keeping you up, am I?"

"Not at all. My bedtime is twelve sharp."

"This place is very relaxing."

"I'm glad you like it."

Randall whimpered in his sleep, twitching at Lake's feet as he chased some dream animal. Mrs. Hayes said, "He's a handsome dog."

"He's probably a bit disoriented right now."

"My Rory passed on last year. I haven't been able to bring myself to get another dog."

"I'm sorry to hear that."

"He was a grand old thing."

"You should replace him. What kind was he?"

"A Newfoundland."

"You might consider a springer. I think they like the sea. Renard has done some sailing."

"Will you be sailing?"

"I hadn't thought about it. How could I do that?"

"You can rent a sailboat. Do you know Nantucket?"

"Only from a travel article. This is sort of spur-of-the-moment visit. I figure we'll just walk around."

"You can leave the dog here as much as you like. He seems very well-behaved."

"Thanks," Lake said. "Tonight we'll stay in. It's been a long day."

She settled back into her own thoughts. The knitting needles were a metronome.

"I wonder if I could ask you a personal question," he said. "I've had something on my mind." He had to talk.

"Certainly."

"You're sure it's all right?"

"I can't very well know, can I?"

"Well, here's the question. Have you ever known someone you

didn't trust at first but later everything was fine? I'm trying to get a woman's point of view on this."

"I'm not sure I understand the question," she said, peering at him over her glasses. She put aside her knitting.

"It's hard to explain. I mean, someone gets off to a bad start with you. A man. He made some mistakes. He was kind of misleading. But then maybe you discovered that he wasn't so bad."

"That happens between people quite often, don't you think?"

"I guess it does. Unfortunately, we're talking about me."

"I see."

"Not big mistakes. In fact, the other person doesn't even know about them. But she can tell that they're there."

"Do you like this person?"

"Sort of. I mean, I could. But it's not in the cards. Basically, it's a dislike problem. I just want to get rid of the dislike."

"Have you known her long?"

"A few weeks."

"Time often helps with these things."

"I hope you're right, Mrs. Hayes."

"That's a very important part of it, of course."

"What is?"

"Hope. Caring about it."

"I'm not too hopeful. I think it's a lost cause."

They were silent for a few minutes.

"Tell me about how time helps, Mrs. Hayes."

"Well, take Alfred, for example—my husband."

"There was a trusting problem?"

"There was."

"I don't want to ask you specifics about that, but tell me about the first time he asked you to go out with him. What did you say?"

"I said no."

"Right. My experience exactly. But obviously he asked you out again, since you married him."

"I said no a number of times."

"For how long?"

"For two years."

"Two years," Lake said.

"Yes. Perhaps a little less."

"Can I ask why? I don't want to pry, but was there a really serious problem?"

"I believed he was attached to Amelia Roberts. Certainly *she* thought so."

"So you felt he was not being completely straightforward?"

"Yes, I did."

"Maybe it wasn't that simple. Maybe he sort of got himself in a tangle."

"You might put it that way."

"But you got past that problem. Alfred straightened everything out, right? At the end of two years, he asked you one more time, and you said yes. Was everything okay after that? Obviously it was."

"No, it wasn't."

"What happened?"

"I'm not sure I should be telling you all this."

"Just the ending, the part where everything was okay."

"That took a while. Alfred sometimes had trouble with the truth in those days. He didn't value it as much as he should have."

"But you married him."

"Three years later."

"Three years," he said. "How long were you married?"

"Forty-seven years."

"So, two years until you agreed to go out with him, three more until all of the misunderstandings were cleared up, and then forty-seven. The ratios aren't that bad, when you think about it. If you take the long view."

"Alfred was a fine man. But a handful."

"It all worked out in the end," Lake said.

"Sometimes it does," she said. She gathered her knitting things together. "Breakfast will be available from eight to ten."

"I'll be up bright and early. On the go."

*P*atience. Maybe it didn't suit his temperament very well, but it was worth a try. As midnight passed and he descended toward sleep, he made a decision: the next time he asked Jennifer to go out with him would be July 11, exactly a year from today. The glacial pace of Alfred and Mrs. Hayes was not necessary: Philadelphia had a warmer climate than Nantucket; life was lived at a quicker tempo. A one-year waiting period was a good plan, a patient plan. If Jennifer got involved with someone else in the meantime, too bad. You have to take risks in life.

Dreams reached for him, but he held them off a little longer, reviewing the plan. Even a year seemed excessively long. He changed the schedule: the next time he asked Jennifer to go out with him would be exactly three months from today, on October 11. All of the problems about the house would be gone by then, and impressions of his evasiveness would have faded. Three months was a better plan.

But common sense suggested that the three-month waiting period should run from yesterday, July 10, since that was when he had first asked her out. That gained him a day.

But since he had asked her out in the early morning and had been regretful ever since, yesterday should count as part of the waiting period. That gained him another day. October 9 would be the date for trying again—if he felt like it. He dropped off to sleep.

The next morning, he clipped on Randall's leash, and they went for a walk, meandering through the town. After a while, he sat on a bench and watched people stream along the sidewalk. A pack of kids on high-tech bikes hurtled into view and shot up a hill, out of sight. Randall's nose twitched as he registered smells of coffee and doughnuts.

Later, Lake strolled down to the waterfront, dawdled in a small art gallery that sold scenes of rose-covered cottages, then wandered through the marina—a sea city, bristling with masts and outriggers and radio antennas, where residents ate and played cards and watched television in public view, like creatures in a zoo. He stopped near a burly man standing in the stern of a big powerboat; its transom bore the name *Heartthrob*.

"Morning," said Lake. "Good name for a boat. Throbbing engines, right?"

The man puffed his cigar and shrugged.

"How did you decide to leave out the hyphen?"

"Shit, I don't know."

The sight of all the outriggers gave Lake an idea. He found a fishing-tackle store, rented a surf-casting rod, bought some lures, and asked directions to the nearest beach beyond the harbor.

"You're not going to catch much there," the man in the store said.

"I'm practicing patience."

After a fifteen-minute walk, he reached the top of stairs that led down a bluff to the beach. A world of water stretched into the distance, light-spattered and wind-ruffled, with a long, slow underbeat of waves rolling from the horizon. He could feel the curve of the planet. He sensed storms whispering a thousand miles away, a rocky continental shelf diving down into darkness, lobsters clicking their claws and whales thrumming. He knew his trip here had been the right thing to do. Jennifer didn't have a monopoly on instinct.

All morning, he cast for bluefish that weren't there. He took off his sneakers, rolled up his pants, and waded into the water up to his knees so that he could feel the sea rhythms. In time, the rod became part of his arms, and he was able to loft the plug far out into the sunshine; it arced across the blue sky, kicking up a little fountain of spray when it landed, and danced back in as he cranked the reel. Randall curled up on the sand and slept briefly. Then he moseyed off, sniffing seaweed and driftwood and other items of interest. A mother and a little boy came down the beach. She called Randall over, and the boy timidly stroked his head. A jogging couple stopped to pat him. Lake continued casting. His lips turned to salt. His eyes were stuffed full of sunlight. Hundreds of times, the plug came skipping back in, fishless—but he didn't care about fish. He was tuned to the earth, stitched into the terrestrial fabric, needing nothing more.

Then he felt hungry. He gathered up his gear, put on his shoes, called Randall, and climbed up the steps with the sea beat fading behind him. As he stood on the bluff, he checked his watch. It was almost one-thirty. He noticed the July 11 date on the face of the watch. October 9 didn't seem very far away—the merest blink of time for someone who took the long view.

*P*hysical exertion was exactly what he needed. That afternoon, he and Randall jogged miles to the South Shore, and Lake swam in the ocean while Randall stood guard. When the sun was a few inches above the horizon, they started back, taking their time. Later, Lake explored on his own. He listened to a street musician's guitar, revisited the marina and watched people idling away the evening in their big powerboats, had a beer at a bar, then went home to the bed-and-breakfast, where Randall, exhausted by the day's activities, was sound asleep on Lake's bed. Lake kicked him off, but gently.

The next morning was clear and bright, with enough of a breeze to give flags a postcard ripple. Lake took his coffee to a rocking chair on the back porch and viewed the day. Gulls carved the sky, and climbing roses shivered on a shingled wall. Mary would be in the office by now. He considered calling her to find out what was going on, but he didn't particularly want to know. Instead, he walked with Randall to the lighthouse that stood on a sandy point in the harbor. The channel ran close to shore there, and boats of every kind paraded past—outboards, a rumbling ocean racer that looked like a knife, yachts showing their bottom paint as they hissed by, a rusted trawler, a sail-board leaning against the wind and skittering across the wavetops. Lake had an urge to go to sea. A half hour later, he had located a place that rented small sailboats.

His sailing experience consisted of a few hours of fooling around with friends five years earlier, but he figured that close observation would provide the requisite nautical knowledge. He stood at a distance from the floating dock where the rental dinghies were berthed. The wind was steady and blowing directly offshore, out toward the fleet of big yachts moored in the harbor. Getting away from land would be easy—a matter of setting the dinghy's single sail out wide and letting the wind push. Getting back would require tacking. He wasn't exactly sure of the technique but knew that the sail had to be kept close in.

Just then, a man and a small boy walked over to one of the tethered dinghies, unfastened it, hopped aboard, hoisted the sail, cast off, put the tiller over so that the boat turned, and glided away. Lake observed every step with an eagle eye and locked the sequence into memory, confident he could replicate all the moves. A few minutes later, another rental dinghy supplied the necessary lesson in home-coming. A suntanned girl was sailing it by herself. She executed a series of zigzags, then let the sail flap as the boat covered the last few feet to the dock. Again, Lake memorized every detail. He approached the proprietor. "I'd like to take a boat out for a couple of hours," he said.

"Can you sail?"

"Sure."

"You've sailed before?"

"Of course."

"You a pretty good sailor?"

"About upper intermediate, I'd say."

"I'll need a deposit or credit card number."

"Fine."

"You have to wear a life jacket."

"It's not necessary."

"It's required. Don't take it off."

"Okay, fine, but what about a life jacket for my dog?"

"The Coast Guard doesn't care about dogs."

"No problem, he's an experienced sailor," Lake said. "I'll take that one." He pointed to the boat the girl had just brought in. Its sail was still up, so he wouldn't have to figure out how to raise it while the proprietor looked on. He lifted Randall onto the fiberglass seat that adjoined some sort of slotted contraption. But Randall had his own ideas about where to sit and immediately jumped down into the bottom of the boat.

Carefully imitating the steps he had observed, Lake unfastened the dinghy from its cleat, stepped in, and put the tiller over to one side. Under the pressure of the wind, the boat slipped backward and turned. The sail went out on its own. He grabbed the rope attached to the boom. He straightened the tiller and gave it a couple of professional jiggles, as if trying to get the feel of this perky little craft. The dinghy zoomed along, with a wake burbling behind and unknown destinations up ahead. It was, he felt, an exceptionally skillful departure.

Randall seemed tense. Lake decided not to try any experimental maneuvers for a while, at least not until Randall had settled down and the skeptical proprietor was far astern. He stretched an arm along the side of the boat and turned his face to catch the full rays of sun. When he opened his eyes an instant later, he saw that he had veered off course; he made a quick correction. Evidently, alertness was important, but he expected to soon master the forces of wind and water. This was the sort of challenge he liked. Improvisation, learning by doing—it made a person feel alive.

They were headed toward the edge of the fleet of moored yachts. Opting for a safer course, he pushed the tiller over. Suddenly strange things began to happen. The boom lifted up. The sail bulged. The boom swung across the boat like a great scythe, missing Lake's head by an inch as he ducked. The boat pivoted, tipped. The sail shot all the way out on the opposite side and began to flap thunderously. While trying to make sense of these events, Lake noticed Randall cowering in the bottom of the boat. "No problem," Lake said.

The next few seconds passed without further incident. Lake pulled in on the rope that controlled the boom. The sail filled, and the boat picked up speed again. He concentrated on making the dinghy go straight, and soon they had passed the yachts, with no more obstacles ahead.

After a while, he deduced that the wind had whipped the sail across the boat because he had turned the tiller the wrong way. Very gently, he pushed it toward the sail, simultaneously pulling on the boom rope, as he had seen the suntanned girl do. The boat was now pointed in a new direction, mostly sideways to the wind. Yet it was still going downwind rather than sailing forward. Was it possible the boat was broken and lacked the capacity to tack? He pushed the tiller further over and trimmed the sail. The dinghy continued to skid sideways and downwind, and it became hard to steer. He eased back onto his original course. Apparently, the boat was going to take him downwind no matter what he did.

He began looking around for instructions. None had been supplied. He was still having an outwardly idyllic sail, still crossing bright water with birdlike ease. But an inability to change course might make this trip a long one. Instructions would have helped.

Warning: Take provisions on any voyage, no matter how short you expect it to be. The sea is unpredictable.

He peered ahead. No end to the harbor was yet in sight. Randall's eyes were fastened on Lake.

To either side, sand and low hills slid by—possibly within reach, if he could figure out some different way to set the sail or steer. Then an outboard approached at high speed. He waved his arms, and the outboard slowed and drew near. Four shirtless teenage boys stared at him. "Yo," said one.

Lake pointed in his downwind direction of travel. "What's out there?" he said.

"Wauwinet," said the kid standing at the boat's center console.

"What's Wauwinet?"

"A town."

"How far?"

"Coupla miles."

"This boat only goes in one direction."

"Is the rudder busted?"

"I don't think so."

The kid glanced at his buddies. "Listen," he said, "we'd give you a tow but we haven't got time. I'll tow you to shore if you want, but we gotta go."

Lake waved them away. "I've always wanted to see Wauwinet."

The kid hit the throttle, and the boat raced off, soon shrinking to a speck. Lake and Randall sailed on into the blue distance.

A half hour later, the end of the one-way trip loomed. The dinghy bore down on Wauwinet, with the sail bellied out and the rope straining in Lake's right hand. The town appeared to be no more than a handful of houses lined up along a beach. A few boats bobbed at moorings near shore, and a long dock extended out from some sort of seaside inn. He steered to the left of the dock, aiming for an opening between boats. His plan was to run right up on the beach; once ashore, he might be able to rent a Jeep and a trailer and haul the dinghy back to where the voyage began. As he contemplated his options, the boat slipped steadily sideways, refusing to follow the leftward course. He was bearing down on the dock, in danger of ramming it. He flung the tiller over. In a way that was now familiar, the sail bulged. The boom lifted and then slashed past his head. The rope caught on something, and the sail filled again. As though swatted by a giant hand, the dinghy lurched, dipped its nose, and teetered sickeningly. Water poured over the rail. Lake flailed for a handhold, missed, and toppled overboard, amazed. When he refocused, the dinghy lay capsized, its sail awash. He didn't see a dog.

"Goddammit, goddammit." He spun in the water, searching. Suddenly he realized that Randall might be caught under the sail. He tried to dive, but the lifejacket held him up. He wrenched it off and lunged under the sail, fumbling around, feeling for the body of a dog in the dimness. Finally he had to come up for air. He filled his lungs and prepared to go down again. At that moment, he glanced toward shore, less than a hundred feet away. A dog was standing there, watching him.

Lake righted the boat, grabbed the bow line, and began to swim. His feet soon touched bottom, and in five minutes he and the swamped boat reached land. He stood panting on the beach. A man in paint-covered pants came over. "I see you've got a problem."

Lake wasn't in a mood to talk. "It depends on how you look at it."

"Where are you coming from?"

"Nantucket."

"How are you going to get back?"

"Helicopter."

"I could give you a tow." He pointed to a battered white skiff. "That's my boat."

"Hey, I would appreciate that."

"For fifty dollars."

"Ten," Lake said with disgust.

"It'll be fifty."

"I've got a friend who'll give me a tow."

"I might take twenty-five, but that's it."

"Okay," Lake said. "My dog here is probably shaken up. I ought to get him back home."

"Shaken up?"

"I wasn't sure he could swim," Lake said.

"Hell, he's a spaniel. He could swim all the way around this island if he wanted to. He was out of the boat and on the beach in about ten seconds."

"That's typical."

"Done much sailing?"

"Some."

"How come the centerboard is up? Not a good idea when you're jibing."

"Ah."

*W*hen he got back to the bread-and-breakfast, he called Karen. "How about if I dropped by?" he said.

"When?"

"In a few hours."

"Where are you?"

"Nantucket."

"You're ahead of schedule. I thought you said in a couple of weeks."

"I'm a man in a hurry."

"It's not especially convenient. Will you be there for a while? Stephen will be here on Friday. Why don't we make it for the weekend?"

"I'd like to come now."

"Is anything wrong?" she said.

"Not really, but I'd like to drop by for a quick visit."

"Come on, then."

Lake thanked Mrs. Hayes, hustled into town and caught the ferry to Oak Bluffs. From there, he took the long taxi ride across the island with Randall sitting beside him. The taxi left them in front of an old white-shingled house in the middle of a big lawn. He rang the bell. Karen opened the door, welcoming. Then she saw Randall.

"You brought the dog."

"Of course. We go everywhere together."

"So you decided to keep him."

"This isn't Randall," Lake said. "This is Renard. Sort of a substitute."

"You got another dog?"

"To fill the hole in my heart."

"You can't bring him inside. We're not allowed to have pets in this house. Take him to a kennel."

"We're coming in."

"Put him in the garage."

"We're coming in."

"Well, hurry up before the neighbors see."

Lake followed her in. The house was airy and light, with children's toys on the floor and pictures of ships on the walls. "This is nice," he said. "How do you like Aunt Ilsa's house in Maine, by the way?"

"I love it," she said. She studied Randall. "He's matted."

"I like the look. Sort of casual macho."

"What happened to his hair?"

"He had a boating accident."

"His head—it's a kind of two-tone brown."

"I think he has some cocker spaniel blood."

She inspected with her fingers, parting the hairs. "You didn't," she said.

"You'll hurt his feelings."

"You dyed him," she said. She gave a yelp of laughter.

"You're wrong. This is Renard."

She sank into a chair and looked at Lake in wonderment. "You're completely nuts."

"This is Renard," he said.

"Okay, it's Renard."

"Where are the kids?"

"In the kitchen."

Lake went into the kitchen. Emily, dressed in pajamas, sat at a table, playing a mommy-and-daddy game with a spoon and fork. Steebie was in a high chair, grudgingly accepting spoonfuls of white stuff from a babysitter. His chin and bib were covered with globs.

"Hi, I'm Lake," he said to the babysitter.

"Hi."

"Sort of a messy eater you've got there."

"He's not very cooperative."

Karen came in. "Margaret, did you meet my brother Lake? Emily, say hello to Uncle Lake."

"Hello, Uncalake," Emily said, without looking up from her game. Lake was glad he had come.

Later, when the kids were in bed and the babysitter had gone home, he sat with Karen and talked. "Sometimes I feel like I'm programmed for disaster," he said. "Like father, like son."

"Not really," she said.

"There's a difference, though. Dad does whatever he feels like doing and doesn't even bother to conceal it. I do whatever I want, but I hide it. Afraid of the uproar, I guess."

"There are many differences, Lake."

"I wish Aunt Ilsa had never left me the house. It's screwed up everything."

"Did you tell Jennifer about the will and her grandfather?"

"No."

"You have to. Maybe it won't bother her, or maybe she'll see some way around it. But you have to tell her."

"I was going to. But I didn't handle it right."

"What do you mean?"

"I asked her out. I wanted to talk to her in relaxed circumstances. I thought maybe it would be easier that way."

"I knew it."

He shrugged.

"That was really dumb," Karen said angrily. "She's selling the house. She's the agent. Asking her out puts her in a very difficult position professionally—not to mention the difficult position she doesn't even know about."

"Something was already bothering her."

"It's your own fault, Lake."

"Maybe in three months she'll feel differently. You've got to be patient about these things," he said.

Karen didn't say anything.

"I've been very busy at work anyway."

"You like her."

"Yes, I like her."

"She's not your type."

"What's my type?"

"You were smitten with Charlotte, for example. She's the exact opposite of Jennifer, running around and organizing everybody, always being outrageous."

"Charlotte's okay. She just burns a little brighter than most."

"You had a thing for her."

"It wasn't serious," he said. "Anyway, she's married now."

"If you can call it marriage. Frank Sibley is the ultimate creep."

"We were talking about Jennifer, not Charlotte."

"Jennifer isn't the kind of person you can use," Karen said.

"You think I'm using her?"

"Aren't you?"

"I wasn't looking at it that way."

"No one ever really gets away with using people, even if they think they do," Karen said. "But Jennifer would always know. She's very perceptive, Lake."

"I can tell, unfortunately."

They were silent. Lake was afraid the conversation was over. He would have to go to bed and return to Philadelphia tomorrow, no better off than before.

"Am I Jennifer's type?" he said. "I mean, if I wasn't using her."

Karen shook her head.

"I was afraid of that," Lake said. "Anyway, I'm not going to see her for a long time."

"That's good."

He looked out into the darkness beyond the windows. "I messed this up," he said. "I really did."

"Maybe you should talk to her grandfather. There might be some flexibility with the terms of the will. Or I could talk to him. I could sound him out."

"It's my problem," he said. "But thanks."

"I'm glad you still have the dog."

"The dog is a troublemaker," Lake said. He headed upstairs. Behind him, Karen said, "She may be your type, Lake."

9

*P*erhaps time would erase Jennifer's memories of his sly-
ness, but only if he proceeded no further down the present
road. He would not sell the house through her. Maybe he
would sell it later—some other way—but she would not be a part of
it. If he did ask her out again and get to know her better, he would
try to tell her everything. It was good that he wouldn't see her for a
long time. Explaining would be hard.

The next morning, he struggled out of a dream-sea crowded
with swimming dogs and Steebie in a high chair and a powerboat
that kept running in circles. After Karen and the babysitter and
the children left for the beach, Lake sat beside the telephone in the
living room. It occurred to him that this would be an easier call to
make if he had a car phone: the words would be spoken on the
fly.

He dialed Jennifer's office, preparing to hang up on her voice-mail message. But she picked up her phone.

"Jennifer Dee."

"This is Lake."

"Hi," she said in a flat voice.

"How are you?"

"Fine."

"That's good. Listen, I won't take up much of your time. I have just two things to say, but first I want to stress that they are in no way connected."

"Hold on a second, would you?" she said. She put her hand over the mouthpiece. He could hear her talking to another woman but couldn't quite make out the words. Then she came back on the line. "Sorry," she said. "What were you saying?"

"That I have two things to say."

"Hold on." Her hand went over the mouthpiece again. He heard a muffled word that sounded like "counter-offer." Then she came on the line again. "Sorry," she said. "We have a crisis here."

"And they are in no way connected."

"What?"

"In no particular order, they are—"

The woman's voice could be heard in the background again. Jennifer said, "Can I call you back?"

"This'll only take a minute," he said.

"Okay. What is connected?"

"They are in no way connected."

"What is in no way connected? I'm glad you called. I wanted to give you a report."

"In random order, the two things are: First—about the other day—I realize I was definitely out of line and never should have asked you to have dinner with me. It was wrong, and I apologize. I'm temporarily sorry, I really am. I wish I hadn't done it. I hope you'll forgive me."

"You're temporarily sorry?"

"Yes."

"I don't get that."

"Don't get what?"

"How do you mean temporarily sorry?"

"Never mind. I'm just trying to say two simple things as honestly as I can. The second thing is, I want to take the house off the market. I have to. I'm not ready to sell."

"Are you absolutely sure?"

"Nothing's absolute, but I'm sure."

"Do you remember the Dankmyers, the people who looked at the house on Saturday?"

"Yes."

"I think they're going to make an offer. I can't guarantee it, but I think they will. If you take the house off the market, they may disappear. There are lots of problems with taking a house off the market and putting it back on."

"I've got to."

"Can we talk about it?" she said. "Are you free for lunch tomorrow?"

"I'm in Martha's Vineyard," he said.

"What are you doing there?"

"Visiting Karen."

"I thought you were planning to go to Nantucket in two weeks."

"I changed my mind."

"Oh."

"About lunch," he said.

"Maybe I could call you later," Jennifer said. "What's your number there?"

"Ask me about lunch again."

"We can't exactly have lunch if you're on the Vineyard. I could call you tomorrow."

"I'll be back in Philadelphia on Wednesday."

"Can we discuss it then?" she said.

"About lunch."

"Are you free for lunch on Wednesday?"

"Yes. But I'm still taking the house off the market."

"I just want you to understand what's at stake."

"I'm beginning to understand what's at stake."

A call came into the office as he was leaving for the restaurant, and he had to listen to an engineer's explanation of how the valve on a propane tank works, but he was too distracted to pay attention. When he arrived, Jennifer was sitting at a table along one wall, looking cool and professional and sipping iced tea. "Sorry I'm late," he said. "Some engineer thought we were going to incinerate thousands of innocent consumers."

"How was your trip?" she said.

"Good. I did some sailing, but that part didn't go too well."

"What happened?"

"I sank."

"That sounds pretty drastic."

"It wasn't so bad."

"Was the weather nice?"

"Excellent. How was the weather here?"

"It was bad all Monday and part of yesterday."

"The garden could use some rain," he said.

"How's Karen?"

"Fine. Are you a gardener?"

"I don't have a garden."

"Would you be, if you did?"

"Probably," she said.

"It looks like it's going to rain this afternoon," he said.

"It does look that way."

"How do you feel about vegetable gardens? Maybe I should mix some vegetables with the flowers in my garden—make it more productive."

"Let's talk about the house," she said.

"We are."

"I mean about the possibility of keeping it on the market for a little while longer."

"The impossibility."

"Can you tell me why you want to withdraw it now?"

"I'd rather not."

"Did word get out that it's for sale? We've been very careful."

"I'm sure you have."

"You realize you'll have to notify us in writing that you're withdrawing it from the market."

"I'll put a letter in the mail this afternoon."

He waited for her to get up and leave. But she stayed. "Jennifer, I just can't sell it now," he said. "I have a problem."

"Is it a big problem?"

"I'm not sure. Believe it or not, it has something to do with a dog, but that's all I'm going to tell you."

"It doesn't sound so big."

He didn't answer. He sat fiddling with the silverware, remembering Emily playing a private game with a spoon and a fork—a game that could never go wrong.

"I have a suggestion," she said after a while.

"I'm sorry about this," he said.

"Here's my suggestion. We won't show the property to anyone else. If the Dankmyers decide to bid, I'll communicate their offer to you. They're on the verge of bidding. All you have to do is listen. Then you can say no if you want. But if you decide the offer is a good one and your problem can be worked out, you might want to accept. That would automatically reactivate the contract. We would get our commission, and you would sell your house."

"That's not fair to the Dankmyers, since I'm going to say no."

"You have nothing to lose by listening, and at this point, neither do the Dankmyers. They've done their thinking. I showed them the house again yesterday."

"You mean, no matter what, I just say no?"

"Unless you decide to say yes or to negotiate."

"You think I might not say no?"

"People sometimes change their minds when they have a good

offer. It happens. The Dankmyers aren't under any illusions. I told them you were considering taking the house off the market."

"What did they say?"

"They seemed to feel you were negotiating in advance."

"I'll never understand real estate. It's like a hall of mirrors."

"A lot of it is trying to keep everyone's mind open. You have to keep the dialogue going."

"I'm in favor of that part, the dialogue."

"Good," she said.

"It's a form of playing for time, I guess."

"In a way."

"I believe in playing for time," he said. "The Dankmyers like the house?"

"Very much."

"How do you feel about it? I mean, not as an agent, just as a regular person."

At that moment, the waiter arrived and asked if they were ready to order. They studied the menu. "The fish here is usually very fresh," Lake said.

"I'm having a salad," she said.

"They've got bluefish."

"Salad."

"Bluefish are hard to catch," he said. "It requires great patience."

"Salads take a long time to grow."

After they ordered, they talked about sailboats, and she explained jibing. "Personally, I prefer powerboats," he said. He described Karen's house on the Vineyard—but not to her satisfaction. She wanted to know specific information about rooms, and square footage, and windows and appliances. He couldn't tell her where the washing machine and dryer were located—if they existed at all.

When they were almost finished, he said, "Do you think my house is a mausoleum?"

"Not at all. It's special."

"What I'm really asking is, do you think it's ridiculous for a person like me to be living in a house like that?"

"I don't know you very well. But I don't think it's ridiculous."

"I'm mostly what I seem to be," he said. "A few flaws, but I'm planning to repair them. I'll tell you one thing I've discovered. I like Victorian paintings. I can't believe it. I actually like them. Aunt Ilsa had good taste." A silence descended. "How's your salad?" he said finally.

"Very good."

"How's your grandfather?"

"My grandmother, you mean?"

"Right, your grandmother. How is she?"

"Fine, I think."

"I met this wonderful older woman in Nantucket named Mrs. Hayes. She's about seventy. She has a very long view of everything, as if she lives on a completely different time scale."

"Maybe that's what happens when you get old."

"She was that way when she was young. She was telling me about how she married her husband Alfred. Their courtship lasted five years."

"They weren't sure about each other, I guess," Jennifer said.

"Alfred was sure."

"Do you know that for a fact?" Jennifer said.

"Well, he was very persistent," he said.

"Even then, people aren't always clear about what they're feeling," she said. "They believe they care about someone, but the feelings aren't necessarily what they think."

"Has that ever happened to you?" Lake said.

"Yes."

"Me, too," he said.

After a moment, he said, "I didn't mean to get into all this serious stuff."

"It's okay."

"Do you want coffee?"

"No, thanks." She was thinking about something. "I was kind of rude the other day, on Saturday," she said.

"No, you weren't."

"I could have handled it better."

"Don't say that." He suddenly began to feel strangely upset, or strangely something. "You handled it exactly right."

She shook her head.

He told himself that he should consolidate his gains with Jennifer. This lunch had brought the beginnings of a friendly relationship between them. He should settle for that. It was enough. Perhaps it was as much as there would ever be, although he hoped that someday there could be more, because he sensed that they had things in common, points of resonance.

Her eyes were cast down, her mind far away. He became weak. The weakness spread through him. He told himself: Don't do it. But he was going to do it; he was going to ask her out.

"Jennifer," he said, "I swore I wouldn't, but I will anyway.

Would you have dinner with me sometime?" But even as he said it, he knew he couldn't face her amazement and disgust. "On October 9," he said. "In three months. But forget that. I'm just being stupid. No one plans that far ahead. Listen, did you get enough to eat? A salad isn't very much."

"Let me see," she said. She pulled a leather-bound calendar book from her bag and leafed through the pages until she came to October. "It looks like I'm free." She took out a fountain pen and made a small notation: Lake Stevenson.

"I'll pick you up at eight," he said.

She made a notation of the time.

"I made an ironclad resolution not to ask you out again until then," Lake said. "That's what I meant when I said I was temporarily sorry."

"I see."

"But would you have dinner with me sometime sooner? We could go to a movie."

"Okay."

"You will?"

"Yes."

"Tomorrow?"

"All right."

She sipped the last of her iced tea. Then they were outside.

"And we're agreed about everything?" she said.

"Maybe not everything."

"But you've agreed to listen to an offer if the Dankmyers make a bid in the next few days."

"My mind is closed," he said.

"It's a little bit open," she said.

"When do I get to close it?"

"Soon," she said.

When he rang the doorbell of her house in Merion, a curly-haired guy opened the door. "Is Jennifer here?" Lake said.

"Jennifer!" the guy shouted, then: "Come in. I'm Mike. Have a seat." He gestured toward a worn sofa and left the room. Lake poked through the magazines and catalogues piled helter-skelter on the coffee table. A can of Coke rested beside the telephone.

Jennifer came downstairs. She wore a dark skirt and a blue sleeveless silk blouse. He stood. The words in him were: You are more beautiful than anything in the whole world.

"Ready," she said.

He held the door for her.

"That was Mike Rankin," she said as they walked to the car.

"How many people did you say are sharing the house?"

"Six, but two are getting married. I don't think we'll go back to six, though. It looked messy, didn't it?"

"Not very."

"We've scheduled a big cleanup for this weekend. I'm doing the kitchen."

"Do you like having housemates?"

"Most of the time. We all get along, but it can be kind of chaotic."

"My house is the opposite. Just me and my dog."

"Reynolds, is that his name?"

"Renard."

"But he's not your dog, right?"

"At present, he is."

He opened the car door for her.

"I thought you told me you didn't have a car phone," she said.

"I was jealous of yours."

She laughed. He realized that he wanted to sit beside her in a movie theater. "Why don't we go to the movie first and eat afterward?" he said.

"All right."

*A*s a car chase flashed and leaped on the screen and the theater filled with the screams of tires and terrified pedestrians and torn metal, Lake paid no attention whatever. He was content to be beside her, with her bare arm so near that he wondered if perhaps some tiny particles of self were crossing the gap in quantum excursions.

Later, at the restaurant, he said "I remember you when you were about thirteen."

"I remember you," she said.

"Do your parents live in Haverford? Maybe we were neighbors."

"They moved to Florida a few years ago."

"But you have family in Philadelphia."

"Just an aunt and uncle and some cousins. And my grandparents."

"Did you and Karen see each other much after she went to Greenwich?"

"We've always stayed in touch," she said. "You didn't move to Greenwich, did you?"

"I didn't have to. I was about to start college when my mother died."

"That must have been a hard time."

"It was," he said.

"Karen said she felt like the family was coming apart."

"I couldn't live with my father. Karen could, but I couldn't. It made me crazy whenever I visited. But I never knew she felt that way. About the family coming apart, I mean."

"She did."

"I wish I had known that."

"What did you do after college?" she said.

"I worked for a publishing company. Then I started my own company."

"You like your work, don't you?"

"Very much."

"You were a photographer. Once Karen and I snuck into your darkroom. We thought we spoiled your pictures when we opened the door."

"You probably did."

She smiled, impish.

"You were a chatterbox. I remember that," he said.

"I wasn't."

"You talked all the time."

"I was never a chatterbox."

"Now you're a sphinx."

"I'm not."

"So what are you?"

"I'm balanced," she said. "Actually, I'm not perfectly balanced."

"How are you not in balance?" he said.

"I don't think I'll tell you."

"I love talking to you," Lake said.

"Why?"

"I just do."

They talked about people in her office—a woman named Binky whose son had been having trouble at school, a friend named Harriet who had been a mentor, a man who was angling for the top position. "What's his name?" said Lake.

"Robert Tinley."

"Bob. It figures."

"He's very good."

"Beware of anyone named Bob," he said.

"Are you speaking from experience?"

"Not direct experience."

"What did Bob do in your case?" she said.

"I'll never know exactly, but I'm sure he doesn't obey all the Lord's commandments. Also, he likes clothes too much."

"Robert Tinley is a very natty dresser."

"See, they're all alike."

"I used to go out with someone named Bob."

"Was he like the rest of them?"

"No."

"It was a serious thing?"

"For a while. Then it had to be more serious or less serious. He's in California now."

Lake waited.

"But your Bob theory is wrong," she said.

"My theories usually are."

"People named Amanda, that's different. They're the ones to beware of."

"Did it become less serious?" he said.

"What?"

"Bob. The one who went to California."

"It stopped being anything at all."

Lake saw that it was so.

"I know an Amanda," he said. "Not much of a dresser, but you may be right about Amandas."

Later, he said, "The idea I mentioned the other day about mixing vegetables with the flowers in my garden, I don't think you approved."

"No, not really."

"It's not the usual thing, but why not?"

"Why would you want to do that? It's a lovely garden."

"I could grow salad things, for example."

"Or you could go to the supermarket," she said.

"Vegetables would help attract wildlife. I've been spending a lot of time watching what goes on back there. I've got a mockingbird who's always giving speeches, but I can't figure out who he thinks his audience is."

"Guarding his territory."

"From what?"

"Other mockingbirds."

"Ah."

"Do you have a park near your apartment or a backyard or

anything?" she said. "We have a backyard, but we've never done anything with it."

"I'm giving up my apartment. But I wouldn't have moved back there anyway if I sold the house. It's a very inhospitable place."

"Where will you go if you move?" she said.

"I don't know."

"Another apartment?"

"A house. But I'm not planning to move."

She turned thoughtful.

"Are you picturing a house that might suit me?" he said.

"Trying."

"What does it look like?"

"I can't picture anything."

"There must be someplace where I would fit," he said. "Invent one for me."

"Why would I do that? My mind doesn't work that way."

"Mine does. Inventing sort of enlivens things, if the circumstances are right."

"Like how?"

"Well, like a really small example would be at your grandparents' party, when some woman was talking about her trip to England and asked me in a snotty way if I had been there recently. I said no. But I could have said that I had returned from London that very day. Then we might have had an interesting discussion."

"But that would have led to more lies."

"Adjustments. If she asked me where I stayed, I could invent a place, the Green Ox or something, and if she put on the pressure, I would make a good fighting retreat. No harm done."

"That's terrible," she said.

He saw that he had blundered into a bad place. "I don't do it much anymore," he said.

"Why do you do it at all?" she said.

"I don't know," he said. "But I'm stopping. I've stopped. I would never tell the smallest lie to you."

"How could I know, if that's the way you think?"

He saw how right she was. "I don't know how to answer that," he said.

She was silent.

"Do I have to answer?" he said.

"No."

"Old habits," he said. "Changing is hard."

"It's not that hard. Not if you want to."

"It seems hard."

"It's not."

"You're very nice, Jennifer."

"You're nicer than you think you are."

Then, since he felt something closing in on him, he asked her if she liked sports, and she said she liked tennis, and he asked her if she liked baseball, and she said she didn't know anything about it, and he asked her what she liked to do when she was free to do anything at all, and she said she liked to read. The subject of the truth was safely behind them, forgotten for the moment.

They talked about favorite cities, favorite climates, her bicycling trip in Canada, the best mountain bikes, the feeling of mountains, the psychology of mountain climbers. "I've been learning about dog psychology," he said. "Dogs consider themselves indispensable. It doesn't occur to them that they're anything except terrific."

"It must be nice."

"I suspect they hold humans in slight contempt."

"Are you talking about Renard?"

"Maybe not contempt," he said. "But they're highly independent thinkers. Also quite subtle. You have to stay alert when you're dealing with Renard. Do you think dogs are upset when they have to move to a different house?"

"Without their owner, you mean?"

"With or without. Either way."

"I think what dogs care about is their owner, not where they live."

"But dogs are very concerned with territory."

"Their territory is where their owner is."

"Maybe it's as simple as that," he said.

They talked about the virtues of a slate roof and the performance of the mayor. Then he saw her suppress a yawn. "You're tired," he said.

"A little. It's been a long day."

"I'll get the check."

"This was delicious," she said.

Outside, he stood quietly beside her as they waited for the car. He didn't feel the need to talk anymore. Before tonight, he could never find the right words to say to her. Now they were gathering inside him, an inexhaustible supply.

"What a nice night," she said.

"It is."

On the way back, they listened to a classical music station. "Here we are," he said when they pulled up in front of her house. At her front door, she said, "Thank you very much. I had a lovely time."

"Me, too," he said. "Good night."

"Night."

He kissed her on the cheek. Friends now.

10

*J*ennifer phoned the next day, late in the afternoon. "Lake, I have to tell you something."

"What is it?"

"I just got a call from Lydia Dankmyer. Her husband went to your house. She called me because she was feeling guilty about it."

"Start again."

"She told me her husband went to your house this morning. To look at the outside. They're about to make an offer and he was worried about the condition of the shutters or something—she wasn't sure what—and he went over there to make a last-minute check. They know the house can't be shown on Fridays. I told them that weeks ago, but he went there anyway."

"Of course," he said.

"What do you mean?"

"What were your exact instructions about Fridays?"

"I said the owner doesn't want the house to be shown on Mondays or Fridays."

"That explains it. Him going there on a Monday or Friday was inevitable. I'm surprised he didn't go on both days."

"I don't understand."

"This is my field. This is what I do for a living. For any procedure, you have to spell out the rules so that there is absolutely no room for maneuver. You have to say: Do not, under any imaginable circumstances, for any reason of any kind, go to the house on Mondays or Fridays; do not approach it or enter it, upon pain of scuttling the whole deal. If you don't cut off every possibility for disobedience, it's guaranteed to happen. It's a law of human nature."

"He didn't go inside."

"Well, it's probably all right then."

"But your housekeeper came out."

"Ah."

"She saw him walking around and came out and asked him what he was doing."

"What did he say?"

"Lydia wasn't exactly clear about that. But I think her husband told your housekeeper that he was thinking about buying the house and had to be sure of its condition."

"In other words, he told her it's for sale."

"Apparently."

"Here we go," Lake said.

"I never dreamed he would do anything like that."

"It's not your fault."

"I hope it hasn't upset your housekeeper."

"I'll explain it to her somehow," he said. He tried to imagine a diversionary story: Maybe he could convince her that Dankmyer was a wily tax inspector and was doing an assessment of the house; after all, he had half persuaded Mary that the dyeing of Randall was just an aesthetic experiment. But he was sure it was too late. Mrs. Lundquist had probably alerted Vere the minute Dankmyer left.

"I'm very sorry, Lake. I'll speak to Mr. Dankmyer."

"Don't bother. He was just doing what came naturally. I'll take care of everything."

"Lydia Dankmyer says they're going to make an offer tomorrow."

"It's pointless."

"But you'll listen?"

"I said I would. But my answer will be no."

"Just listen. That's all you have to do."

"Will you have lunch with me tomorrow? I know a really nice restaurant out in the country. They have great salads."

"I'm busy all tomorrow. Weekends are the busiest time. I wish I could."

"Someday soon, then."

"Bye."

*H*e was sitting on the terrace with Randall the next morning when he heard the telephone ring. A hummingbird was darting among the flowers, and patches of shadow stirred on the lawn. He reached the phone on the fifth ring.

"It's me, Jennifer," she said.

"I was sitting in the sun."

"I have an offer from the Dankmyers."

"I'm listening, but my mind is made up."

"I'd like to tell you about it in person so I can answer any questions."

"Is that what real estate agents do, present offers in person?"

"They usually do, yes. It helps."

"It's a nice policy."

"When is a good time?" she said.

"Now would be good."

He returned to the terrace and stretched out on the chaise and closed his eyes and waited for her to come visit him in his house. After a while, the phone rang again. He hurried in, hoping she hadn't changed her mind.

"Mr. Stevenson?" said a deliberate voice.

"Yes."

"This is Billington Vere."

"Good morning, Mr. Vere."

"My wife has just received a very puzzling telephone call from Mrs. Lundquist. She asked about the possibility of working for us full-time. She said that she will be available because you are selling the house."

"I see."

"Are you selling the house, Mr. Stevenson?"

"No. I thought about it, but right now I'm not selling the house."

"You do remember that you agreed to take the property on a

particular condition? The condition was that you keep and maintain the house as a home for your aunt's dog for the rest of its natural life. Do I need to remind you of that?"

"Didn't Mrs. Lundquist tell you that Randall disappeared? Didn't she mention that?"

"Randall is the dog?"

"Was."

"I don't talk to Mrs. Lundquist about dogs, Mr. Stevenson, or about anything else, for that matter. It's hardly her concern. You say the dog is gone?"

"Unfortunately, yes."

Just then, the doorbell chimed. Randall barked.

"Mr. Stevenson."

"Yes?"

"Did I hear a dog bark?"

"Possibly. Not the dog you think."

"I'm coming over, Mr. Stevenson. Stay right where you are. And I want that dog to be there when I arrive." He hung up.

Lake stood thinking. This was a time for great ingenuity; this called for perhaps his greatest fighting retreat ever. He could grab Randall, and together they would make their escape through the garage and not return for several days. He could sell him to the Dankmyers along with the house, thus fulfilling the spirit of his aunt's will. He could—

The doorbell chimed again. He went into the hall and studied his reflection in the mirror. The person there had the appearance of a decent, honest individual—a bit strained, perhaps, but surely not a criminal.

He opened the door. Jennifer smiled at him, holding up a manila envelope—the offer from the Dankmyers, no doubt. "You've got to leave," he said. "It turns out this isn't a good time after all."

"What's the matter?"

"A small difficulty. Can you come back in a half hour?"

She grew solemn. It hurt him to watch her expression change. He heard a car approach. "Quick, come in," he said, and pulled her through the door, thinking he would rush her out the back, or possibly hide her in the attic—but all the while knowing that there was nothing he could do to extricate himself this time.

The doorbell chimed. Randall barked. Lake opened the door and was pinned by Vere's prosecutorial glare. To buy time, he said, "You are well, I trust?"

Vere ignored him for the moment. "Jennifer, what are you doing here?" he said.

"Hello, Granddad," she said. "I'm here on business."

"I see," he said. He thought for a moment. "Does it have anything to do with selling this house?"

Jennifer turned to Lake.

"The house isn't for sale, Mr. Vere," Lake said.

"But you were considering selling it," Vere said coldly. "According to Mrs. Lundquist, some man she encountered yesterday believes he might buy it."

"It's not for sale now."

"This is most interesting," Vere said. "Jennifer, were you aware that Mr. Stevenson's aunt left him this house on the condition that he keep it as a home for her dog for the rest of the dog's life?"

"No, I wasn't," she said.

"You did agree to that condition, didn't you, Mr. Stevenson?"

"I'm afraid I did. And I must say that I admired Aunt Ilsa's concept. She was a bold thinker."

"You agreed to what you choose to call her concept," said Vere, "and yet I find that you have taken steps to sell the house while the dog is very much alive."

"Ah, you think this dog is Randall. No, this is Renard."

"I believe this is your aunt's dog."

"I can prove he's not. I have a photograph of Randall in the living room to prove it."

"Why do you have this dog, then?"

"He's a replacement."

"Were you perhaps afraid of having someone find out that you managed to lose your aunt's dog within weeks of becoming its guardian? I won't ask you what sort of carelessness or thoughtlessness brought that about. A dog whose well-being was vitally important to her. A dog she went to great lengths to provide for. I won't ask how you managed to fail your responsibility to such a degree in so short a time. But I will say that you had good reason to be afraid of people finding out."

"Such things happen, Mr. Vere."

"So you got another dog."

"As good as the old one. My aunt would have liked him."

"No doubt," Vere said. "Although perhaps she might have preferred not to make a change."

"One never knows."

"And in regard to the house that she so generously left you, along with a sum of money more than ample for your expenses, you decided to make a change there as well."

"I said I was thinking about it. It wasn't working out."

"Quite so. And I now learn not only that you are selling the property through my granddaughter but that you have concealed from her critical facts in the matter. Facts that I would describe as shocking."

Lake could not look at her. "I did conceal them, Mr. Vere," he said.

"Are you going to lose this dog, too, when it suits your purposes?"

"No, but he can do whatever he wants. We believe in free choice in this house."

"That's very convenient, isn't it?"

"I don't believe a dog can stand between a person and what they want to do with their property," Lake said.

"No, but honor can."

Lake didn't respond. He knew he had already gone too far, unable to resist the thrust-and-parry of battle.

"I told your aunt we shouldn't have set it up this way," Vere said. "I told her it should be a trusteeship for the dog. She wouldn't listen to me. She said she knew you. She said you would do what's right. It seems she didn't know you well enough."

"I guess not," Lake said quietly.

Vere said, "Is your sister in on this?"

That was it. That was the end. Vere knew exactly how to get to him. "No," Lake said. "No, she is not. She doesn't know anything about it." Rage gathered in him. "But let me tell you something, Mr. Vere. I'll do anything with my house that I want."

"In spite of your aunt's wishes."

"My aunt is dead."

Vere turned away from him in a fury. Lake ignored his existence. He wanted to say: Mr. Vere, the Stevensons are like Vishnu; we possess powers of destruction you cannot even imagine.

Then Vere was gone.

Jennifer was still there. "Now what?" Lake said.

"You seem to make all the decisions around here," she said.

"That's right, I make the decisions."

She tossed the envelope on the hall table. "Do whatever you want," she said. "But you'll have to deal with my partners. I won't have anything more to do with this house."

Then she was gone, too, and he stood among the ruins, feeling a thousand feet tall in the greatness of his wrath, not caring that everything was smashed.

On Monday morning, still angry, he met Mrs. Lundquist at the door, informed her that he no longer needed her services, and handed her a check for two weeks' wages. "Wait, Mrs. Lundquist," he said as she turned to go. "I have something for you." He went to the hall table and returned with the portable television he had readied for her. "Think of it as a parting gift from my aunt," he said.

She backed away.

"No, no, take it," he said. "Who more deserving than you?"

"Thank you."

"You're extremely welcome. Goodbye now."

At the office, he concentrated ferociously on his work. But before noon, Mary said, "What's wrong, Lake?"

"Everything."

"Is there anything I can do?"

"You could shoot me."

"It can't be that bad."

"It's worse. Shooting would be too merciful."

"Can I get you some lunch? How about from that Chinese place you like?"

"Mary, whatever you do, don't be nice to me. I'm not worth it. It's a complete waste."

So they all worked grimly through the day, with none of the usual wisecracks, and the hours creaking by.

*T*he next morning he heard from Jennifer's office. "Mr. Stevenson, this is Binky Foster," a woman said in a bouncy voice. "I'm calling about the Dankmyers' offer on your property in Chestnut Hill."

"I have the offer."

"They were hoping you would respond to it. We received your letter about withdrawing the property, of course. But my understanding is that you might be willing to consider a bid from them."

"I am considering it."

"We feel it's a very good offer."

"Who's we?"

"We at Mayhew, Foster."

"I am considering it."

"Do you know when you might make a decision?"

"Very soon."

"I'll tell the Dankmyers. They're quite eager for a response. Can I answer any questions about the bid?"

"No questions. I'll get back to you sometime this week, as soon as I make up my mind." He hung up.

He looked out the window. All he had to do was say yes. He didn't know why he delayed, since he had already decided to accept. The offer was higher than he had ever expected, and it had no contingencies. Jennifer would get a commission so big that, at least in financial terms, she might not think of him as the worst person she had ever met. His life would be restored to its former simplicity. He didn't know where he would live. Probably closer to the office. He would be able to afford anything at all, with plenty of money left over for the expansion of InstruX.

He thought about calling Karen. He wanted her to take her pick of the silver and china; it should stay in the family. But at this moment he couldn't even face talking to Karen, the one person who might understand.

*J*esus came in the night. Lake was in the office of some law enforcement people, and Jesus arrived, entering quietly. His hair was long, He was dressed in a white robe, and He wore a crown of thorns. He stepped into the room, gazed thoughtfully at Lake, and shook His head, indicating that forgiveness was out of the question. Cooperation between Jesus and the FBI seemed quite natural in the dream. Lake wanted to say he was sorry, but no words would come out.

A light rain fell the next day. That evening, he didn't bother to grab a snack in the kitchen or to turn on the seven o'clock news. He went straight through the house to the garden and walked around the flower beds, memorizing their layout and colors. He wanted a small flower garden at the next place where he lived. Flowers were good, a gentle transaction between people and the planet.

Droplets clung to the petals and leaves, and bees were still at work. He liked the blue flowers that resembled bells. He liked the tall white things. He liked them all. As he walked around with Randall trailing behind him, he saw that the days were already growing shorter, and he decided that even if the Dankmyers didn't want to move into the house right away, he would move out as soon as possible.

In the library, he put on Bach to cleanse his mind, then opened the mail. One letter was addressed to Mrs. Ilsa Grinnell. It bore a return address of Green Grove Memorial Park, Haverford, Pennsylvania. He had forgotten about the almost-illegible note Aunt Ilsa had left in her desk drawer:

Lake Green Grove Mr Witter

Inside was a single sheet of notepaper, with a brief message typed on a manual typewriter:

Dear Mrs. Grinnell:

This is to remind you that we await your instructions about the stone.

Sincerely yours,
Louis Witter

A memorial park. A stone. A stone that evidently involved a promise or obligation. He tossed it aside, tired of entanglements, no longer interested in the bizarre workings of his aunt's mind.

Again, he tried to muster the strength to call Karen. He didn't know what he would talk about. Maybe he would ask her about the time when she felt that the family was coming apart. Maybe she would want to tell him about her feelings at that time, if he asked. But he didn't call.

*A*t work the next day, he noted the top entry on his calendar book: Call Binky Foster. But he didn't call.

Later, to put off that conversation a little longer, he looked up the number for Green Grove Memorial Park. An elderly man answered. "Green Grove. Louis Witter."

"Mr. Witter, this is Ilsa Grinnell's nephew. Your letter came to me. My name is Lake Stevenson."

"Uh-huh," he said. "You're house-sitting for the summer?"

"My aunt is dead, Mr. Witter. I'm living in her house."

The phone went silent. Finally, Mr. Witter said, "I'm sorry to hear that."

"She died in early April."

"I'm real sorry."

"You mentioned a stone."

"Yes, your aunt ordered it back in February. She said she'd let me know about the arrangements for it later, but I never heard from her."

"What kind of stone is it?"

"Marble. The very best. Made for us in Georgia."

"It's a gravestone?"

"That's right."

"Mr. Witter, what sort of memorial park is Green Grove?"

"A pet cemetery."

"Did she indicate what arrangements she was thinking about?"

"I seem to remember her saying she had to explain about the stone to someone. I had trouble understanding her when she ordered it. She didn't sound well. Sounded very bad."

"She had several strokes."

"I'm sorry to hear about her passing. I've known her for a long time. She was a good friend to me."

"Could I come out there?"

"Sure."

"I'd like to come right away." He wrote down the directions. Then he said to Mary, "I'll be gone for an hour or so. If someone named Binky Foster calls, tell her I'll be in touch this afternoon. Come, on Renard."

"You can leave Renard here, if you want."

"I'll take him. I need the company."

*G*reen Grove was surprisingly small—a grassy acre shaded by a few old trees, with an ornate iron fence around the perimeter. He parked in the gravel lot beside the office building. Instead of going in, he followed a winding path out through the cemetery. Randall watched from the front seat of the car.

Grave markers and monuments were everywhere, hundreds of

them. Flowers had been left at some of the graves, and offerings of pet food, and little American flags. Beside one grave was a tattered Snoopy doll. In a few places, plastic windmills twirled festively in the breeze. Lake began reading inscriptions:

Lisalee
1970–1982
Our Little Darling
The McNair Family

Donny
Until We Meet Again
Anna Strong

Jinx
1951–1965
My best friend in this selfish world
Goodbye
Joe

Trinket
Sleep Well My Angel
Mommy

Tiger
1985–1986
We Will Love You For All Eternity
God's Will Be Done
The Beardsley Family

On the grave marker for Tiger was a plastic-sheathed photograph of a tiny fluffy white dog with bright eyes and a black button of a nose.

Many of the graves were gathered in family clusters. Anna Strong had buried three dogs side by side. Joe had owned a sequence of three Jinxes. Lake wandered, hunting for his aunt's name. He knew he would find it, and he did. Under an oak tree, five grave markers were lined up in a row. The first was a simple brass plaque.

Rudy
1927–1939 Beloved Pet of
Ilsa Stevenson

The second was slightly larger, also of brass.

Risa
1939–1951
My Darling
Ilsa Stevenson

The rest were marble and undated.

Roland
My Beloved Friend
Ilsa Grinnell

Rima
My Beloved Friend
Ilsa Grinnell

Rosy
My Beloved Friend
Ilsa Grinnell

Lake stood there for a while. Then he walked to the office building and pushed through the screen door. An old man was sitting behind a desk littered with papers.

"I'm Lake Stevenson, Mr. Witter," Lake said.

"Mrs. Grinnell's nephew, you said."

"All her dogs are buried here."

"Every one," Mr. Witter said.

"She must have been young when she buried the first one."

"Just a girl. Not even grown up. I remember when she came because I was starting the business then. I still remember her. Just a child, and she came by herself. She knew what she wanted to do and she had saved up her money."

He looked as though he had been crying, but maybe it was age. "She was a good friend to me," he said. "She helped me out one time. And she's always brought every one of her dogs here. I believe she would want to be laid to rest here herself, if she could."

"I believe she would."

"I'll bring you the stone," he said. He went into the back room and emerged with a flat rectangular package. "It's good that you've come," he said. He pulled the brown wrapping paper off and handed him the pinkish marble stone. It said:

Randall
Our Beloved Friend
Ilsa Grinnell
Lake Stevenson

Lake looked at it for a long time.

Finally, Mr. Witter said, "Do you have her dog?"

"Yes."

"She wanted his stone to be ready for him when his time comes. Wanted their time together to be remembered."

"Yes."

"Well, here it is."

"Keep it at Green Grove, Mr. Witter, if you would. Is it paid for? Can I pay for the storage?"

"No, no charge."

"When the time comes, he'll be buried here."

"I'm glad of that."

Lake held out his hand. Mr. Witter shook it. "Thank you, Mr. Witter," he said.

*H*e called the real estate agency from his car phone, remembering the number, dialing as he waited at a red light. When Binky Foster came on the line, he said, "It's Lake Stevenson. I've made up my mind. I'm not selling the house. Please tell the Dankmyers I can't accept their offer."

"You're sure?"

"I'm sure."

"Do you think there's any possibility you might reconsider? The Dankmyers might be open to discussion."

"No possibility. But it was a very good offer."

"I'll tell them."

"Could you switch me to Jennifer Dee?"

"I'm afraid she's not here."

"Where is she?"

"She asked me to handle this, Mr. Stevenson."

"I don't want to talk to her about the house. It's about something else, and it's important."

"I'll tell her that you want to speak to her."

"Where is she now? Please, there's something I have to tell her. It's personal."

"She just left to view a house in Merion. I don't believe they have a telephone there. I'll have her call you."

"Could I have the number of her car phone?"

"I'll have her call you."

"Please," he said. "It's important."

He heard rustling. She gave him the number. He dialed as he drove.

"This is Lake."

"Yes?" she said in a toneless voice.

"I need to tell you something."

She didn't reply.

"It's about why I wanted to sell the house. And something else."

"You don't have to explain anything to me."

"Yes, I do."

"Well, be quick."

"I'm not far away. I'm driving. It's strange to talk car-to-car. You're moving, I'm moving. Too much moving."

"What did you want to tell me?"

"One thing is that I misunderstood my aunt," he said. "Her will said I could have the house if I also took the dog."

"I know all that."

"It was the way she intended it that I didn't understand. I thought it was entirely about her—her dog, her house, setting up things so her world would go on the way she wanted even after she died. But I was wrong. She was sharing the thing that mattered most."

"What was that?"

"Her dog. I just found out."

"Found out?" she said, sounding puzzled.

"She wanted him to be buried with all the dogs she ever had in her life, and she wanted her name to be on the grave in remembrance. She had a gravestone made for him in advance, for when he dies. But she put my name on it with hers, so he would belong to both of us. I saw the gravestone. That's how I found out."

"Lake, I'm almost at this place."

"Can you sit in the car for a minute? I have a couple more things to say."

"Just for a minute."

"I'll be quick. My mistake about her isn't the important part."

"What's the important part?"

But the words about lying wouldn't come.

"Are you there?" she said.

"Yes."

"What's the important part?"

Finally he said, "Now I know why real estate agents like to present offers in person."

"Why?"

"Because of the importance."

She was silent for a moment. Then she said, "Are you saying you want to tell me this in person?"

"Yes, I am," he said, and tears crept into his eyes.

"Where are you?"

"I think I'm on Jansen Street," he said. "I'm parked."

"I'm at 3214 Highfield Avenue. I'll be sitting in my car outside. But I have to go into the house soon."

"Thank you," he said. He hung up.

Three minutes later, he pulled up behind her car, got out, and slid into the passenger seat beside her. "I'm getting rid of my car phone," he said. "I didn't mean to do this to you. I had to talk to you, but I didn't mean to do it this way."

"It's okay."

"I called Binky Foster and told her I couldn't accept the offer."

"All right," she said.

"It was a great offer. You did a fantastic job. I think you had the Dankmyers in mind right from the beginning, from the very first time you came to the house."

"I did."

"I'm sorry about your commission."

She shrugged.

"Have you spoken to your grandfather since Saturday?"

"He called me."

"What did he say?"

"He said I should have no further dealings with you, but I had already decided that."

"Did he talk about honor?"

"Yes."

"He's right," Lake said. "I wanted to tell you about the will, but I was afraid of what you would think of me."

"It's not all your fault," she said. "You tried to take the house off the market. I kept pushing. I thought you might change your mind when you heard the Dankmyers' offer. I knew it was going to be good."

"I have to tell you about a lie, Jennifer. Another one. The last one."

"Okay, tell me."

"Your grandfather will actually feel better about it, but I'm never going to be able to talk to him."

She waited.

"Do you see the dog in your rearview mirror?"

She looked and nodded.

He said, "That's my aunt's dog. His name isn't Renard. I made that up. It's Randall."

"I thought so."

"My aunt's picture of him in the boat gave me the idea. When I was interested in photography, I did a lot of retouching. I retouched Randall."

"I see."

"Pretty dumb."

"Very."

"That's everything," he said. "Thank you for listening to me."

"Thank you for saying it in person."

"It clears the air."

"It does," she said.

Then, because the air was clear: "I'd like to call you sometime."

"All right."

"But not on a car phone."

"No."

He slipped from the car, with the No reverberating in his mind.

11

It was too late in the year to produce a lettuce crop, but a gardening textbook informed him that cabbage was still possible. Anyone who liked salads was bound to like coleslaw, he figured; maybe cabbage cultivation would be his fall gardening project.

In the meantime, work rose like the tide. Derek Kast sent a stream of requests. He wanted a four-color version of some old black-and-white instructions for a pruning tool; he wanted to turn a diagram of sprinkling patterns into an enticing landscape; he wanted a visual sequence on how to dig a flower bed; he wanted a whole new look. A start-up bicycle manufacturer called to see if InstruX would be interested in producing all their sales literature. Danny's work on the software project brought a feeler from a Texas computer company. The workdays began to stretch into the evenings.

Lake had to ask everyone to work on a Saturday, and even then they couldn't catch up.

Toward the end of July, a friend of Paul's appeared in the office—thin, alert-looking, dressed entirely in black, with wire-rimmed glasses. Paul approached Lake's desk and said in his usual cryptic way. "Got a minute?"

"Sure."

He left. His friend came over. "I'm interested in a job," he said. "Paul said you might be looking for someone."

"I wasn't, but maybe one of these days," Lake said. "Are you a designer?"

"A writer."

"What kind of writing do you do?"

"Plays. They're kind of experimental. None have been produced yet."

"The writing we do is real dry stuff. I'm Lake Stevenson, by the way."

"Robert Dickey."

"Do people call you Bob?"

"Rob."

"That's good," Lake said. "I can give you an instant test if you want. At least it'll show you the kind of things we deal with."

"Sure."

Lake searched his desk drawer for the instructions that had come with his new digital watch. He handed the little booklet to Rob, along with the watch. "Last night I was trying to set the time," he said. "These instructions are fairly typical of what we get. Edit a few sentences and see if you can find a way to improve them. You can sit over there."

Rob retired to a chair near the wall, fiddled with the watch, and wrote on a pad Mary gave him. After a while, he handed the watch back to Lake, along with the original instructions and a short rewritten section.

> *When function status of watch is normal time mode (indicates PM or AM), pressing set Button 4 will cause seconds to flash. Pressing Button 3 will cause hours to flash. Pressing Button 1 will cause hours to advance. Pressing Button 3 again will cause minutes to flash. Pressing Button 1 will cause minutes to advance. Pressing set Button 4 will return function status to normal mode.*

had become

> *Your watch is telling normal time when PM or AM appears beside the digits for hours, minutes and seconds. To enter the mode for normal time, press Button 1. To set the time, begin by pressing Button 4; the seconds will begin to flash, indicating that you can now proceed. To set the hours, first press Button 3; the hours digit will begin to flash. Advance to the desired hour by pressing Button 1 again as many times as necessary. To set minutes, press Button 3 again; the minutes digits will begin to flash. Advance by pressing Button 1 again as many times as necessary. Then return to the mode*

for normal time by pressing Button 4 again. Your watch is now set.

"What are your plays about?" Lake said.

"Well, I just finished one that takes place in a manned space capsule that's floating out of the solar system after the navigational gear malfunctions."

"Uh-huh."

"The characters are an astronaut and a computer. Except the computer has malfunctioned, too and it has a kind of speech impediment. It starts talking in code whenever the astronaut says anything in the past or present tense. It will only converse in the future tense."

Lake nodded, wondering if there was a link between writing experimental plays and being an instructional genius. "What you did on these directions is good," he said. "Actually, it's better than good. How about trying a full-scale test assignment? I'll give you part of a project we're working on, and you can bring your edit in whenever it's ready. We'll pay you."

"I set your watch ahead by a minute, by the way," Rob said. "It was slow."

By the end of the week, he had been hired. Office productivity soared. Randall had his old name back. When Lake explained that it had been a case of mistaken identity, Mary raised her eyebrows but didn't pursue the matter.

Bill called. "How's the pet-book business?" he said.

"I'm still thinking about pet videos," Lake said, "but right now, things are cooking here. Incidentally, the chief-operating-officer slot is still open. Pays well. Many fringe benefits."

"Maybe we should talk."

Lake could tell he was serious. He made an inward wager that Bill would be part of InstruX before the year was out.

But other parts of the future wouldn't come into focus. Each time he thought about calling Jennifer, he veered away, thinking he should let a few weeks or maybe a few months pass. He had ambushed her with the car phone, even though he hadn't meant to. He felt awkward about it in a way he couldn't define. The days went by, and he continued to work late into the evenings. Randall turned out to have a taste for Chinese food.

When Lake arrived home one Monday and checked for messages on the answering machine in the library, Steve's voice said, "Trivial Pursuit tournament at my place this Friday at eight. Be there. Bring Ellen."

He called Steve. "Friday sounds good," Lake said, "but no Ellen."

"I was wondering about that."

"Why?"

"I saw her and a guy having lunch last week," Steve said. "There was something about the way they were talking."

"He looked like an Italian movie star?"

"Right."

"It's not a surprise," Lake said. "There were other problems. I'd like to bring someone else, if she'll come."

"Sure," said Steve. "But no Ph.D.s."

He called Jennifer. Two people answered at the same time. "I've got it," Jennifer said; then, after a click: "Hi."

"I was wondering if you might be free on Friday night. A

friend of mine has these regular Trivial Pursuit tournaments, and they're quite enjoyable. Very casual."

"Sure," she said.

"I'll pick you up at eight."

"Fine."

"You don't have a Ph.D., do you?"

"No."

"Okay then."

*S*he was a star in the arts-and-leisure category. "Where did you learn all that stuff?" he said as they drove back to her place afterward.

"I like to read. Where did you learn all that geography?"

"I like maps."

"You knew the capital of Finland, and you were the best person on science," she said. "That was fun. Steve's very nice."

"We grew up together."

The car rolled through the evening, almost steering itself as it traced the ups and downs of the land. Insects floated around streetlamps. A hillside of trees lifted away to the left, gray in the moonlight. As they talked, words and silence made a single easy flow, a spell.

They pulled up in front of her house but sat in the car. "Do you have any brothers or sisters?" he said.

"No, why?"

"You're so self-contained."

"You more than me."

"No, no," he said. "I'm notorious for erratic behavior—as you know."

"That doesn't mean you're not self-contained. Would you like to come in?"

Two of her housemates arrived home ten minutes later. "Mike, you remember Lake," she said. "Lake, this is Terry."

They were bursting with news, still caught up in the mood of a softball game they had played that night. Jennifer listened attentively. Camaraderie was strong in this house, Lake saw.

Mike and Terry retreated to the kitchen to continue their discussion. Lake said, "This makes my house seem so quiet."

"It's never dull here," she said. "And someone else is moving in next week."

"I thought you weren't going to fill the vacancies."

"It's a friend of Terry's. Terry has the lease."

Mike came into the room. "Sorry to interrupt," he said. "Who was the famous knuckleballer who used to pitch for the Baltimore Orioles?"

"Hoyt Wilhelm," Lake said.

"That's it," said Mike. "Hoyt Wilhelm. I'm working on a softball knuckler."

"Ask him a geography question," Jennifer said.

"Where is Belize?" Mike said.

"Central America," Lake said.

"See," Jennifer said, pleased.

Mike returned to the kitchen and his conversation with Terry, but Lake was conscious of their presence, and after a while he got up. "Promise me you'll be my future Trivial Pursuit partner."

"I promise."

———————

*T*he following Wednesday, he kept her to himself. They went to a bistro for dinner. She ordered a salad for her first course. "How do you feel about coleslaw?" he said.

"I like it. Why?"

"I thought you might. By the way, did I tell you that I hired a housecleaning agency? Three people come to the house every Friday. It's like a military operation."

"The housekeeper is gone?"

"Yes. She was part of the bad old days."

"Lake," she said after a pause, "I'll mention this only once, just so you know, and then I won't say anything about it again. The Dankmyers still want the house. Lydia Dankmyer asked me to tell you that if you ever change your mind about not selling, they would be very interested."

"I haven't changed my mind."

"I'm just transmitting a message," she said.

"I've been wondering if I should get a decorator. Do you know Sarah Beasley?"

"No."

"She goes out with a friend of mine. I have a feeling she would completely redo the place if she had her way. Do you think it needs a major overhaul?"

"You have to make up your own mind about that."

"My mind is a blank about decoration."

"Sometimes you have to live in a place for a while."

"I suppose," he said.

She sat quietly.

"I love the way you say nothing," he said. "You can say nothing in a very nice way." He looked out the window. "Summer's winding down. It's almost dark outside."

"I'm going away next week," she said. "For three weeks. I'll be back the day after Labor Day."

He nodded, watching her.

"My Uncle John and Aunt Isabelle have a place in the Adirondacks, and they asked me to come. I used to go every summer."

"What do you do there?"

"Canoe, hike, lots of things. It's right on a lake."

"Sounds great," he said. It also sounded far away. Later, when they reached her house in Merion, he walked her to the front door. Through a window, he saw that the television was on and two people were watching.

"Would you like to come in?" she said.

"Not tonight, thanks," he said. He took her hand and lifted it and kissed her fingers, and then somehow he was holding her and kissing her. He made himself let go. "Up early in the morning," he said. "I'll call you."

"Night," she said.

"*W*hen does your flight leave?" he said over the phone the next day.

"Early Sunday."

"Can I see you before you go? How about dinner Saturday night?"

"I don't think I can, Lake. I'm going to be frantic with shopping and packing. Work is crazy right now, and Saturday looks like the worst."

"I want you to send me a postcard," he said.

"I will. I'll try to send you one with mountains in it."

"Why mountains?"

"One night we were talking about mountain climbers, and you said you thought they came the nearest of anyone to understanding the earth. I liked that. Do you remember saying it?"

He did, but what mattered was that she remembered such a little thing.

"But don't be disappointed if I send you pine trees," she said. "The Adirondacks aren't very high. I think pine trees might be more authentic. I'm going to send you pine trees."

"I'd like that."

*H*e hardened himself to her absence. But late Saturday morning, she called him at home and said, "One of my appointments fell through. Would you like to play tennis this afternoon? With me and Maggie and Bruce, just for an hour or so."

"I haven't played for while."

"That's okay. Maggie hasn't either."

"You've finished your packing and shopping?"

"Not quite," she said, "but Maggie and Bruce want to play, and Mike and Terry dropped out. I said I'd play if you would. Can you do it? The court is near you. We could pick you up on the way."

"Who's Bruce?"

"Bruce McClellan. He moved in last week. His parents have a court."

"Does he have a brother named Peter?"

"Yes, do you know him?"

"Not really," Lake said. He wanted to ask: Does Bruce have a loud laugh?

"Can you do it?" she said.

"The strings in my racquet are busted."

"We'll find you a racquet."

*T*hey honked at exactly three o'clock, three faces in a Cherokee, with Bruce at the wheel, his hair slicked down like his brother Peter. The seat beside Jennifer was empty. "Lake, this is Maggie and Bruce," she said as he slid in.

"I hope you're in a forgiving mood," he said. "I'm rusty."

"You get Jennifer," Bruce said. "I've seen her play. You live in that big place by yourself?"

"Yep."

"Whew."

"Plus a dog," Lake said.

"Jennifer said you inherited it. What's it like?"

"What?"

"Living there."

"It's fine. I've always liked space." He turned to Jennifer. "I'm painting the garden furniture white. That's what I was doing when you called. It looks good."

"What color was it before?" said Maggie. She had soft, almost babyish features and very fine blond hair tied with a velvet ribbon. She was perfectly turned out in tennis whites, complete with wristband. Jennifer wore a yellow tee shirt with her tennis skirt.

"Sort of blackish green," he said. "I'm brightening things up."

"White shows the mildew," Maggie said.

"I have a large paint supply," he said.

"Here we are," said Bruce, pulling into the driveway of a Tudor-style house. "My parents are away and everything is shut up, so I can't invite you inside. They want me to use the court. Keeps away the burglars. I've got a racquet for you, Lake. It's a midsize with a five-eighths grip. Hope that's all right."

"That's fine."

Lake knew what was going to happen—knew that Bruce would be a good player and that Maggie would turn out to be better than advertised. But he didn't care, since he would get to play with Jennifer. As they walked around the house to the court, he tapped the racquet strings and said, "You hit the ball with this part, right?" She glanced at him, startled. He said, "I'll have to go on raw athletic ability."

Bruce was very good, with long, smooth strokes and an effortless touch at the net. When they were rallying, Lake hit a shot deep to his backhand, and Bruce took it with ease, driving it back with heavy topspin. He cracked the practice overheads and volleyed like a machine. But Lake saw that Jennifer's game was almost as polished, and he saw that Maggie had no backhand at all.

Almost as soon as the match began, it settled into a battle between Bruce and Jennifer. Bruce hit most of his shots toward her, and she usually went right back at him—both of them enjoying the rifled exchanges of ground strokes and deft lobs and angled volleys. Lake focused on just getting the ball back when a shot came in his direction: Hitting a ground stroke winner against Bruce was almost impossible, and Maggie was so frustrated that he didn't want to add to her troubles.

As they switched sides after the third game, Bruce said to him, "You're playing well." What he meant was: You're not in our league. But Lake had speed, and he began to use it. By the middle of the first set, he was sprinting to the net at every opportunity and punching away anything within reach, surprising himself with his successes.

He watched Jennifer with fascination. She was relentlessly aggressive, even ruthless. At 4–5, ad-out, she charged the net and hammered a ball at Bruce's stomach from close range. He returned it past her with a lucky stab, winning the set for them, smirking.

They rested for a while in the chairs at courtside. "You're quick," Jennifer said to Lake.

"You're incredible."

"I used to play a lot," she said.

A half hour later, when they dropped him off, he said to Bruce and Maggie, "Thanks, I enjoyed it." He said to Jennifer, "Have a wonderful trip."

"Bye," she said.

He walked up the path thinking about the last point in the match, when he had lunged for a forehand drive from Bruce, and Jennifer had flashed out of nowhere to intercept it, feathering the ball back over the net with control so perfect that the shot seemed like a piece of sculpture.

————

Summer made its last push, the August sun sailing through a bleached sky, the streets and soil breathing heat—too hot for cabbage cultivation, so hot that Randall lay panting in the shadows, hot into the evenings, and the residue of heat present when he awoke and listened to the peeping birds and sank back into sleep again. She was far away, in a cool place, without him, perhaps not even thinking of him.

Sometimes in the lullaby zone between wakefulness and sleep, he imagined nights at her northern lake—the water a rippled mirror, an arrow of moonlight leaping across the darkness and into the eye. Loons called. She slept in a cabin, soft curves under the blanket. Her hair spread on the pillow. He watched her.

Sometimes he imagined her days—green mountains and high clouds, a long shining V behind a canoe, small cousins running on a lawn. She sat by the water, reading. She walked barefoot on the rocks. He watched her.

Sometimes he ached for her, recalling how they stood at her front door and he kissed her and felt the faint press of her body against his, infinitely alluring. He wondered what was happening to him. But he knew what was happening, really.

At times he would see her on the tennis court, sprinting back for a lob and lofting it over the flailing Maggie, banging a shot past Bruce, everyone shaking hands at the end. He remembered her in the car coming back from Steve's or in a restaurant, the conversation straying through parts of their lives, so free that the talk seemed like children whispering in the dark.

Once they stumbled into a place of pain. At the bistro, he had asked the waiter for the wine list, then changed his mind and said, "We'll skip it."

"Why?" she said. "Go ahead."

"Would you like wine?"

"I'll just have mineral water."

"We'll skip it," he said to the waiter, who left.

"Why did you assume I wouldn't want wine?" she said angrily.

"You don't."

"But why did you assume it? I've never said that. How do you know whether I like wine or not?"

"I don't."

"Did Karen say something about it?"

"No."

"Then why did you assume it?"

"Because you were drinking water at your grandparents' party, and you barely touched the wine when we went to a restaurant before, and you drank ginger ale at Steve's. But I shouldn't have assumed."

"No, you shouldn't have."

Slowly the anger passed.

"It was a problem at home, Lake," she said finally.

"I know about those," he said.

"My mother had trouble with it for a while. Sometimes just the idea of drinking bothers me. It shouldn't, but it does."

"Don't say that. Maybe it should."

"I might have a little wine."

"All right."

She said no more then, but he sensed that they could come back to it someday, when the trust was deeper.

Now, however, she was a world away. Here, heat and haze; there, his imaginings of her star-peppered nights and crystal days and the tang of wood smoke. Then a postcard came, connecting them. On the front was an aerial photograph of a lake set among endless pines. On the back was her handwriting, firm and fast.

Dear Lake,

It has been raining almost nonstop for a week and everyone is sharing a cold, but I'm having a lovely time. Have finished 2 books, one 700 pages about life in the Middle Ages which was grimmer than I realized, especially what they ate. We're doing a 10 mile hike tomorrow and I hope I don't slip off the mountain in this rain. My Uncle John has just arrived from Phila and says it is very hot there. You can see our camp in the postcard, the group of houses on the long point in the top right hand corner. Miss you. Jennifer

She missed him. It was there in her own writing, a blue fountain-pen track made by her own hand. He took the postcard with him to work the next day and looked at it surreptitiously from time to time. Then Mary noticed that he had a secret pleasure, and he put it away and only read it in his thoughts.

———

Charlotte called. "Lake," she said, "can your company make up rules for things? Like a game. I need some game instructions, just on one little sheet of paper."

"I don't understand."

"I'm giving a pool party, and the theme is fishing. I thought it might be fun to have some fishing games."

"Frank would be better at that than me," Lake said. "He knows everything about fishing. I don't know very much."

"This party is kind of in honor of Frank," she said. "Here's my idea. Frank has some old fishing poles that can be used in the game, and there are some old wading boots lying around the house. I thought maybe we could make up a casting contest. Like you try to hit something in the pool when you cast your hook, and if you hit it, you get a glass of champagne. Like that. If you miss five times in a row, you have to wear the boots for a while."

"Sounds pretty simple," he said. "It seems like overkill to have the rules printed up. Why not just tell people how the game is played?"

"I thought it would be fun to do the rules as a fishing license. Everybody who wants to play gets a license. I mean, that's what happens when you go fishing, right?"

"It's a nice idea," Lake said.

"I'll pay you, of course."

"No, you won't. I owe you a favor. Remember when you told me about the lousy directions for your programmable sprinkler? The company that makes the sprinkler is one of our clients now."

"Great," she said.

"I'll draft something and get back to you. I wouldn't let anyone cast with a hook, though. Maybe you could tie a cork or some kind of plastic bobber on the end of the line."

"Frank has boxes full of fishing junk," she said. "I'll find something without hooks."

That afternoon, Lake spent ten minutes on it.

1 FISHING LICENSE

Issued by the Department of Game and Fisheries for the Pool of Sibley; not valid for other Pennsylvania waters. Season opens at [Get hour from Charlotte]. Good for one day only.

Pennsylvania's sparkling streams and spring-fed lakes provide some of the finest fishing in America. The catch to be had at the Pool of Sibley has a liquid beauty famed among anglers everywhere, but it presents certain special challenges.

Equipment:	Fishing rod, line, and bobber. Inner-tube target floating in Pool.
Rules:	On each turn, angler gets 3 tries to cast bobber into inner tube.
Prize:	A successful cast of bobber into the target entitles angler to 1 glass of champagne or other beverage of his/her choice.
Penalty:	An angler who fails to make a successful cast during his/her turn shall be required to put on waders and wear them until another angler has incurred the penalty.

Proprietors reserve the right to limit any angler's catch so that the natural balance of the Pool of Sibley is preserved.

It wasn't particularly good, and, anyway, Lake had a feeling Frank would nix the idea. Fishing was sacred to him, the purest of sports; Frank would hate this game.

He showed Paul the rough draft. "This is for someone's party," he said. "The idea is that it's supposed to look like a fishing license. Could you design a border for it, sort of official-looking? Don't spend much time on it."

Paul took the draft without comment and began working on his computer. Fifteen minutes later, he gestured for Lake to come over; his design resembled the engraved border of a stock certificate, but leaping fish were sprinkled through it. "Perfect," said Lake. "I'll run it by the people giving the party and then we'll print as many as they need. I'm returning a favor."

Paul returned to his work, having uttered not a word.

*W*hen the software manual was finally printed, bound, and shipped, Lake announced a celebratory Chinese lunch. At twelve-thirty on the appointed day, everyone put aside their work and prepared to leave. Lake observed the proceedings. By one route or another, Mary, Danny, Paul, and Rob each found their way to where Randall sat in state; each gave him a farewell pat, along with a fond message. Paul, in a Terminator voice: "I'll be back." Danny: "Okay, Randall, you're in charge." Rob: "You be a good dog, Randall." Mary, forever driving wedges between Randall and his master: "It's not fair that Lake won't take you. I'll bring you some food."

People could not control themselves when it came to dogs, Lake reflected. A dog's expectations of attention and love were so absolute that no human could resist. It was a form of mind control: a dog simply looked at you, and suddenly you were aware of nonnegotiable obligations to confer a pat and a kind word. Lake walked over and stroked Randall's head. "I'm doing this under protest," he said. Randall wagged.

At lunch, they discussed projects that had passed through InstruX in recent months. They talked about developing a stable of freelancers to help in a crunch and trying out new photographers. Paul wanted a new computer; he wanted to explore animated instructions. Mary wanted to investigate a change of accountants. Danny wanted to travel to Texas to meet with a prospective client there. Lake said yes to everything. They were a family to him, even Rob, already a fixture, more talented than anyone. "I think next year will be a year of changes," Lake said.

They looked at him.

"I don't know what, exactly," he said. "But good changes. We're going to need more space."

The talk shifted away from work. "How's your new house, Lake?" Mary said.

"Very quiet."

"Take notes on everything you do," Danny said. "We'll publish the InstruX Guide for First-Time Homeowners. How to find the right contractors when you redo the kitchen—identifying problems and all that."

"There's not much to take notes on," he said. "It's kind of a static situation."

"Do you miss your old apartment?" Mary said.

"I barely remember it," he said.

"The vanishing past, the invisible future, the roadless present," Rob said.

"What?" Lake said.

"That's a line from my play."

"The one about the computer talking to the astronaut in the future tense?"

"The astronaut says that line. But a friend of mine thinks it's pretentious. She's an actress, so she's probably right."

"It sounds pretty good," Lake said.

"I'm thinking about adding another act. The spacecraft hits some interstellar debris, and suddenly the computer will only talk in the past tense."

"Got it," said Danny. "The astronaut says, 'I see we're approaching a planet. Computer, will its atmosphere support Earth-type life?' And the computer says, 'It did not.' And the astronaut says, 'But will it?' And the computer says, 'The question is meaningless.' "

"*Was* meaningless," said Rob.

Lake refilled his plate, wondering what sort of person had rented his apartment, then thinking about the roadless present. It could lead anywhere at all.

———

A second postcard arrived, this one showing mountains ablaze with autumn colors.

> *Dear Lake,*
>
> *The sun finally came completely out and it's absolutely glorious. Jackie (cousin) and I paddled a canoe all the way around the lake. My arm feels like it will fall off but we had a wonderful time, so peaceful and beautiful and we didn't get back until after sunset. I wish I could stay here forever, but I will probably beat this card home. Anyway, very cold in winter, and the leaves are already starting to turn. J.*

He read it over and over. The postcard said nothing about missing him. What she would miss was being in the Adirondacks, it said. It sounded exactly like a note to a casual friend. Maybe that was what she wanted to be. She was saying: We are postcard friends.

When she returned to Philadelphia in a couple of days, she wouldn't call him. After a week, she might call. I've been catching up on my work, she would say. I meant to call, but I didn't have a minute. How've you been? How's Randall? Maybe we could do some tennis soon. Changed your mind about the house?

Or he might call her. I'm just calling to say hello, he would say. Thanks for the postcards. I've been very busy. Maybe we can get together sometime soon.

But even as he was saying those things, he would be thinking the truth: I've missed you; I've thought about you a thousand times every day; I dream about you; I want to be with you every second. But, of course, none of that could be said. So he wouldn't call her.

———

*L*abor Day weekend arrived, hotter than ever. He took Randall to the park on Sunday, planning to test his suitability for an instructional pet video. They worked on basic commands: Sit; lie down; come; stop. Randall quickly grew bored; he refused to lie down, then refused to sit, then refused to pay any attention at all.

"Hi, Luke," a voice said behind him.

He turned and said, "Hey, Holly. Hi, Tina."

"What are you doing?" Holly said.

"Giving him a screen test. He's not going to make it. I was thinking of putting him in a video, but he ignores the director."

"What happened to his hair?"

"Just some bad makeup work."

Randall and Chloe converged. She received his attentions placidly, even with interest. Tina began throwing a tennis ball for Sable.

"I haven't seen you here in a long time," Holly said.

"No. I've been busy."

"I took your advice. I'm not going back to Missouri."

"That's great, Holly."

"I love it here. I couldn't go back."

Lake was pleased for her. She seemed happy. Her hair was shorter than it had been early in the summer, and she was very tanned. A gold necklace looked good against her skin.

"Have you been to the beach?" he said.

"Most weekends. Too much traffic this weekend, though. Have you?"

"I went to Nantucket back in July."

"I hear that's a neat place."

"It is."

"What did you do?" she said.

"Mostly sat around. I do too much of that."

"You should join my fitness club."

"Mm."

"Skyvane, on Germantown Avenue," she said. "They've got everything, and it's not that expensive."

"I might," he said.

"Look at those two," she said, pointing to Randall and Chloe, who were now licking each other's faces.

Lake smiled at the sight. "Maybe I was casting him in the wrong kind of video," he said.

"They're cute," Holly said.

"Randall has a tendency to press his luck."

"Do you live far from here?" she said.

"About a fifteen-minute walk."

"Tina and I live right there." She indicated a building just across the street from the park. "We have a ground-floor apartment."

"The park is really convenient for you."

"Yes, but you should use it more often. The people are great."

"I think I probably will."

"I'm going to be here this afternoon," she said. "It gets kind of noisy with people picnicking and playing football and everything, but right over by the woods is good for sunbathing. That's where I go. It's nice, if you want to sunbathe."

"I've got a pool party this afternoon," he said. He called Randall.

"Well, have fun," Holly said.

"You, too."

*H*e chose to work on his backlog of magazines instead: Charlotte's invitation had been casual—"an end-of-summer roundup," she had said; "half of the world is away." He sat in the garden and read a series of business articles, but his attention kept straying. He felt sweaty. A dip in Charlotte's pool would be worth the drive, he decided. Besides, it would help pass the time. He grabbed a jacket and a bathing suit and drove out to the Sibleys' farm.

When he turned into their long, tree-lined driveway, an old puzzlement awakened. How had Charlotte ended up here? How had life steered her to this place, with its vast, rambling house, its fields and panel fences holding neighbors at a distance: out here in the country with a husband who was twenty years older and famed for rudeness and his wandering eye? She liked money, but there was something more, something Lake couldn't quite understand. Once she had said to him, "He doesn't care what I think." Maybe that was part of the appeal.

More than a dozen cars were parked along the driveway and in the turning circle. As he got out, a woman's squeal floated from somewhere behind the house. He followed the sounds to the pool. The party was in full swing—people eating at tables, standing with drinks at poolside, stretched out on chaises, a few of them swimming, everyone talking and having a good time. Brazilian music laid down a beat behind the babble. A man with a massive gut bounced on the diving board, then launched his bulk outward with a *blang;* the surface of the pool erupted. "Five-point-nine, Johnnie!" a man shouted. Someone close to Lake said softly, "Two-point-one, fats."

He saw Charlotte. Over her bathing suit she wore a filmy robe, open now; it was silvery, patterned with what looked like fish scales. She held an empty champagne glass and was talking with some women Lake didn't recognize: he knew only a few of the people here.

Some pieces of paper were scattered on the broad apron of the pool: his fishing licenses, already used and discarded. A pair of waders—the penalty for unsuccessful casting—lay near the diving board. The inner-tube targets were still floating in the pool.

He stood, watching. On the lawn near the shallow end of the pool was a drinks table manned by an expressionless bartender in sunglasses; an orange fishing net served as the tablecloth for the bar, and a pair of crossed oars provided maritime heraldry. A woman in a starched blue dress hovered at a table laden with food, including the remains of an enormous salmon. Charlotte had worked hard at her theme. Two short, stout deep-sea rods with glinting brass reels had been planted like flagpoles on either side of the food table; large gray plastic fishes—inflatable children's toys—were tied to the tips of the rods. Inflatable turtles, linked beak-to-beak with fishing line, dangled from the table in a decorative arc. Close to the pool was a kind of billboard, a painted sign that said "FISHING CAMP." One of Frank's mounted trophies, a great gleaming tarpon, had been fastened below it as proof.

Beside the path to the house was Charlotte's supreme display: a male mannequin, seated in a small, flat-prowed aluminum skiff. The mannequin was dressed in full fishing regalia—boots and heavy khaki pants, a flannel shirt and many-pocketed vest, and a cloth hat covered with streamers and artificial flies. What looked like a salmon rod was tied to the mannequin's right hand. Lake walked over for a closer look. An open tackle box lay in the stern of the boat. He saw that condom packets were mixed among the lures in the box's top tray. At the mannequin's feet were some plastic fish and a half-empty bottle of Jack Daniel's whiskey. A piece of paper was pinned to the mannequin's hat. It said: "Frank."

A woman shrieked and fell backward into the pool, and a man jumped after her. A couple danced near the bathhouse. Lake took off his jacket and approached Charlotte. "A trout, I presume," he said.

She turned from the women she had been talking to, threw her arms around him, and pressed her cheek to his. "I'm the catch of the day," she said. "Get out of those clothes. You come fishing with me."

"Where's Frank?" he said.

"Where is Frank always?"

"No Frank?"

"Frank is fishing. Frank is in Canada, naturally. Or maybe it's Alaska. He's getting eaten by mosquitoes, I hope. But we can go fishing, too. We can have our own fishing party. This is a counter-party."

"So I see."

"Do you like it?" she said, gesturing toward the boat and the mannequin.

"Frank to a tee," he said.

"Oh no, uh-uh, Frank's not that good-looking. Do you think I should take a picture of it so I can show it to him?"

"I think not."

"I think not, too, although I'm tempted."

"Where did you get all the plastic fish?" Lake said, because nothing else came to mind.

"I bought out a store," she said. "Put on your bathing suit. You look sweltering."

"I'm going to. How did the fishing-license thing go?"

"Oh, Lake, it was so much fun. Sally Emmett had to wear the boots for practically the whole time, because everyone else was making good casts, and you can imagine how much she liked that. Some people won two or three times on every turn. We couldn't figure out if the rules meant you could only get one drink per turn or one for each hit. I had to make an interpretation."

"What was your interpretation?"

"One drink per turn."

"Very wise."

"But the stupid people broke the rods. They tied some of my plastic fish to the end of the line and started casting the fish. They busted the rods, the stupid people. What kind of fishing is that? You don't cast fish. Even I know that."

"A flaw in the rules," he said. "I should have anticipated that people might decide to cast fish. I should have added a penalty."

"But it was fun," Charlotte said, "and now I want you to get a drink and get some food and put on your bathing suit. The day is young. I think we're going to have some night fishing."

"I just came out for a swim and to make any necessary arrests," he said. "As a warden."

The huge-gutted Johnnie cannonballed into the pool. Charlotte flinched. "Dumb fuck," she said.

"Maybe he thinks he's fishing with dynamite," Lake said. Charlotte took off her trout robe to inspect where she had been splashed. Lake walked toward the bathhouse to change. He paused by the side of the pool. There, flung on the ground, were the two rods used for the fishing-license game, with inflatable fish still attached to the end of their lines. Both rods were fractured near the tip, hopelessly ruined. They were split-bamboo fly rods—delicate, old, beautiful, no doubt worth thousands of dollars. But it was done, and probably more of the same would be done before this particular fishing trip was over. He would just swim and go home.

12

s he sat in the library on Tuesday evening and watched the
daylight die, lesser thoughts receded and left a single, sov-
ereign fact in their place: She's back; she's here, somewhere. More readings of the second postcard had told him that there
could be no mistaking the situation: it wasn't going to work out; he
had allowed his feelings to feed on themselves and lose all connection with reality; he had imagined the whole thing. She was back, a
few miles away, with people who were not him. Or maybe by
herself, but not with him.

> *I wish I could stay here forever, but I will probably beat this
> card home. Anyway, very cold in winter, and the leaves are
> already starting to turn.*

Rob's play about the astronaut and the computer popped into his mind. If everything remained in the future tense, nothing could ever hurt you; that was the essence of Rob's idea. You might worry; you might have reason to be depressed; but you would suffer no actual wound or disappointment. He tested the concept by running a quick mental reel of the future: Lake moves to a town house, with his apartment on the top floor and the offices of InstruX downstairs; Bill joins the company, allowing Lake to take extended vacations in the Caribbean and Europe, where he meets the woman he will marry, a Belgian former Olympic skier with a bewitching accent; Jennifer moves to California and marries her Bob and makes a fortune in real estate; she has two children, named Bob and Jennifer; many years later, she and Lake run into each other in Los Angeles; she says, "I know you from somewhere"; he says, "Yes, you do"; she says, "Your face is very familiar, but I can't place it"; he says, "Philadelphia, one summer years ago. You were going to sell my house"; "Oh yes, now it's coming back. Blake, right? What a pleasant surprise. It's nice to see you, Blake. I'm very happily married, by the way."

It didn't hurt at all. The trick was to stay in the future, where nothing had happened yet, especially the bad things.

But he knew he was going to have to call her. To stiffen his nerve, he made a pilgrimage to the living room and stood in front of Uncle Paul's portrait. Disdain rose in him reflexively. He headed for the phone.

The line was busy on the first try, busy on the second try. When he finally got through, someone who sounded like Mike answered. Lake heard other voices in the background. He said, "Is Jennifer there?"

"Jennifer. Jennifer!" Mike shouted. "Phone for you. No. Right. I will. Someone on the phone for you."

After a while, Jennifer came on. "Hello?" she said.

"Hi, it's Lake."

"Oh, hi, Lake," she said cheerfully.

"Did you just get back? Am I interrupting something?"

"I got in this afternoon," she said. "The airports were crazy. One of my suitcases didn't make it."

"They'll probably deliver it tonight."

"I'm sure they will," she said.

"Coming home is a climate shock, I guess."

"It's a bit disorienting."

"It was a good vacation?"

"Yes, really good. But I'm waterlogged from all the rain. How are you?"

"I'm great, I'm fine, I've been very busy. Working."

"I'm dreading work tomorrow."

"Sounds like you're having some festivities over there."

"It's sort of a reunion dinner. Maggie and Terry both just got back, too."

"Nothing like a little home cooking."

"Bruce is doing all the cooking. He's making pasta primavera."

"With a salad on the side, I hope," Lake said.

"No salad. It's in the pasta."

Lake thought he might write up the Rules of Life.

Rule #1: Do not trust yourself.
Corollary to Rule #1: Especially do not trust your emotions.
Nothing is what it seems.

"Did you get my postcards?" she said.

"Yes. The Adirondacks look like real wilderness."

"I took some pictures," she said, "but you won't think they're very good."

"I'd like to see them," he said. "Actually, it's you I'd like to see." He heard a shout in the background, then an answering shout. He wondered if it would be possible to switch this conversation to the future tense: I will ask you out if you will say yes; we will go to dinner if you will be willing to go. Instead, he said, "Would you be free for dinner tomorrow?"

"I'd love to."

"I'll pick you up at eight, if that's okay."

"That's fine."

*W*hen he saw her, a peace spread through him—an instant, magical easing of strain, just from the physical fact of her being there and being real.

"You're tan," she said.

He thought: You are the face I've been seeing for three weeks. You are the voice I've been hearing.

"I was in the sun quite a bit this weekend," he said.

"I'm pale from all that rain," she said.

"No, you're not."

"See my canoe muscles?" She flexed.

"Wow."

As he walked her to the car, he said, "I missed you."

"Me, too."

Before he started the engine, he leaned over and kissed her, without saying a word, because he had to and because she was glad to see him. At the restaurant, the peace deepened minute by minute, and soon they found their way back to where they had been before—talking without thinking, a cocoon around them both.

He told her about work and the arrival of Rob, who could effortlessly turn confusion into clarity. "I should be working for him," Lake said. "My greatest fear is that InstruX will lose him, and he's only been with us for about a month."

"You think he might not stay?"

"He's an artist."

"Everyone else has stayed," she said. "You told me they've all been with the company almost from the beginning. Maybe it's the kind of place that people don't leave."

"I hope so," he said. "Do you feel that way about your real estate firm? Can you see yourself still working there ten years from now?"

"I'm not sure. Sometimes I think I need a change."

"Ten years is a long time," Lake said. Then the thought turned upside down, and he said, "I met you ten years ago."

"Eleven."

"Time," he said.

"Time," she said.

"It's strange stuff."

She looked at him in a way he couldn't read. "I thought you were cute," she said.

"What?"

"When I was thirteen."

"Cute?"

"In a way."

"Now what do you think?"

But her thoughts were elsewhere. After a while, she said, "You're different."

"Good. I wouldn't want to be seen as cute."

"Different from a few months ago."

He couldn't answer that.

When they reached her house, she said, "There's a good movie on TV. Want to watch?"

"Sure."

She brought potato chips from the kitchen and settled beside him on the sofa. He put an arm around her. Then he heard footsteps upstairs. "Who's that?" he said.

"Maggie."

They watched the second half of the movie. Mike came in close to the end, waved, and went straight upstairs. Then violins swooped and the camera pulled back until the hero was just a speck, debonair to the last. Lake said, "Got to go." She nodded. He kissed her lightly at the door.

"Night," she said.

*A*nother night: dinner, talking about her cousin Jackie, talking about Karen, talking about nothing, feeling that they were on a raft together. Then another night: dinner, a movie. Ten minutes into the story of a homicidal teenage boy and his brain-damaged mother, he whispered, "I hate this."

"So do I."

"Can we leave?"

"Yes."

Outside the theater, he said, "We could go back to my house."

"All right."

"We could go to your place, if you'd rather. Or we could go to a jazz place I know. Your place is closest."

"Let's go to your house."

Randall greeted them at the door. "See, he remembers you," Lake said. "Actually, he remembers practically everything. But only if he wants to. If I tell him he can't get up on the beds, he doesn't remember that."

Lake led her into the living room and walked around switching on all the lamps. He turned on the light over Uncle Paul's portrait. Then he went into the dining room and switched on the lights there. "Sorry for all the darkness," he explained. "I never use those rooms."

"What rooms do you like?"

"The attic is good."

"I mean downstairs."

"The library and the kitchen. I'm never in the others."

"They seem too formal?"

"I don't know. I don't feel particularly comfortable in them yet."

"Then turn the lights back off," she said.

"But then I feel them as empty spaces."

"Then close the doors. Or close the door to the living room, anyway. You have to go through the dining room and pantry to get to the kitchen. You'll just have to hurry through."

"Close the door?" he said, amazed.

"Until you feel like opening it," she said.

"You would do that?"

"All you'd be doing is turning off lights and closing the doors," she said. "You're not knocking down walls, but you could do that, too."

"Let things develop, you're saying."

"Right."

"Patience," he said.

"It's hard to figure out everything about a house right away. Sometimes it's a mistake to rush it."

He returned to the hall. Slowly, experimentally, he swung the living-room door shut. The latch gave a loud click. The room was gone.

"How does that feel?" she said.

"Not bad. Quite good."

"See?"

He reopened the door and walked around the living room shutting off lights, then closed it up again.

"Can I get you something to eat or drink?" he said.

"No, thanks."

He shut the door to the dining room. "That leaves the library," he said. "We're getting near the minimum."

"How do you feel about the library?" she said.

"I love it." He led her in. "That's Randall's chair," he said, pointing. On cue, Randall came into the room and hopped up on the leather chair, making himself into a ball. "Want to watch television?" he said. "I'm not sure what's on."

"What do you usually do in this room?"

"Listen to music mostly, if I'm not reading or working."

"Let's listen to music," she said.

Lake selected a Mozart piano concerto, turning the volume low so they could talk. She settled against him. "Tell me about canoeing," he said.

"It's wonderful."

"Now tell me about the exact feeling of the paddle going in the water."

"It's wonderful."

"Now tell me about the sound the canoe makes as it goes through the water."

"A nice sound."

He kissed her hair and sank back against the cushion and let thoughts of canoes mingle with Mozart.

*M*idway through the second movement, she fell asleep, her head against his shoulder and her lips parted ever so slightly. He stayed very still, in a spell of contentment—everyone asleep except him. The present was not roadless; the road was sleeping against him.

She stirred after a while. "Are you awake?" he said.

"Yes." She curled against him.

Then desire rolled over him like an avalanche. She was in his arms, clinging to him, and he was lost in the taste of her skin and the sound of her breath, unable to get enough of her, wild for her. He could hardly speak, but he said, "Come upstairs with me." They walked upstairs, stopping on the way for kisses that couldn't wait, standing dizzy with the universe echoing all around.

Then sitting together on the bed. Then falling together into an unimaginable deepness, holding each other tight as they were carried away, joined for a journey more wonderful than anything he had dreamed in all the time of yearning for her.

*T*he days of a new life went by, with air and earth changing even as he changed. The heat fell away, the sky turned pure blue for a time, and once he saw a wavering formation of geese flying across. Then an armada of cumulus clouds sailed overhead—imperturbable heaps of silvered whiteness, riding an unfelt wind. The dogwood leaves began to turn, mixing green and red like a ripening apple. A few maple leaves yellowed at the ends of branches, and some rocked to the ground. Acorns and beechnuts were falling, too. He bought a rake. The grass was so lush and green that he wanted to keep it clean.

The cricket noise diminished, and the birds spoke less, and some of the flowers wilted, but he savored the descent into dormancy, listening to the changes like music.

"What's with you, Lake?" Mary said one day. "You've been in la-la land all morning."

"Just daydreaming."

She nodded. A few minutes later, he heard a small cough and looked over, knowing he would see a Lake tableau. Her hands were clasped, and she wore an expression of rapture. There were no words on the cardboard sign in front of her, only:

♪   ♪   ♪

She broke the pose and gave him a fond smile and went to work. You see it, Mary, he wanted to say. You're right.

Every day, the feelings grew stronger, expanding under the touch of even the littlest things. One Sunday before work, she came to his house, and they cooked brunch together. He mixed batter and announced that he would make her a perfect pancake.

"There's no such thing as a perfect pancake," she said.

"Watch," he said. "How big do you like your pancakes?"

"Medium."

Lake poured the batter into the pan.

"Too small," she said.

Lake poured some more. She examined it closely. "Still too small," she said.

He added more.

"It's not round," she said. "It has to be perfectly round."

He sculpted the batter with the spatula.

"It should be a little bit thicker," she said. "Also, it has to be exactly the same color on both sides."

"Is it edible, would you say?"

"Yes."

"Edibility is the standard of measurement," Lake said. "This is a perfect pancake."

Then she made a pancake shaped like a four-leaf clover. "It's a good-luck pancake," she said, and he could tell that she was talking about them.

Sometimes when he and Jennifer made love, he felt as if he would drown in the pleasure. Once she said, "Lake is a funny name. It's like 'lick,'" and she licked his ear and cheek and neck and made him mad with desire. Sometimes they traveled softly to where they were going. Sometimes they just lay against each other and talked quietly. He did not try to tell her what she meant to him—not yet. They were both shy that way. But that would come.

Then it would be late, and she would have to get back to her house. He wanted to ask her to stay with him, so that they could wake up together with the peeping birds, but she always said, "I have to get back." He didn't mind the drive from Chestnut Hill to Merion—eleven miles and twenty minutes across the city. The drive back home alone was the hard part. He wondered when he could say, "Let me take you home in the morning," or "Please live with me here."

It was only a small shadow, like the other small shadow of her having to work on weekends. He began going to the park on those days. One Sunday, he saw Holly reading the newspaper on a towel near the trees, with Chloe beside her. She was wearing a man's white shirt and a bikini underneath. When she waved at him, he went over. "How's the world?" he said, indicating the newspaper.

"Boring. Tina said you were training Randall here yesterday."

"It's a losing battle. He only does what he wants."

"Let me try," she said, jumping up from her towel. She went over to Randall and leaned down and looked him in the eye and said, "Sit." Randall instantly sat. He awaited her next command with total attention.

"I don't believe it," Lake said.

"You've got to sound like you mean it," she said.

"Goddammit, Randall, what kind of dog are you?" Lake said.

"Want me to take over his training?" Holly said.

"Well, he and I have worked out a kind of relationship," Lake said. "Everything is totally voluntary. I wouldn't want to change that. Anyway, I've got a trump card. He'll do anything for food. That puts him completely in my power."

"Can I throw the Frisbee?"

"Sure."

He watched. Her technique was excellent. Then she rubbed Randall all over. He basked in the attention, raising his head to make sure she didn't miss any good places under the chin or around the ears. "You like that, don't you?" she said. "Yes, you like it, you like it, you do. People like patting, too, Randall."

She picked up the Frisbee and handed it to Lake and brushed against his arm as she returned to her newspaper. "Want to read a section?" she said.

"I can't stay," he said. He wondered if he should say something casual about Jennifer, but he didn't, figuring that nature probably had subtler ways of sorting these things out. "Bye, Randall," Holly said. "Chloe says goodbye."

*T*hen another shadow fell.

"Lake, your father," Mary said one morning.

Lake picked up the phone and said, "Hello, Dad."

"One moment, please," said a secretary.

After a while, his father came on. "Hello, Lake. Keeping well?"

"I'm fine."

"Good. Listen, I've got a proposal. I'm coming down there for the Harvard-Penn game, and I'd like to see you. Second Saturday in October, the ninth."

"I'll be here."

"I'm coming with Philippa. I don't believe you've met Philippa."

"No."

"She and I have been close for some time. You're too much of a stranger in these parts. Actually, that's one of the reasons for this trip. She's very eager to get to know you. Family and all that."

"I'd like to meet her. There's someone I want you to meet, too."

"She has a boy about eleven. Richie. That's another reason for the trip. Philippa wants to interest him in football. She worries about him, so we're going to have a taste of the gridiron."

"Sounds good."

"Sometimes one has to do it," he said. "How she found out about the football schedule, I'll never know. She's a resourceful woman, as you'll see. How about meeting us at the Racquet Club after the game? Four-thirty, say. Nice place to chat for a few minutes."

"I'm not a member."

"You should be. You'd find it very useful. That's all right, I have a reciprocal. Four-thirty, shall we say?"

"I'll tell you what," Lake said on impulse. "Why don't you come out to my house after the game. We could be more relaxed. There's someone I'd like you to meet."

"To Ilsa's house?"

"It's more familial."

His father was silent for a moment, then said, "I suppose we could do it, but we couldn't stay long. Who is this someone?"

"Jennifer Dee."

"I used to know some Dees. I hope you're not thinking of doing anything reckless."

"I'd like you to meet her."

"Speaking of that," said his father, "I'll let you in on a little something, just so you know the lay of the land, so to speak. Philippa and I are perhaps not quite so . . . not quite so pledged to one another as she perhaps thinks. She has certain assumptions, but things have been a bit ragged lately."

"I see."

"But she has her good points. All right, it'll be Ilsa's place. What's the address?"

"Seventy-three Peal Avenue."

"I gather from Karen that you're required to keep it until the dog dies."

"Right."

"Extraordinary. Although quite in character for Ilsa. She liked to put people on a leash."

"She didn't really intend it that way."

"Well, it will give Philippa a feeling for the family, if that's what she wants. All right then, October 9, sometime before five."

"Bye, Dad."

As he sat in silence, doubts formed: his father, the house, family—pieces of families, like continents drifting, scarred by old collisions and sunderings. He thought about calling back and saying, yes, he would meet them for a quick drink at the Racquet Club. But maybe Jennifer would change the equation and the pieces could assemble into a new pattern.

The date reminded him of something. Then he remembered. He reached Jennifer at her office. "I just got a call from my father," he said. "He's coming down here for a football game on October 9 with a woman friend and her son, and he's going to stop by the house after the game. Do you think you could come over? I'd like you to meet him."

"That's a Saturday," she said.

"Right."

"Saturday afternoon is always bad," she said. "I couldn't get there until about five at the earliest."

"That's fine. And we're on for dinner at eight o'clock that night."

"We are?"

"Don't tell me you forgot," he said. "Do you have your datebook there, the red leather one?"

"Yes."

"Look up October 9."

Pages riffled. "Where did that come from?" she said, surprised. "Oh, now I remember. That was your joke when you came back from Nantucket."

"It wasn't a joke. It's a special day. I stop being temporarily sorry on that day. After that, my conscience is completely clear."

*H*e decided not to think about his father's visit, but he could feel himself tightening. Far in advance, he bought some liquor, cheese, crackers, pâté. He adjusted the position of the furniture in the living room. He went back to the liquor store and bought sherry, thinking Philippa might prefer it. He made a trip to the supermarket for tea, in case she wanted that. He bought Coke for Richie. Then, envisioning the poor kid stuck in the living room with the adults, he bought a new championship-grade Frisbee for Richie and Randall to play with.

Even with Jennifer, he grew tense and distracted. He canceled a date, saying he had to work late; then she canceled one.

It was not too late to switch to the neutral ground of the Racquet Club. He was considering it when Charlotte called on Saturday.

"Lake," she said, sounding rushed. "I'm in town. Can I stop by?"

"Sure."

"I'll be over in fifteen minutes."

Right on the dot, her sporty Mercedes pulled up in front of the house. She was dressed in a blaze of bright linen and looked like a lioness, sleek and golden. She kissed him and said, "Hello, my love."

"The last time I saw you," Lake said, "you were a fish."

Her face fell. He had meant it as a joke and quickly said, "A very beautiful trout."

"Don't remind me. That's why I'm here."

"Come in. We'll sit in the garden."

"What's this?" she said.

"What's what?"

"Why is this door closed?"

"I never use the living room. I don't feel comfortable in there. Maybe someday I will."

"Someday," she said, as though he were an absurd child. "Lake, you dope. This is a marvelous house. You can't close off the rooms."

"Why not?"

"You just can't. How will you ever feel at home in a room if you don't use it. Closing it off is exactly what you shouldn't do."

"Let's go out in the garden."

"We're going into the living room," she said, opening the door. She pulled him into the room and pushed him down in one of the chairs. She sat in another chair. "There," she said. "That's better. This is very cozy."

Lake waited. She kept combing her fingers through her hair and tossing her head and pretending to look around at the pictures and furniture. "Charlotte——" he began.

"We have no secrets from one another, Lake."

"Sure we do," he said, "but not too many, I hope."

"You and I know each other," she said. "We know what the other person means."

"I think so," he said.

"I need a teeny favor," she said.

"Come out to the garden," he said. He led her outside, and they sat in the white chairs.

"It's nothing much," she said. "Do you remember the fishing license and all that?"

"Yes."

"It was a joke. The whole party was a joke. Just a joke."

"Did things get out of hand later?"

"Somewhat," she said, her jaw set.

"How bad?"

"Well, boys and girls will play. That was a playful crowd, for sure. But everyone needs playtime. Frank would understand that part. No one knows more about it than Frank."

Lake waited.

"Nicky Turnbull got a little distasteful, though. He was dead drunk. I never should have invited him. I can't stand him."

"What part wouldn't Frank understand?" Lake said.

"The Frank mannequin," she said. "That was my mistake. It seems you're not supposed to hold your husband up to public ridicule, no matter how much he deserves it."

"Did someone tell him about it?"

"Yes. It went further than I planned. The mannequin was a joke, but some people made a big deal about it. The bimbo who came with Nicky had a Frank connection once upon a time. She decided she would take the mannequin home with her. She told everyone that she and Nicky were going to do some fun things when they got home, and she wanted to make Frank watch."

"Jesus."

"Frank had cheated on her, it seems. This was her notion of revenge. The two of them were so blasted they could hardly carry the mannequin."

Lake pictured it—the hilarity, bodies lurching, Charlotte a proud Valkyrie positioned high above the fray she had created. Then rumors finding their way to Frank.

"Evidently an important issue is how it was intended," Charlotte said.

"It's a factor."

"Lake, if anyone asks you about the fishing license or the idea for the party, tell them it was meant completely as a joke. Like if a lawyer asks—anyone like that. Say that I told you it was supposed to be just a spoof, for fun."

"I will."

"Thanks. I can take care of that fucking Frank, don't worry." Her face was alight: the warrior queen. She rose and went back in the house, and he followed. She looked at the open door of the living room, thinking about something. Then she said, "What about the upstairs?"

"What about it?"

"Did you close off the rooms upstairs?"

"Maybe."

"I'm going to see." She went upstairs. He followed, staying well behind her. When she reached the top of the stairs, she gave a whoop of laughter, genuinely amused. "Just as I thought."

He watched as she walked along the hall, methodically opening all the doors he had closed. She came to his bedroom and looked in. He said, "That door's already open, Charlotte."

"So I see." She went in. He stayed outside, watching her. She went to the window and looked out, surveying the front lawn with approval. Then she strolled around the room with a proprietary air. Something on the dressing table caught her eye. He saw that Jennifer had left a pair of gold earrings there. Charlotte picked one of them up and studied it. She turned to him with a grin. "You do have secrets," she said.

"None that you can't know."

"You're sweet, Lake. You're my friend."

Shadows grew. He and Jennifer went to a favorite restaurant on Monday, but she was remote from the start and, after a while, hardly seemed to be hearing him at all.

"Do you like it?" he said.

"What?"

"The beef stew."

"It's all right," she said.

"The lamb stew, I mean."

"The service in this place is slow," she said.

Before dessert arrived, she said she wanted to have an early night. "Hard day?" he said.

"Not particularly."

When they reached her house, she didn't ask him in. Then he knew something bad was coming. She called later that night. Without preamble or even a greeting, she said, "I have to ask you something," she said.

"Ask away."

"Why was Charlotte Sibley at your house on Saturday?"

"How did you know that?"

"I just know it. What does it matter? How I know it isn't the point."

But an anger surged up in him, and he had his own questions. Who would have seen Charlotte's visit? Who would have felt she had to be told about it?

"I'm going to guess how you know," he said. "My guess is that your grandfather saw Charlotte here."

"Lake," she said, "I'm beginning to wish I hadn't made this call. No, it wasn't my grandfather."

"But you did make this call, and I think you're accusing me of something, so I get one more guess. It was Bruce."

She didn't answer.

"Bruce, right?"

"Yes, it was Bruce," she said.

"Is Bruce watching my house?"

"He was on his way to his parents' tennis court. He saw her car. Bruce knows her."

"Who was he playing tennis with?"

"Why was Charlotte Sibley at your house?" she said.

"Who was Bruce playing tennis with?"

"Terry, I think. Why was Charlotte Sibley at your house?"

"She's a friend of mine," Lake said.

"She was upstairs. Bruce saw her at the window."

"I'm very impressed with Bruce's abilities as a spy. He's good," Lake said. "So what if Charlotte was upstairs? She wanted to look around. She doesn't approve of my closed-door policy."

"You were at that party she had, weren't you? Her famous fishing party."

"How do you know about that?"

"A lot of people know about that party, Lake."

"Do you want me to tell you about it?" he said. Then he heard the hardness in his voice. "Jennifer, I can't believe we're having this argument."

But the question about Charlotte's visit hung between them. Lake knew she would not ask again.

He raged inwardly at Bruce, imagining what he had said to

her: Jennifer, I think you ought to be aware of what Lake Stevenson is up to; Jennifer, it runs in that family. Lake could almost hear him saying it—the helpful hints, the parental history that Bruce might have learned from his own father. He pictured the encounter with Bruce's father at the Veres' cocktail party, Perry McClellan's winked allusions to womanizing.

"Charlotte asked me to design a fake fishing license for the party," he said. "I did it as a favor. I also went to the party for a while, not for long. I'm sorry to hear that it's become so famous. But don't judge Charlotte from that."

"Why not?"

"You don't know her, Jennifer."

She didn't reply. For half a minute, she was just there—a presence on the other end of the line, attached to him by an invisible thread. He said, "I haven't had a silent phone conversation since I was sixteen. It's really very enjoyable."

"I played tennis with Bruce last weekend, but not at his parents' house," Jennifer said.

Lake thought about this. He said, "Who won?"

"Bruce. I almost beat him, though."

"He's beatable," Lake said.

*T*he wariness remained. He felt it when he arrived at her house the following evening. No one else was there. "Let's sit for a minute," he said, indicating the sofa.

She sat at the far end.

"Did we clear everything up last night?" he said.

"I think so."

"How could we have an argument like that?"

"Lake, we still don't know each other very well."

"We do."

"We haven't known each other for very long."

"Do you think I'm hard to know?" he said.

"A little."

"But are you making progress?" he said.

"Yes."

"That's good. I pledge my full cooperation."

She smiled at that, and Lake relaxed. "I like this house," he said. "It's friendly."

"I think Jackie may move in with us," Jennifer said. "She's dropping out of law school."

Lake thought: You are supposed to be living with me, not with your cousin, not with these other people. But there was no way to say it.

Later that evening, he reminded her of his father's visit on Saturday.

"I've got an important appointment in Paoli that afternoon," she said. "It's already been put off twice."

He said nothing. It was obvious that she didn't want to come.

"I'll try to make it," she said.

*T*he visit rolled in from the horizon. Then the day was upon him. At ten o'clock, he took Randall to the park. A big crowd was there—dogs chasing one another, sticks and balls flying, everyone in a Saturday mood. Holly came out of the crowd. "Hi, Luke," she said.

He started to say that his name was really Lake. But he didn't feel like dreaming up excuses for having deceived her in the first place.

"Guess what?" she said. "I'm going back to school. Part-time."

"That's great, Holly."

"My parents won't pay for it, so I'll have to keep working. I can't even talk to them anymore. They just don't get it."

When he didn't pick up on the conversation, she said, "We're giving a party tonight, Tina and me."

He nodded.

"Come, if you can," she said. "It's totally casual. You know where I live." She pointed to her building. "On the ground floor. The buzzer says H. Baker. Will you come? Say yes."

"I can't tonight, Holly. But thanks."

"Too bad. We'll get you next time. I would have called, but I didn't know your last name."

"It's Stevenson. Lake Stevenson actually, but some people call me Luke."

"Lake."

"Or Luke."

"I like Lake."

"Either one. I've been having some identity problems, I think."

"You look tired."

"It's my version of the Missouri situation," he said.

"Remember what you told me: Just say no."

"I already did," he said. "A long time ago."

"*Y*ou must be Lake," said Philippa. "I've heard so much about you." She was a good-looking woman, carefully coiffed, dressed as though for a day in the country, but with a lot of jewelry.

"That's me," Lake said. "Come in. Hi, Richie. How was the game?"

"We lost," Richie said firmly.

"It was a very exciting game," said Philippa. "We might have won if the umpire hadn't called pass blocking right at the end."

"The referee," Lake's father said. "Not pass blocking: pass interference." He seemed older—still very imposing in that haughty way of his, but definitely older. Lake heard an edge of anger in his voice. He wondered if something had happened with Philippa today. She was flushed. She moved past Lake and examined herself in the mirror.

"So Ilsa left you all this," Lake's father was saying. "Well well well. I never would have pictured you here. Never."

"Where did you picture me?"

"Philippa," he said in languid tones, but not even looking at her, "I present to you my son. You will notice that he is never at a loss for sharp reply. Let's see, where did I picture you? To the extent that I was able to form an image of you at all during your years of elusiveness, I pictured you perhaps joining the foreign service, sorting out international disputes, a high-level go-between."

"This is a nice house," Philippa said, finished with the mirror. "It's rather like mine, actually."

"I'm slowly settling in," Lake said.

"I hope we'll see more of you in Greenwich," she said. "We must talk about Thanksgiving. Oof, I'm exhausted."

"Come in and relax," Lake said. He led them into the living room. "Let me get you something."

"Philippa will have tea," his father said. "I'll have scotch, a little water, no ice. We can't stay long."

"Richie, where are you?" Philippa said. "Come in here." But he was gone. "Boys," she said to Lake. "I think he enjoyed the game, though."

"He didn't even see the game," said Lake's father. "He was too busy jabbering."

"Well," she said to Lake, "I'm glad that we finally have a chance to get acquainted. I'm sure your father told you the news."

His father seemed not to hear; he brushed something off his sleeve. Lake said, "He hasn't given me the details."

"We haven't picked a date yet," she said, "but soon."

"Philippa is referring to marriage," his father said.

"We'll be living at my house in Greenwich. It's far more comfortable, really. We'll have room for lots of visitors. I want you to know that you'll have your own room there, waiting for you whenever you can come. Karen visited us last spring, with those two angelic babies of hers. It made me feel almost like a grandmother, although of course Richie is only eleven."

"Ready for boarding school," his father said.

"Don't say that, dear. He might hear you. He's much too young for boarding school."

"Never too young."

"I said you mustn't say that, dear. Your father loves to tease," she said to Lake. "Was he always like that?"

"I believe so."

"I've grown used to it, but perhaps Richie wouldn't always understand, although he's a very intelligent boy."

"A gifted child," said Lake's father.

"Not in the technical sense of the term," she said, "but he does extremely well in school. He wrote the most remarkable essay about a tree growing from a seed and getting old and ending up as firewood—"

"A brilliant boy," said Lake's father.

"He's very interested in ancient history. He told me that the name Philippa comes from the family of Alexander the Great. What an extraordinary thing."

"Exalted forebears. Any boarding school would love to have him."

"I'll get the drinks," said Lake.

"Tea for Philippa," said his father.

Lake went into the kitchen and put some water on to boil. He spotted Richie and Randall on the back lawn, took the new Frisbee out to them, then made his father's drink. When he returned to the living room, his father was saying something about Aunt Ilsa.

"I understand your aunt left you her dog, too," Philippa said.

"The most goddam fool thing," his father said. "Typical Ilsa."

"The dog meant a lot to her," Lake said.

"It's the most harebrained, cockamamie idea I've ever heard of in my life. Who on earth but Ilsa would insist that you take her dog with her house? But she was always like that. I could never understand Ilsa. She was pigheaded from the start. I could tell you some stories about Ilsa."

"Was that her husband?" Philippa said, indicating the portrait.

"Yes," Lake said. "Uncle Paul."

"I don't know why any man would have her," his father said.

"You certainly are a hard-hearted brother," Philippa said to him. "Surely she wasn't that bad."

"She was great," Lake said. All of the muscles in his face were tight.

His father looked at him with slightly narrowed eyes, as though he were a surgeon deciding where to make the first incision and whether it would be a long stroke across the patient's body or a short slice to test the resilience of the flesh. "How's your little business coming, Lake?" he said.

"Not bad," Lake said. "How's everything with you?"

"Instructions, is that what you call it?"

"InstruX."

"Lake has a company that tells people what to do," his father said to Philippa.

"I know that."

"It's a heavy responsibility," his father said.

"What is?" Lake said.

"Telling everyone what to do. It requires always being right, doesn't it? But some people are strong enough to carry the load. Ilsa was one."

"Do you remember any of the dogs you had when you were young?" Lake said.

"No."

"How about Rudy? That's the first one I know about. Probably you were about five. Or Risa. Risa was the next one."

"If there was a Rudy or Risa, it belonged to Ilsa."

"That's what she thought. They were her beloved dogs, she said on the grave markers. It's funny, in most families, dogs are shared."

"Is this a line of reasoning? I detect that you are making some sort of point."

"Not really," Lake said. He turned to Philippa. "What was the score of the football game?"

"Two touchdowns to three, I believe. What's that in numbers?"

"It will come to you, my dear," his father said.

The doorbell chimed. "That's Jennifer," Lake said. "I asked her to stop by."

His father and Philippa looked at one another. Philippa raised her eyebrows. Lake left.

"Hi," Jennifer said as he opened the door. "I finished early."

"They're in the living room," he said. "Richie's out back with Randall." He led her in. "Philippa, this is Jennifer Dee. Jennifer, this is my father." Jennifer shook hands with them.

"He always had an eye for the pretty ones," his father said.

Lake thought: How would you know?

"Now, Jennifer, tell me," his father said, "is your father Reggie Dee?"

"Yes."

"I knew him many years ago. A wonderful tennis player, always club champion. Do you play tennis?"

"Yes, I do."

"You must practice a great deal then," Philippa said. "Practice is so important. Lake—Lake's father—has been passing a football with my son Richie—"

"Throwing a football," said his father.

"—and now Richie can pass it even farther than he can, although age has something to do with that, of course. But even at my age, I can hardly pass at all. I'm hopeless at sports."

"On the contrary," his father said. "You are a superb croquet player."

"Yes, I'm quite good at croquet," she said. "I'm quite good at that. But really, it's not so difficult, is it? You swing the mallet and the ball always seems to go in the right direction. I'm excellent at long shots. My first husband tried to teach me golf, but I could never learn. Yet you would think that the games are very much alike—"

"You've only had one husband, my dear," Lake's father said.

"I'm counting you, of course."

"Impending marriage," his father explained to Jennifer. "Settled this very day. At halftime. Between hot dogs, while Richie was in the bathroom."

"That's nonsense," Philippa said. "It was settled long ago. What he means is that this is a kind of family day for us, and we've been discussing it in that way."

"Congratulations," Jennifer said.

"Now tell me all about you and Lake," Philippa said.

"Philippa," Lake said, "Jennifer just stopped by to say hello. She's a friend of Karen's."

"Do you work, Jennifer?" she said.

"I'm in real estate."

"I've thought of going into it. Everyone says I'd be good at it. It's an instinct. But I'm so busy with other things. Everyone is after me to work on this or that committee, and I find it hard to say no if the cause is worthy, which most are, naturally."

"I'll get the tea," Lake said.

"Have you and Lake known each other forever?" Philippa said as he left.

Lake stayed away as long as he could—longer than he should have, almost ten minutes, because an old despair was in that room. While the tea was steeping, he went outside. Richie had just thrown the Frisbee hard against the trunk of the big oak, evidently as target practice. "How's it going, Richie?" he said.

"Fine."

"Want a Coke?"

"No."

"Where's Randall?"

"He wouldn't catch the Frisbee."

"Yeah, he gets bored with it. You want to watch television?"

"No."

"It's right through there, if you change your mind. Also, you could try the attic."

"What's in the attic?"

"Lots of great things."

"Attics smell," he said. He flung the Frisbee at the tree again, missing.

When Lake returned to the living room with the tea tray, they were still on the subject of real estate. "I can't bear houses with old bathrooms," Philippa was saying. "You have to have nice bathrooms and big closets. Nothing is worse than too little closet space."

"It should be noted that Philippa's closets are immense," Lake's father drawled.

"You ought to be grateful," Philippa said. "In your little closets, all the clothes get wrinkled. But Jennifer can tell you about closets. Closet design is quite the thing, isn't it? Rebuilding is expensive, of course, but it's an excellent investment. Isn't that so?"

"It can be," Jennifer said.

Lake put down the tea tray. "Jennifer, I forgot to ask you if you would like something."

"Just tea."

"What a lovely tea set," Philippa said. "Did it come with the house?"

"Yes."

"A dowry, as it were," his father said.

"What?" Lake said.

"For the dog."

"The dog is male," Lake said.

"An endowment, then," his father said.

"Yes, an endowment."

"My fortunate son."

"It seems a pleasant enough dog," Philippa said. "But more to the point, does this suit you, Jennifer?" With an expansive gesture, she indicated the house, living here.

His father intervened quickly. "What exactly did Ilsa's will say, Lake? There must be some way you can sell this place."

"Perhaps they want to be here, darling," Philippa said.

"She isn't—" Lake started to say.

His father interrupted. "You haven't been listening, Philippa." He addressed himself to Lake again. "Is it a trusteeship?"

"It wasn't set up that way."

"So if the dog happens to disappear, you can do whatever you want," his father said. "Maybe Jennifer would sell the house for you. Nice commission."

Jennifer's eyes went from Lake's father to Lake and back, connecting.

"That's a very inappropriate suggestion which I'm sure you don't mean," Philippa said. "I'm surprised you would suggest it to your son, but I suppose you're teasing again."

The despair was reaching for Lake now. He decided to tell the truth, no matter what. "I already thought of it," he said.

"You didn't consider it, for a minute, I'm sure," Philippa said.

"I considered it for about a month," Lake said. "Family minds work alike, it seems."

"It's all foolishness," Philippa said. "You men get the most preposterous ideas. Luckily, you have us."

"Thank God," Lake's father said. "Who knows what we might do?"

Philippa fiddled with her rings, pleased at something. "Be grateful," she said. Her eyes swept around. "I do think we make a very attractive family," she said.

When no one responded, she said, "Jennifer, you never answered my question."

"What was the question?"

"Does this suit you?"

Jennifer sat upright in her chair, tense.

"Here. This," said Philippa, explaining. "Of course it does."

"No," Jennifer said. Her eyes flicked toward Lake. He saw sadness but no wavering. Philippa stared at her.

"No, I'm afraid it doesn't," Jennifer said with finality.

Lake's father leaned toward her. His mouth drew into a thin, bitter line. He broke the silence. "I commend you for your honesty," he said.

Lake was by himself now, far away. More than anything, he had wanted to know what Jennifer felt about a future with him in this house. He had never expected to find out in such a terrible way. But sooner or later, the moment of truth would have come. His father was right about her honesty. She would not evade a direct question.

"Well," his father was saying, "it's been an interesting and eventful day. I wish we could stay and continue our chat, but we have a long drive home. Philippa, my dear, I'm sorry to hurry you at your tea. We have to start or we'll never get back. Jennifer, it's been a pleasure meeting you."

Jennifer nodded.

"I'll round up Richie while you finish, Philippa. It'll give me a chance to see what further wonders have befallen my son. Ilsa did have an eye for art. Who knows what else I'll see. Perhaps a large kennel in the back." He wandered away.

Philippa finished her tea. "Now remember," she said to Lake as she got up, "I'm expecting you to visit us. Remember what I said about your room. I hope we'll see you at Thanksgiving."

"Sure," Lake said.

"Goodbye, Jennifer," she said. "Things usually work out."

———

*T*hey stood in the hall after his father and Philippa and Richie had gone. Lake was adrift, fading. He thought of how fragile dreams are. One word can shatter them, one unpremeditated word, like a stone dropped into still water. He forced himself to speak. "A day for truth," he said.

"What do you mean?"

"What you said to Philippa."

"She had been drinking. She's like all drinkers. They destroy things."

"Yes, they do."

"Do you expect me to like her?" she said coldly. "Am I supposed to like your father?"

"No, I don't expect that."

"He's an angry person. He enjoys it."

"Being in this house made him angry," Lake said. "He was never welcome here."

"I'm sorry I was so blunt. I didn't want to hurt you, but she kept pushing."

"It was my mistake. Neither of us was ready for this."

"Do you want to talk about it?"

"No." He couldn't face hearing why she had decided that he didn't suit her. He didn't want her to spell out whatever it was—problems of trust, problems of behavior, of connections and associations, of a millstone house.

He thought of his days as a miler on track teams in high school and college. In a race, you had to know where you were every instant. The worst mistake a runner could make was to misjudge the balance between the past and the future. That was what he had done, and now there was only the past.

He couldn't bear to say goodbye at this moment. "I'll call you tomorrow," he said. "I have to clean things up." He headed for the kitchen, moving blindly.

*A*s he stood in the kitchen, he decided it was better to know the truth now rather than later, when the hurt would be worse. He saw that events had been moving this way—a pulling apart, a fraying of the old ease and closeness. And she had been making her reservations clear all along, keeping her distance from the house, never spending a night here, careful to signal her attachment to her own place. She had never misled him.

He and Randall went for a walk, heading for the park. Halfway there, his mind tripped over something invisible—probably something about how families die, or how they sometimes aren't even born—and his mouth twisted like a child's. But he would not surrender to those feelings. He turned another corner. Randall trotted briskly beside him. Lake envisioned himself walking through a winter snowstorm. If snowflakes landed on him, they would not melt. That was how people would be able to tell about the coldness of his nature, those who didn't already know.

He came to Holly's building. Music was thumping inside. He walked past the door, not even slowing, yet aware that in other, earlier times, on a day of losses like these, he might have gone in and joined the party and maybe even ended up in the darkness with Holly, forgetting everything for a little while, losing himself behind a locked door, with the music thudding beyond.

Rule of Life: Do not inflict your troubles on others

The park was deserted, a hole in the glow of the city. He walked to the center of the field and looked up at a sky seeded with stars. Once when he was young, he had tried to count the stars, but he stopped before he got to a thousand. Their manyness had frightened him then. It soothed him now. Under such a profusion of worlds, all people were lonely. Losing someone you cared about, hearing words you had feared—these things were insignificant under the billions of stars. And the words never spoken—the father who walked away without saying it hurt him to leave, the son who couldn't ask him to stay, the words of true love that a man and a woman would say to each other when they knew they belonged together—all those words, even if they had been spoken, would have been meaningless against the shout of the stars.

It soothed him. He sat on the wet grass and opened his eyes wide to the fields of starlight. Randall moved about in the gloom, a vague shape. Lake wondered where Jennifer was. Thinking about her recalled the scent of her skin, the very essence of life to him. Tears rolled down his cheeks, flowing freely now, because he had the stars to help.

Humans would go to those stars. They would fling themselves into the blackness and ride toward a dot of light lifetimes away, then toward the next dot of light, and the next, trying to master them somehow, as he had tried with his star count. It was a brave thing in its hopelessness.

Randall came over and sat beside him. Lake thought about what he would say to Jennifer in the morning. He would apologize for Philippa and her presumption, but he would not apologize for his father; he would not deny his father. He and Jennifer could be friends.

That thought broke him. He lay down on the grass, weeping silently for a long time. He covered his face with his hands. He couldn't even let the stars in.

Afterward, he walked for miles, and he would have kept on walking, but Randall grew tired. They returned to Peal Avenue, and Lake sat on the terrace with his chair facing the dim garden. Probably he would never learn the names of the flowers now.

*H*e called her the next morning. "I guess we should give it a rest for a while," he said.

"Don't you think we should talk, Lake?"

"You said what you felt."

"Yes," she said.

"That's always best."

"We could have lunch today," she said. "I could meet you somewhere."

They were back to lunch. They had moved three months backward in a single day. But going backward was no answer. "I can't do it today," he said. It wasn't a lie. Lunch would have killed him.

13

Thanksgiving approached, and Lake prepared to go to Greenwich for the family gathering promoted by Philippa. She said she wouldn't take no for an answer; Karen was coming and he had to be there, all of them together. She had pressed the invitation as a claim, as though Thanksgiving dinner at her house was a family ritual of long standing. Of course he had to come; it was expected.

Lake said yes. He needed to go somewhere, anywhere.

The house hardly existed for him now. He worked late most nights and went into the office on weekends. When work didn't fill the time and he and Randall had to be at 73 Peal Avenue, they lived in the library, the kitchen, and his bedroom. Even those three rooms were more than he wanted. Sometimes he went to sleep on the sofa in the library, but the pressure of a wet nose against his face would always wake him and urge him upstairs. Randall seemed to object to people sleeping on sofas; he liked the bedroom at night.

Any excursion into other rooms only reminded Lake of the strength of his prison. The old regime remained intact. Furniture, curtains, rugs, books, lamps, the little objects and adornments—all were still there, silently defying any impulse to dislodge them. The living room and dining room drove him away with their Chippendale-and-velvet grandeur, their mahogany moods, their paintings of European cities and seascapes from other centuries. Winter darkness gathered early in those rooms and never fully drained away. If he turned on the lights, gilt and brass and silver exploded, and when the shrapnel of light had fled, a tomb remained.

Sometimes he tried to find a new path through the world. In late October, he drove to Cape May because he had heard it was a good place for bird-watching, but he and Randall spent the day walking on the beach, beside a gray ocean. Holly called and asked him to another party, but he said he had a business trip and couldn't make it. At Steve's, he spent part of an evening talking to a girl whose name he couldn't remember. She was very interested in emotions. She seemed to be saying that modern loneliness was invented by the French. Lake drank and nodded. Quite possibly, he said; that's interesting. But maybe it was invented by Hollywood, he said. Later in the conversation, he said that people always associate loneliness with emptiness, but really it's more like compression. It pressed you into a smaller and smaller space. It collapsed you into a black hole. Your only hope was that you might pop out in another universe. That's interesting, she said; that's a good metaphor. They drank and nodded. After a while she was gone. Then Lake talked to Megan, Steve's girlfriend. She asked about the house. It'll work out,

Lake said. You can always sell it, Megan said. He shrugged. He liked Megan, but he couldn't tell her what selling the house would prove: that he was still who he used to be.

He tried not to think of Jennifer. The trick was to nip every thought of her in the bud and force his mind in another direction— toward plans for leasing new office space, or the problem of where to go for lunch, or any issue at all. That usually didn't work, but as the weeks went by, the feelings of loss seemed to shift toward something more like regret. So when Philippa called and called again, he decided he could handle Thanksgiving in Greenwich.

The roads out of Philadelphia were jammed on Wednesday evening. An accident on the turnpike produced a massive tie-up. At the George Washington Bridge, traffic was backed up for miles in a stop-and-go line. Philippa's house was mostly dark when he finally reached it after eleven o'clock. But she met him at the door and greeted him warmly. "Everyone's in bed except your father," she said. She led him into a large paneled room where his father was watching the news.

"Hi, Dad," he said.

His father grunted. He pushed himself up out of the chair and shook hands. "Glad to see you, Lake." He said it almost as if he meant it, and Lake felt that they might be able to get through Thanksgiving without fighting.

"Where shall we put the dog?" his father said.

"He sleeps with me."

His father grunted again and said, "Fix yourself a drink. Philippa, you go up to bed. You've got a big day tomorrow."

"I'll show Lake to his room," she said. "Then you two can talk."

"I think I'll just turn in," Lake said. "It was a tough drive."

Philippa led him upstairs and along a hall to a room with a huge canopied bed. She said good night. A mountain of pillows covered almost a third of the bed; Lake removed all but one, put the pink quilt on a chair, and lay down. He stared up at the canopy, thinking that this was like sleeping in a hut.

Breakfast brought everyone together in the dining room: Philippa and his father; Richie subdued and polite; Stephen hearty and talkative; Karen distracted as she tried to keep tabs on Emily and Steebie. Karen was the one he wanted to see; she was his family.

Later, Lake found her in the living room reading a magazine as Emily played a game on the rug.

"How are you doing?" he said.

"You were nice to come up from Philadelphia," she said. "It means a lot to Philippa."

"What about the wedding plans?"

"Soon, I think."

"Philippa seems to be mellowing him."

"She'll be good for him," Karen said. "So how are you?"

"Not bad. Working hard."

He watched Emily, a miniature Karen. She was playing with some small plastic figures—different-colored cylinders with balls for heads. He stretched out on the rug near her. "Can I play with you, Em?" he said.

"Yes."

He touched one of the plastic figures. "Who's that?"

"That's the mommy."

"And who's that?"

"That's the daddy."

"Who's that?"

"That's the nurse."

"Why is there a nurse?"

"The baby is getting shot."

"Shot? Who shot the baby?"

"The baby is getting *a* shot."

"Oh, *a* shot. I'll bet the baby doesn't like that."

"With a needle."

"Can I be the baby?"

"Yes."

"I'll be the daddy, too," he said.

This seemed to be an acceptable division of labor. Emily pushed two of the figures toward him, and they began to play.

After a while, Karen said, "Lake, how are you really?"

"Fine, I said."

"Something's bothering you. I can tell," she said.

"I think I make a very good daddy. I make a good baby, too."

"You do."

That pierced him deep. But he trusted Karen, and he said, "An affair of the heart."

"Who?"

"Jennifer."

"I thought so. She called me in September and asked when your birthday is."

"March," he said. "Too late."

"Why?"

"Because we broke up. It wasn't going anywhere."

"That's what you decided?" Karen said.

"She did. I'll get over it."

Karen didn't say anything. He smiled at her, comforted in a small way. He turned back to the game with Emily. "What happened while I was away?" he said to her.

"The baby is at the store," Emily said.

"Daddy will buy the baby a toy," he said.

*T*hanksgiving dinner that afternoon was ceremonious and lengthy, and Emily vanished early. Randall appeared in the doorway, ready for turkey, but he remembered the manners taught by Aunt Ilsa and halted on the far side of the threshold. Lake's father, too, was on his best behavior and told stories of colorful Wall Street characters and teased Karen about being a softhearted parent. Philippa discoursed on the roots of America and offhandedly claimed heavy ancestral representation on the *Mayflower*. Then she said to Lake, "Poor Randall. He looks so unhappy."

"That's not unhappiness," Lake said. "It's fear warring with greed."

"We'll save him some turkey," she said.

Lake stood and lifted his glass and said, "Philippa, if I can speak for the out-of-towners in this family, including Randall, may I say that we would travel any distance to eat this way. But what matters is coming together. Thank you for providing a center, and thank you for the best stuffing any turkey ever had."

Philippa beamed and Stephen hear-heared and Karen said, "It's all so lovely, Philippa," and Lake sat down thinking about Jennifer and the Veres, united and festive far to the south.

He noticed Karen's earrings, graceful spirals of tiny emeralds and diamonds. Later, he said to her, "Those are beautiful. Did Stephen give them to you?"

"They're from Aunt Ilsa. She left me a lot of jewelry."

"They're truly beautiful."

"Thank you," she said, touching them.

A week later, a package arrived from Boston. Inside was a small jewelry box, and in the box were Karen's spiral earrings. A note said, "Give them to someone."

He telephoned her that night. "Karen," he said, "I wasn't hinting that I wanted your earrings."

"I want you to have them."

"I don't know what to say."

"Say thank you like a nice boy."

"Thank you. Thank you very much."

"You're welcome," she said sweetly. Steebie yelled in the background. "Gotta go," she said.

*H*e threw himself back into his work. InstruX was flourishing. Danny talked about a software division; on his desk was a cardboard sign that said VICE PRESIDENT SOON. Rob was more productive than ever. He turned out crisp copy effortlessly, playing with rhythm like a doodling drummer.

Release the brake. Let the spool run free.

Or:

Extremes of temperature will weaken the bond. Avoid heat and cold alike.

One day, Lake saw Rob and Mary leave together at lunchtime. He didn't think anything of it, but later that week the two of them lunched together again. After that, he watched, and he detected little signs—gazes that drifted across the room and settled on the other person like a butterfly on a flower, Rob putting a note on Mary's desk without a word, Mary unconsciously plucking something off his sleeve as they stood close. They made an incongruous pair: Rob, thin and dark and intense; Mary, tall, her red hair flying wild. But they had the same quickness and confidence. Lake was pleased for Mary; in the past, she had always been attracted to people she ended up despising.

He asked Rob to have lunch, and they went to the Chinese restaurant. "How's your play coming?" he said when they sat down. "The one about the astronaut and the computer."

"It didn't work out."

"Too bad. It was a good idea. Are you doing anything new?"

"Not now."

Lake decided to come straight to the point. "How are you feeling about InstruX?" he said.

"I like it more than I expected."

"InstruX feels very good about you," Lake said.

"Is this an evaluation? I've never had an evaluation before."

"No, it's an appreciation. You're doing a fantastic job. I'm giving you a fifty percent raise, effective today. You've got a tremendous future, Rob. I hope you'll stay."

He seemed startled. "Thank you," he said.

They talked about politics for a while. Then, as though it had been on his mind all along, Rob said, "Lake, theater is still the most important thing for me. That's still number one."

"That's fine. InstruX likes its employees to have balanced lives."

Rob relaxed. "How about you?" he said. "How's everything going with you?"

"Pretty good."

"Are you still in your aunt's house?"

"Still there," Lake said. "I'll be there for the foreseeable future."

"You don't want to be?"

"My aunt would have done well as a playwright," Lake said. "She scripted my housing future."

"I wouldn't mind having an aunt like that," Rob said.

"She had imagination, too. Well, let's just say she imagined things. She believed she had psychic powers. Apparently the powers didn't apply to people, though."

"What did they apply to?"

"Dogs," Lake said. "She would pick a puppy from a litter by listening to an inner voice. I know this because last summer I came across a box of letters from someone who runs an organization called the Institute of Animal Understanding. Ernest Jeffords, that was his name. He liked her money. No idea was too crazy for Ernest Jeffords, as long as she kept sending money to his Institute. He egged her on, even when it had nothing to do with animals."

"What besides animals?" said Rob.

"Aunt Ilsa had psychic powers about houses, too. She told Jeffords that she bought her summer house in Maine because she heard the call of some spirits there. Jeffords had no problem with that. He even had some suggestions about what the spirits were. He said maybe they came over from Ireland before Columbus reached America. An Irish monk named St. Brendan supposedly sailed across the Atlantic back then—he and a bunch of other monks—and all sorts of magical things happened when they landed."

"Catholics don't believe in spirits," Rob said. "Except for the Holy Ghost."

"Maybe a few Celtic spirits were hitching a ride on the boat," Lake said. "They jumped off in Maine and went looking for a grove of oak trees."

Lake meant it as a joke, but Rob became serious. He was nodding, tapping his fingers on the table. "That's interesting," he said. "That's very interesting."

"I'd say it's nuts."

"It has real possibilities," said Rob. "It could make a play. Listen to this. Suppose there was a Druid stowaway in the boat. Let's say one of the monks is a Druid in disguise. Christianity is driving the old Celtic magic out of Ireland, and this Druid is looking for a new place to start. So he passes himself off as a monk and catches a ride to America."

"How does he know America is out there?" Lake said.

"He doesn't. But he's sure they'll find someplace new."

"It could be a barren rock, covered with bird droppings. No oak trees."

Rob ignored him. "Out in the ocean, everybody says Christian prayers and makes the sign of the cross and all that, but this one monk sometimes mutters strange words that the others can't understand. He's saying Celtic magic spells, but the others don't know that."

"Right," said Lake in his most neutral tone.

"Now here's what happens," Rob said. "They land. The Druid thinks America is virgin territory. He summons a little army of Celtic spirits with magic words. The Druid plans to fill the whole continent with Celtic spirits. What he doesn't know is that America is already taken. Indian spirits are living in the rocks and woods, and they're not about to leave. The result is a spirit war. The Celtic spirits try to fight their way out of the beachhead in Maine, but they're trapped, because the Indian spirits are too strong. They can't get back to Ireland, and they're blocked from expanding beyond the place where the boat landed."

"So a little Celtic spirit colony still exists on the coast, you're saying."

"Right," Rob said. "Sensitive humans like your aunt can detect them, but for most people, they're partitioned off."

"How come?"

"They exist outside of normal time, like all spirits. They have their own separate time."

"Mm," said Lake.

"Would you let me take a look at your aunt's letters?"

"Sure."

"This is great," Rob said, "I can do something with this."

———

*I*n the library that evening, Lake located the box of letters from the Institute of Animal Understanding. He pulled out those that dealt with Aunt Ilsa's urge to buy Pinecroft and set them aside for Rob. He read a few more and saw that Ernest Jeffords had managed to insert a hint about financial contributions in every single one. He jumped to the end of the sequence, curious to see if the money-wheedling had continued until Aunt Ilsa's last days. It had.

Dear Mrs. Grinnell:

I am deeply distressed to hear that you are worried about your health. I trust and hope that your concerns will quickly be allayed. What you say about the fragility of life is undeniable, but I feel that one sort of immortality is available to everyone. If each of us commits a portion of our resources to the ongoing pursuit of knowledge, we will have achieved something lasting. The nature of the commitment is not the point: those who make continuing research possible with their financial generosity are no less meritorious than the researchers themselves. But you have always understood this, of course.

It is entirely characteristic of you to be concerned about the welfare of your dog at a time when your health is worrisome. I am hesitant to express an opinion about your plan for your niece and nephew; surely the need to face such matters is very far off. However, you have asked me for my thoughts, and I must answer. My views concur entirely with yours. I agree that, in the unthinkable event that you are no longer with your dog Randall, an ideal arrangement would be for him to retain his present homes.

Ideals are sometimes unattainable, of course. It is a blessing that you have a niece and nephew who might welcome such an arrangement—one that I trust will be unnecessary but that, by the very fact of it being considered, proves once again your rare and wonderful feeling for animals.

Yours sincerely,
Ernest Jeffords

Lake reread the letter. This greedy, parasitical man had colluded in sentencing Lake to five or six or seven years in a prison of stone. Without Jeffords's encouragement, Aunt Ilsa might have dropped the idea.

Then Lake remembered Vere. As Aunt Ilsa's friend and lawyer, Vere could have talked her out of it. He should have stopped her from drawing up such a will, but he didn't. Nor would he consider any change in the arrangement later. He had tethered Lake with principle. He had said: You either have honor or you don't. And Jennifer was there listening.

Lake looked at the letter and thought about Jeffords and Vere, one on each flank of Aunt Ilsa, complicitous. An idea stirred to life.

He pondered. It was an extreme long shot, yet worth a try. For the first time in weeks, he felt a flicker of his old pleasure in combat.

———

At the office the next day, after everyone had left for lunch, Lake dialed the number of the Institute of Animal Understanding. A reedy voice said, "Ernest Jeffords."

"Mr. Jeffords, my name is Lake Stevenson. I'm the nephew of Ilsa Grinnell, the late Ilsa Grinnell."

"Yes?"

"I am in fact her heir," Lake said.

"Oh, I see. Yes, I see. Mrs. Grinnell was one of our most . . . she was a great friend to the Institute."

"I know why."

"Why is that, Mr.—"

"Stevenson."

"Why is that, Mr. Stevenson?"

"I've taken the liberty of reading your letters to my aunt. It's clear how much your organization meant to her. And your advice."

"That's very kind of you."

"I believe the Institute received a bequest from her estate."

"Yes, we did. A most generous one."

"That was her way. I'm calling to say that I hope you will keep me informed about the activities of the Institute."

"I certainly will. With the greatest pleasure."

"My address is her house in Chestnut Hill."

"I'll send out some materials this very afternoon. The Institute is supporting some very promising research activities at present. I'm quite sure they would have interested Mrs. Grinnell."

"I look forward to receiving them. Speaking of the house in Chestnut Hill, that reminds me of something. I would appreciate your advice about it. Here's the problem: I'm not married and haven't got a family. I suppose you could say I'm quite young to be living in a house like this. As you know, my aunt wanted her dog to suffer minimum disruption when she died. The house was left to me with the understanding that it would continue to be the dog's home for the rest of his natural life."

"Yes, I am aware that those were her wishes. I wrote to her expressing my sense of . . . well, the selflessness of it."

"I read your letter and admired it. You also seemed to suggest that what mattered most of all was that Randall, the dog, continue to receive the care and love that Aunt Ilsa had always given him."

"Yes, certainly."

"I would never claim to be the equal of my aunt when it comes to the care of a dog, but love is another story. I can hope to match her there."

"Of course."

"Randall has become very precious to me."

"I'm pleased to hear that."

"The difficulty is the house. It's much too large. I'd like to sell it, if I could. The money could be put to worthier uses, as I'm sure you'll understand."

"Certainly I do."

"Now here is where I need your advice—and your help, too. I think we agree that the love and care of the dog is the main thing and the house is of secondary importance. Its value could be applied to worthier causes. I would go further; I would argue that a dog is happiest in a house that makes his master happiest. It stands to reason. If the master isn't comfortable, the dog won't be comfortable."

"Quite true."

"The only difficulty in all of this is that the executor of the estate expects me to stay in this house. His name is Billington Vere."

"Surely he would wish the dog to be happy."

"You'd think so, Mr. Jeffords, but I have the impression that he prefers the status quo. He looks at things from a lawyer's point of view. It doesn't occur to him that Randall would be better off if I moved."

"No, a lawyer might not see it from a dog's vantage point."

"Here's how you could help me. You're an authority on animals and how they think, so Mr. Vere would pay attention to you. You would be doing me a great favor if you wrote to him. I'll give you the address. You could tell him that you have no objection to me selling the house. In fact, you consider it to be a desirable solution. You might say that my aunt consulted you on matters related to her dogs over a period of many years."

"I believe she did value my opinion in such matters."

"I know she did. And I have no doubt that Mr. Vere would as well."

"You are very good to say so, Mr. Stevenson."

"Do you think you could write to him?"

"Yes, perhaps I could."

"You might say in the letter that I called to ask your advice in the same way she often did."

"Yes."

"Just say it came up in the course of a conversation. You explored the situation with me, and you feel that, in the light of your long relationship with my aunt, you should express an opinion. Moving to a smaller house is in Randall's interest. It's exactly what my aunt would have wanted, if she were able to weigh all the facts as they presently stand."

"I'd be happy to write the letter."

"I'm very grateful for your help, Mr. Jeffords. Would you also ask Mr. Vere to drop me a note letting me know if he accepts your recommendation?"

"Of course. I'll write to Mr. Vere this very day."

"And don't forget to send me the literature about the Institute. I want to know all about your current projects. My aunt and I shared many interests."

A note arrived in the mail a few days later.

Dear Mr. Stevenson:

I recently received a rather baffling letter from a Mr. Ernest Jeffords. My impression is that he is somehow acting on your behalf, although he included a number of press clippings about dolphins and chimpanzees and seems to regard me as an animal activist. Please inform him that I have no interest in contributing to his organization.

Mr. Jeffords had the temerity to ask that I give you my

*permission to sell the house which your late aunt so gener-
ously left to you. I will confine myself to the legalities of the
matter. At this juncture, there is nothing to stop you. The
only possible obstacles are your sense of honor, your respect
for the wishes of your aunt, and the fact that you gave your
word. Perhaps these do not carry much weight. In any event,
what you choose to do is entirely your concern.*

Sincerely,
Billington Vere

Vere was a hard man, but a worthy foe. Lake taped the note to
the refrigerator door so that he would see it every day. There was a
certain fascination in studying your death sentence.

Then Charlotte called him at the office. "Lake," she said, "I
wanted you to know that Frank and I are splitting."

"That's too bad, Charlotte."

"It's not too bad. It's good."

"What will you do? I mean, what's the plan?"

"I plan to get a life."

"If there's anything you need, let me know. Is Frank moving
out?"

"The farm is Frank's. Besides, I can't stand it. I'm a city girl.
I'll probably rent something for a while. I'm considering Chestnut
Hill, in fact."

"I don't recommend it."

"You still don't like it there?" she said.

"Not especially."

"Well, actually, that's what I'm calling about, Lake. I thought you might still feel that way about your house. Would you consider renting it to me?"

"Rent it?"

"Rent me your house, Lake. Rent it to me furnished. I love it. It's perfect for me."

"I can't."

"Why not? You're rattling around with all the doors shut. You'd be happier somewhere else."

"I have to live here," he said. "I'll rent it to you five years from now, maybe a little more."

"You won't change your mind?"

"Honor forbids," he said.

*C*hristmas approached, and he worked late every day. The lease on the new office space was signed. In January, InstruX would move into a modern building and gain a conference room and a studio area and plenty of room to grow. Lake figured that the company would double in size within a year. He would be very busy; life would be simpler.

He watched Rob and Mary circling one another delicately, and it made him glad. One day Rob said, "I have to thank you for that idea about the Druid stowing away on St. Brendan's boat. The play is going well."

"What's the first scene?"

"The monks put up a cross at the spot where they've landed in Maine, but the Druid hangs back. We hear Indian music mixed with the monks' chanting."

"How do you end it?" Lake said.

"I'm thinking about some sort of peace treaty between the Celtic spirits and the Indian spirits. A magical Appomattox."

"It sounds great," Lake said. "I'm going to send a ticket to Ernest Jeffords."

That day, Lake bought Christmas presents: a doctor game for Emily, a small stuffed bear for Steebie, books for Karen and Stephen and Philippa and his father, a dart game for Richie. He sent the packages northward. On the way home, he stopped at a pet store for Randall's present, a mixed assortment of dog treats.

*H*e knew he should spend the holidays somewhere far from Chestnut Hill. But he hadn't taken the time to plan a trip, and now it was too late. He decided to continue coming into the office every day; the long Christmas weekend could be used constructively.

Six inches of snow fell on Tuesday. Trucks roared by, clearing the roads and scattering salt. He worked until ten o'clock, then drove home and watched a talk show until midnight. He came in early the next day and submerged himself in captions. Randall was bored and wandered from person to person, looking for action. Finally, he went to sleep at Mary's feet. When he began to snore, she jabbed him with her foot to make him stop. After that, the only sound in the office was the clicking of computer keys.

In midmorning, his phone rang. Mary took the call. Lake heard her say, "Mayhew, Foster? Hold on." She looked over at Lake, hesitant, knowing something, even though he had never mentioned his troubles to her. Almost sadly, she said, "For you." He thought: Be Jennifer, be Jennifer.

He picked up the phone. "This is Binky Foster of Mayhew, Foster, Mr. Stevenson," said the voice at the other end. "We spoke a few months ago."

"I remember," Lake said. "You gave me the number of Jennifer's car phone. Please don't call me Mr. Stevenson. It's Lake."

"Lake then. Do you have a minute?"

"Yes."

"This is somewhat out of the blue," she said. "In fact, it's a little unusual, but perhaps you won't mind. Do you remember the Dankmyers, the people who made an offer on your house?"

"Sure."

"I'm calling to say that if you've changed your mind about not selling, they're still very interested," she said. "In fact, I believe they would be willing to pay full price."

"It never rains but it pours," Lake said. "Someone else just asked me if they could rent it. My house is hot."

"It's special," she said. "It's exactly what the Dankmyers want. They fell in love with it."

"Unfortunately, the answer is still the same, Binky. It's not for sale. Maybe in five or six years. It depends on a dog, and he's not very cooperative."

"I see. Well, I hope you don't mind that I asked."

"Not at all."

After he hung up, Lake gazed out the windows in puzzlement. Mayhew, Foster was not the kind of firm that approached people who hadn't expressed an interest in selling their house.

He called her back. "Binky," he said, "is there a reason why you had this idea?"

"We're still working with the Dankmyers," she said.

"But you wouldn't have called me unless you believed that I'm leaning toward selling."

She hesitated. "That's true," she said. "Normally I wouldn't."

"So why did you think I've changed my mind?"

"I must apologize, Lake. Clearly it was a mistake."

"Don't apologize," he said. "It's fine. In fact, you were not totally wrong. For a while, I was wavering. Maybe you're a mind reader."

"No."

"No, I know you're not," he said. "Is Jennifer there?"

"Yes."

"Please transfer me to her. I need to talk to her about something."

Jennifer came on the line. "Hi," she said, cautious.

"Hi," he said. "I'm curious about something, and I have a feeling you can tell me the answer."

"What's that?"

"Why did Binky Foster ask me about selling the house to the Dankmyers?"

"That's what real estate agents do."

"No, they don't," he said. "At least, that's not the way your firm operates. She thought I would be interested. Why did she think that?"

"I told her you might be."

"I'm listening," he said.

"I was with my grandparents over the weekend," she said.

"My grandfather showed me a letter from some animal person. This person said you had discussed the house with him. About selling it."

"I thought so."

"My grandfather said he wrote to you after he got the letter."

"Did he tell you what he said?"

"That it was your choice whether to sell the house or not."

"And that it was a question of honor and keeping my word and abiding by my aunt's wishes."

"All that," she said.

"How did your grandfather happen to share this stuff with you?"

"Well, he knew I used to go out with you," she said. She hesitated, then said, "It was one of his little moral lessons. He never misses a chance to give a moral lesson to anyone in the family."

"I see."

"He said he was sure you would decide to sell the house. He said there was no doubt about it."

"So you had Binky call me so she could earn the commission."

"Not exactly," she said. Lake heard a strange note in her voice.

"How not exactly?"

"It doesn't matter."

"It does matter," he said.

"I told my grandfather he was wrong."

"You told him that? You said I wouldn't sell?"

"I said I didn't think you would."

"But you weren't sure."

"I bet him you wouldn't."

"How much did you bet?"

"Five dollars."

"That's not much," Lake said.

"You don't know my grandfather," she said. "To him, five dollars is high stakes."

"There's something I don't understand. If you didn't expect me to sell, why did you have Binky call?"

"I wanted to see if I would win my bet," she said.

Lake was drowning in her voice. He said, "That wasn't very patient of you, was it?"

"No, I suppose it wasn't."

"It verges on the unscrupulous."

"I don't care," she said.

He listened into the phone, trying to hear the meaning. Then the answer bloomed bright and huge, filling the space between them: What I do matters to her.

He could tell that she was listening for the meaning, too. "About that lunch," he said.

"What lunch?"

"We were supposed to have lunch. Back in October, to talk, but I couldn't do it then. Now I want to have lunch."

"When?"

"Now. Right now."

"Lake, it's not even eleven o'clock."

"Twelve, then."

"I have an appointment at twelve forty-five, and I have to prepare for it."

"We'll go to the McDonald's near your office. From twelve to twelve-thirty. Twelve to twelve-fifteen."

"All right."

She was shy when she sat down at the table. He was nervous. They went to the counter to get food and stood beside one another, saying nothing. Back at the table, he pushed his food away. He didn't know how to begin. He looked out the window. A stray snowflake floated by. "We're going to have a white Christmas," he said. Then: "What are you doing for Christmas? Florida?"

"I'm going skiing with Jackie and her parents. They have a place in Sun Valley. What are you doing?"

He couldn't say that he planned to work; it would sound pathetic. "Philippa asked me to come up to Greenwich," he said. It wasn't a lie; she had.

Jennifer nodded.

"You remember Philippa," he said.

"Yes."

"I'm sure you don't want to talk about that, though," he said.

"Do you want to talk about it?"

He didn't, but there was no escaping. "The day with Philippa and my father, that was terrible," he said. "I shouldn't have put you in that position. I misjudged the way things were with us."

She watched him, armored and remote. Lake sank into himself. He said, "When my father is around, it's trouble."

But he knew that his father and Philippa were only bystanders: Jennifer had made up her mind about him before she came to the house that day. "I was blind," he said. "I didn't realize where things stood. When you told Philippa that you didn't see any future for us, it was hard for me to hear it. But I want to try again, if you'll let me."

"I said what?"

"What you said about us not going anywhere. You were just being honest."

"What are you talking about?" Jennifer said.

He looked at her.

"I never said that," she said.

"You did," he said.

"What exactly do you think I said to her?" Jennifer said.

"You remember," he said. "Philippa somehow got the idea that we were making plans—I guess because she was making plans—and she asked you about the house. About living there. About whether it suited you."

"I didn't say anything about the house."

"It was a bigger question, really. It was none of her business. It was outrageous that she asked you."

"I don't believe this," Jennifer said. "She asked me how I liked being there. She said, wasn't it nice, all of us together, aren't we having a nice time? That's what she said. And she was half drunk and your father was totally destructive. I hated it. I've seen too much of that. I've seen it in my own mother. I hated being there. That's what I said."

"You don't have to take it back. I'm not asking you to take it back."

"I never said anything about the house or us. How could you think that, Lake?"

He felt the blood drain from his face.

"But I could," he said. "I did. How could you think I would care so much if that's all you were saying?"

"I said your father was vicious," she said.

"You can say anything you want about him. You don't know the half of it."

But he saw that there was more. She sat rigid. Pain gathered around her eyes. "Then later I figured maybe it was something else," she said.

"What else?"

After a moment she said, "I thought maybe you wanted to break up, and what happened that day just made it easier."

"Jennifer, why would I want that?"

She shook her head.

"Why, *why?*" he said.

"I've got to go."

He reached for her hand, but she pulled it away.

Cars were collecting outside; people streamed into the restaurant. The answer came to him. "Charlotte," he said. "You thought something was going on with Charlotte. You thought I lied to you about her."

She was up, moving.

"I didn't," he said as he rose.

He hurried to catch up, staying close as she crossed the parking lot. They reached her car. She wouldn't look at him. He put his arms around her. "I didn't lie to you. I would never lie to you."

"Don't talk to me, don't talk to me," she said.

He held her for a moment, very tight. Then he opened the door for her and stood and watched as she drove off. He thought: We'll start again, and we won't stop.

———

*F*rom that moment on, he focused on having a nice Christmas. In his mind, it was already January and Jennifer had returned from skiing. On the way home from the office that day, he bought a large supply of groceries for the long weekend. That night he made repeated trips to Aunt Ilsa's firewood supply in the garage. He laid a fire in the living room and stacked plenty of extra wood close by. He moved a chair to a position directly in front of the fireplace. Then he carried Randall's leather chair in from the library and put it beside his. Every night over the weekend, he and Randall would have a roaring fire, and the house would be filled with choral music. He arranged his Christmas presents from Philippa and Karen on the living-room table. He found Randall's stocking in the cellar and hung it from the fire screen; Randall watched with interest, recognizing the stocking as a good portent.

Thursday brought leaden skies. He was supposed to meet the manager of the new office space, and he wore a business suit to work, but the manager called and rescheduled the meeting. After he put down the telephone, Lake declared that the holidays had officially begun.

Paul handed out computer-generated Christmas cards purportedly from Randall and signed with a pawprint. Danny played a tape that sounded vaguely like a dog barking out the words of "Jingle Bells." At noon, Lake opened a bottle of champagne and wished everyone a merry Christmas. Snow began to fall. "Look," said Mary, and they all looked, pleased.

They ordered in a big lunch and dove into it, talking nonstop.

At one-thirty, Danny left to do some shopping. After a while, Rob and Mary followed. Paul sat at his computer. "Go home," Lake said. "We're closed."

"What about you?" Paul said.

"I'll leave in a few minutes."

"I'll leave when you do," Paul said.

"I'll be out of here soon," Lake said. "Go on."

"I'm not leaving until you do. It's my assignment."

"Who assigned you?" Lake said.

"They all did."

Lake had to leave.

The snow had stopped, but the sky was darker than ever. He took his time driving home, enjoying the sight of people scurrying about on errands, visibly caught up in a holiday mood. Even Chestnut Hill was festive in its way, with wreaths and lights and a caterer's truck preparing for a party. His house looked like something out of a postcard, its stony mass gentled by drifts and lesser brushstrokes of snow.

The house had a chill inside, and he headed straight for the thermostat. But he didn't reach it. On the hall table were two packages, both of them wrapped with red paper and green ribbon.

Keeping his distance from the table, he worked on the problem. Only the cleaning service had a key to the house. Maybe gift-giving was one of their customer-relations policies. It didn't seem likely, however. There were two presents.

He went to the table and examined the cards strung from the ribbons. One said: "To Lake, with love, Jennifer." The other said: "For Randall xxx."

With love, his card said.

Lake went into the library and sat down. He read the card. With love, it still said.

He called Jennifer's house in Merion. Maggie answered. "Hi, Lake," she said. "Jennifer's not here."

"Has she left on her ski trip?"

"Tomorrow morning. She's at work now, but she should be back around five."

"That's okay," he said. "I just want to drop something off. I'll be there in about a half hour." He checked his watch: it said 3:20.

"Drive carefully," Maggie said.

He raced upstairs, fumbled beneath the socks in the top drawer of the bureau, and retrieved the little box that held the spiral earrings. He found wrapping paper and ribbon in the cellar, scissors in the library. Randall watched him as he wrapped the box. "Want to come?" Lake said.

Randall wagged and followed Lake out to the garage. Snow had begun to fall again, and the wind jabbed through his overcoat. Randall sniffed the air with a connoisseur's keenness. They roared out of the garage and away from Chestnut Hill. The roads awakened memories of September nights, and at first he was hardly conscious of driving.

But the traffic was thick, an early preholiday rush hour, slowed to a crawl by the swirling snow. He sat at one intersection for twenty minutes as the windshield wipers thumped. Ahead, taillights pulsed as cars advanced a few feet, braked, advanced, braked. Finally he was through the choke point and in motion again, but still trapped in a cautious caravan. The daylight faded. The wipers batted at smears of neon. A traffic light flared green and yellow and red in the murk, letting just a few cars past at a time.

At another intersection, a car five positions in front of him had trouble gaining traction. Two boys jumped out and pushed it up the slight incline. The car slewed, screeched, and finally gained level ground. The boys jumped back in, high-fiving.

As he waited for the line of cars to begin moving again, Lake picked up the little package, held it in his hand, and imagined Jennifer putting on the earrings. Perhaps it was an inappropriate gift; perhaps it would seem odd when she opened it in a condominium in Idaho with Veres all around and the giver unknown to them. That was unimportant. He saw the tilt of her head as she fastened them on. He saw her private smile.

He reached the outskirts of Merion at 4:45 and swung out of the line of traffic and onto a back road that he sometimes used as a shortcut. A gust lifted a cloud of flakes in front of him. When he tapped the brake, the car skidded slightly, then caught itself and straightened. He eased his way down a hill and accelerated as the road sloped upward again. The snow was untracked, pristine.

Headlights leaped out of the whirling snow just ahead. They bore down on him, too fast; the driver hadn't expected to meet another car on this road. He saw the headlights wobble. Then they were aimed elsewhere and the oncoming car was crazily askew, sliding down at him in slow motion, wheels locked. He caught a glimpse of a woman's frightened face. At the last instant before impact, he wrenched the steering wheel over. His car bounced across the curb and through a low ridge of snow left by a plow; it stopped with the front wheels on someone's lawn. The other car glided by in silence, still half sideways. Lake turned in his seat to watch. The woman managed to regain control before she reached the bottom of the hill. She kept going.

Randall had tumbled off the seat, but he climbed back and seemed unflustered. Lake gave him a pat and said, "Always buckle up."

He put the car in reverse. The front wheels spun, but the car hardly budged. He tried going forward; it didn't help. He rocked back and forth, and the car worked its way a few inches through the ridge of snow behind the front wheels, then bogged down again.

He got out to inspect. The problem was not big: The front part of the car was hung up on the ridge. If he cleared away some of the snow from beneath the engine, he would be able to back out. But that would take time.

He checked his watch: 4:48. "Come on, Randall," he said, and Randall scrambled out. Lake reached into the car for the little box and pocketed it.

He calculated. Jennifer's house was about a half mile away. She was due back around five o'clock. He wanted to give the present just as she had given hers—left for him, a loving hello. He figured he could make it to her house and away before five. He could and he would. This would be a race, and Lake was a runner. A thought came to him as he buttoned his overcoat. Maybe speed was his natural condition. Maybe that explained why he wasn't much good at patience.

He heard a starter's gun in his head and took off. His loafers were almost worthless on the fresh snow, but after a few strides he learned how to keep his balance and make the most of the minimal traction. The snow was blowing in his face, melting on his skin. He focused on good arm motion and breathing. Now he was at the crest of the hill. The road curved gently to the left and down. He moved into the center of the white track and lengthened his stride. The only sounds were his breath and footfalls. It was like the track meets years ago: Even in these clothes, even in these shoes, he was a person who conquered time and distance.

He glanced over his shoulder. Randall was galloping effortlessly behind him, and he had a runner's look of concentration. Lake recognized it and was proud.

It was all coming back now. This was his pace, the miler's pace, smooth and sensuous and tied to some deep inner current. It swept you past a blurred world, sped you around the curves and along the straights, legs and arms metronomic, the track unrolling, the laps completed one by one. As the white road led him on, he remembered races he had run. Midway through the last lap, he would be close to the lead, striding easily, waiting. He would move up. The runners would begin to separate, and some would drop far behind. But usually at the final curve there would be at least one still ahead. Then Lake would reach inward for the strength he had saved. It would be there, ready for him, and he would surge, his legs driving. The leader would sense him coming and press harder. They would swoop around the curve. As the track straightened, they would be alongside one another. Lake would reach into himself for just a little more. He would see the signs of struggle beside him. He would kick hard—all the way, everything. And he would be gone, moving away, stretched out, flying across the line in a dream of wind and noise.

The road passed over a stone bridge and entered a section of woods, dark, with flakes sifting down from the maelstrom high above. He looked over his shoulder. Randall had dropped back about twenty yards and seemed to be laboring a bit. "Come on," he called. He saw Randall reach for his reserve of strength and close the gap. At that, Lake filled with gladness. The dog had a runner's spirit.

They pounded along, with snow spraying underfoot and the woods scrolling by. Lake descended deep into his mind; his body would do the running. He thought about the runner's spirit. He remembered discovering his gift when he was seven or eight. Something would come over him when he was playing tag or capture the flag. At times like those, he felt that no one could ever catch him if he chose to stay free: He was faster than anyone; he could float; he could fly. Later, in competition, he still had the feeling—a wild optimism, the cheetah's heart, an animal joy.

But track had taught him that speed wasn't enough. You had to know where you were at every moment, what was behind, what lay ahead. It was a lesson he must not forget.

Breathing hurt, though his legs were still strong. The woods gave way to close-packed houses. Barking began off to the right. A black dog ran toward them, stopped with legs planted for battle, and raged at the intruders. Randall veered but didn't slow.

They ran on. He checked his watch: 4:55. They were going to make it. He pushed himself. He couldn't get enough air. But he knew he still had that extra bit of strength, the good kick. He checked over his shoulder. Randall had disappeared.

Then he saw him—fifty yards back, casually sniffing at something beside the road. Lake skidded to a stop. "Randall!" he shouted. "Come on."

Randall looked up, then resumed his sniffing. Evidently he had decided the race was over.

Lake looked at his watch: 4:56. The house was just around the bend. This was incredible; this was not the runner's spirit at all. "Let's go, let's go," he yelled. Randall looked up, considered his options, and resumed the sniffing.

Lake ran back. "You're messing up, Randall," he said as he neared him. But Randall paid no attention.

"Okay, you asked for it." He grabbed the dog under the chest and lifted him. When Randall tried to fight free, Lake wrapped him in an iron grip. He began to run, but it was impossible with such a weight. He settled for a fast walk.

He was gasping now, and he couldn't feel his feet because his shoes were full of snow, and his arms were giving out. He rounded the last curve. He mentally designated the front path of the house as the finish. Ten yards before he reached it, he accelerated to a lumbering run. He crossed the imaginary line, leaning slightly forward in good form, and dumped Randall beyond. His watch said 4:58:33. Technically a victory—but Jennifer's car was in the driveway.

He bent over, eyes closed, his head full of brightness, his chest heaving. After a while, the gasping slowed. He brushed himself off. Standing on one leg at a time, he emptied the snow from his shoes. Finally he was ready. He would stay a minute, no more.

A thought formed. "Come here, Randall," he said. Randall approached, suspicious. Lake knelt and unfastened the collar buckle. He took the little box from his coat pocket, slipped the leather strap of the collar through the ribbon, and, working with numbed fingers, refastened the buckle. He stepped back to examine the effect. It was good. Randall definitely looked like a miniature St. Bernard on a rescue mission in the Alps.

He rang the doorbell. Jennifer opened it. "I was getting worried," she said. "Maggie said she expected you an hour ago."

"We made all possible speed," he said, but he directed an accusing glance at Randall.

"Let me have your coat," she said.

He stayed close to the door. "This was supposed to be a sneak visit," he said. "I'm just dropping something off."

"You look frozen."

"Not at all," he said. He gestured toward Randall. "This, in case you don't recognize it, is a small St. Bernard."

"What's that around his neck?"

He reached down to undo Randall's collar. His hands were swollen and red, and his fingers hardly functioned. He got the box free and gave it to Jennifer. "Merry Christmas," he said softly.

"Why is Randall covered with snow?" she said.

"It's coming down hard."

"Did you have trouble getting here?"

"Not really," he said.

"Take off your coat. Look at your hands."

He hid them in his coat pockets. Then he felt ice in his eyebrows and hair and brushed at it.

"I'll make some hot chocolate," she said.

He shook his head. "I can't stay," he said. "The roads will be bad soon." He smiled at her, filled with love. In spite of his resolution, in spite of Maggie watching them and Mike coming out of the kitchen with a beer, he hugged her and pressed his face into her hair and let himself have one small moment of holding her—just one moment, enough to tide him over until he could hold her again.

She touched her hand to his face. "You're frozen," she said. "Sit down."

He shook his head. "I know you're busy packing. I've got stuff to do too." By way of farewell, he said, "Merry Christmas, everyone."

"Merry Christmas," said Maggie and Mike.

Lake stooped to refasten Randall's collar. As he fumbled with it, Jennifer left. Finally the collar was on. He said to Maggie, "I think Randall is a tropical dog. I know for a fact that he has Spanish ancestry."

Jennifer came back. She was wearing a parka.

"What are you doing?" he said.

"I'll walk you to your car."

"It's too cold," he said. "Stay here where it's warm."

"I want to talk to you."

"Okay," he said, waiting.

"In private," she said. She opened the front door and went out into the falling snow. He had no choice except to follow. Randall plodded behind.

On the front path, she said, "Where's your car?"

"Go back inside," he said. "You'll ruin your shoes. I'll call you tonight. I want your number in Sun Valley."

"We'll talk in your car. Where is it?"

"I also want several postcards," he said. "Mountain scenes would be good."

"Which way is the car?"

He gestured vaguely and said, "It's too cold. Go back."

She took his arm and walked with him. The snow was falling straight down now in great heavy flakes. On the sidewalk, he stopped and said, "You have to go back."

"Why?"

"The car is a few minutes from here."

"Why?"

"Randall and I needed the exercise."

"What happened to the car, Lake?"

"Nothing much."

She waited.

"It's stuck," he said, "but I can get it out with no trouble. It'll take me thirty seconds."

"I'll help you. Mike can help."

"I'll be fine," he said, smiling at her. "I'm already fine, except for the fact that we're going in different directions for the moment. I'd prefer to get that over with quickly."

"Your direction is Greenwich?"

"The family hearth," he said.

"Where exactly is this hearth?"

"Actually, Philippa has quite a few hearths."

"And you're going to Philippa's for Christmas?"

He shrugged. "Greenwich should be pretty in the snow," he said.

"You're not going to Greenwich," she said.

"What makes you think I'm not?"

"I'll tell you: When I went over to your house today, I saw the Christmas stocking and the firewood. And in the kitchen, I saw all the groceries. I checked the dates on the food. You just bought those groceries. You're not going to Greenwich."

"I decided not to."

"You never were going to Greenwich," she said.

"I'm too busy at the office," he said.

"We'll get the car in the morning," she said. She seized his arm and turned him back toward the house. Their feet skidded in the snow. "You can't do this," he said.

"I can."

He tried to wrestle free. His feet went out from under him. She released his arm, and he went flying sideways, landing on the lawn in a white explosion. He was up quickly. "A slip, it doesn't count," he said. But before he could make a move, she had darted close and grabbed his arm again.

"It wasn't a lie," he said. "I never actually specifically said I was going to Greenwich. The record will show that I never said it."

"Stop talking," she said.

*M*uch later, she led him into her bedroom. There were puffy pillows, books on a table, three trophies, a picture of a tennis player who had to be her father, a picture of herself with someone who had to be Jackie, a Monet print, a small sofa with orange-and-green fabric, a bureau made of bleached wood, flowered curtains, a patterned brown-and-beige rug. He explored with his eyes, learning.

When she had turned out the lights and they lay in the narrow bed, he said, "I need to know exactly when you'll get back from skiing. I want the flight number."

"I'm not going," she said. "I canceled it an hour ago, when you were in the kitchen talking with Maggie."

"Jennifer," he said.

"I'd rather be here."

"How did you get into the house?" he said.

"I kept a key from when it was for sale," she said. "It's been in my desk since last summer. I should have given it back. Maybe I knew I would need it someday."

*O*n a night in late February, they had dinner at the fish restaurant they liked. Lake said, "Last summer, I made you invite me to lunch here when I called from Martha's Vineyard."

"I believe lunch was my idea that time," she said.

"I helped you."

"How?" she said.

"You suggested lunch so you could talk me out of taking the house off the market."

"So it was my idea," she said.

"But you didn't persist," he said. "You were ready to drop it. I made you ask me again. I couldn't do the asking, because I had sworn that I wouldn't—not for three months."

"Was it hard?"

"What?"

"Getting me to ask you again," she said.

He tried to remember. It seemed so long ago. He remembered being afraid that she disliked him. He remembered wanting a second chance. When she mentioned lunch and then dropped it, he kept saying, "About lunch, about lunch," and tried to transmit a mental message across the miles: Ask me, ask me.

"I don't know," he said.

"It wasn't hard," she said.

"What do you mean?"

"I wanted to ask you."

The talk trailed away. He watched her eat. He thought about how lovely she was, how fine, how much she meant to him. As he was thinking, she looked up from her salad, straight into his eyes, and flushed. Then they talked a little more—about crocuses, about when the grass turns green. Then they sat quietly.

After dessert, he took her hand across the table and held it. His mind emptied of everything but the touch of her. Just to be able to hold her hand—that was all he wanted. Just to be able to reach out and find her there.

He became aware that this was a strange silence, very deep, somehow not an absence of words but instead a presence of things almost heard, yet not quite. He thought of Rob's idea about spirits living hidden among the rocks and trees along the coast of Maine. They exist in some different part of time, Rob had said. That's why you can't see them or hear them, although you know they're there.

This silence was charged in the same way. He could almost hear things that hadn't happened yet. They lay ahead, waiting for him.

The check arrived. Even in the car, the silence held.

Lake thought about magic being brought across an ocean to a new home. He had traveled a long way, too. He was still traveling, he and Jennifer, driving through the Philadelphia night, along quiet streets, through pools of lamplight, past traces of old snow.

Then it was time to stop. The car was so full of feeling that he couldn't drive any further. He pulled over to the side of a dim street whose name he didn't know. He reached toward her, but she was already reaching toward him. "Marry me," he said. "Please marry me." And she said that she would. She would.

about the author

George Constable has written books on subjects ranging from prehistoric humans to the modern Olympic Games. He and his wife live in Washington, D.C.